DON'T EVER TELL

DON'T EVER TELL

BRANDON MASSEY

PINNACLE BOOKS
Kensington Publishing Corp.
www.kensingtonbooks.com

PINNACLE BOOKS are published by

Kensington Publishing Corp.
850 Third Avenue
New York, NY 10022

All Kensington titles, imprints, and distributed lines are available at special quantity discounts for bulk purchases for sales promotions, premiums, fund-raising, and educational, or institutional use. Special book excerpts or customized printings can also be created to fit specific needs. For details, write or phone the office of the Kensington special sales manager: Kensington Publishing Corp., 850 Third Avenue, New York, NY 10022, attn: Special Sales Department; phone: 1-800-221-2647.

ISBN-13: 978-0-7860-1993-9
ISBN-10: 0-7860-1993-X

First printing: July 2008

10 9 8 7 6 5 4 3 2 1

Printed in the United States of America

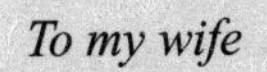

To my wife

Prologue

On the morning of the day he would taste freedom again for the first time in four years, Dexter Bates lay on his bunk in the dimly lit cell, fingers interlaced behind his head, waiting for the arrival of the guards.

He did not tap his feet, hum a song, or count the cracks in the shadowed cement ceiling to pass the time. He was so still and silent that save for the rhythmic rising and falling of his chest, he might have been dead.

Incarceration taught a man many lessons, and chief among them was patience. You either learned how to befriend time, or the rambling passage of monotonous days eventually broke your spirit.

He had long ago vowed that he would not be broken. That he would use time to his advantage. The day ahead promised to reveal the value of his patient efforts.

Resting peacefully, he thought, as ever, about her. About her supple body, and how easily he bent it to his will. Her soft skin, and how it bruised beneath his fists. Her throaty voice, and how he urged it toward raw screams of terror. . . .

Pleasant thoughts to dribble away the last grains of time he had left in this hellhole.

Soon, the metal cell door clanged open. Two correctional officers as tall and wide as NFL linemen entered the cell.

"Let's go, Bates," Steele said, the lead guard. Sandy-haired, with a severe crew cut, he had a wide, boyish face that always appeared sunburned. He had a green parka with a fur-lined hood draped over his arm. "Hurry up or you'll miss your last ride outta here."

Dexter rose off the narrow cot. He was nude—he had stripped out of the prison jumpsuit before their arrival. He spread his long, muscular arms and legs.

"All right, open that big-assed cum-catcher of yours," Jackson said. He was a stern-faced black man with a jagged scar on his chin that he tried to hide with a goatee. He clicked on a pen-sized flashlight.

Dexter opened wide. Jackson panned the flashlight beam inside his mouth, and checked his nostrils and ears, too.

"Now bend over," Jackson said.

"But we hardly know each other," Dexter said.

"Don't test me this morning. I ain't in the mood for your bullshit."

Dexter turned around and bent over from the waist. Jackson shone the light up his rectum.

"He's clear," Jackson said.

"How about one last blow for the road, Jacky?" Dexter grabbed his length and swung it toward Jackson. "You know I'm gonna miss that sweet tongue action you got."

"Fuck you," Jackson said.

During Dexter's first month in the joint, Jackson had tried to bully him. Word of Dexter's background had spread quickly, and there were a number of guards and inmates who wanted a crack at him. A shot at glory.

Dexter had repeatedly slammed Jackson's face against a

cinderblock wall, fracturing his jaw and scarring his chin. Although assaulting a guard would normally have resulted in a stint in the hole and additional time tacked onto his ten-year sentence, Jackson had never reported the incident. He had his pride.

Jackson searched Dexter's jumpsuit and boots for weapons, found nothing, and then Dexter dressed, shrugging on the parka that Steele gave him. Jackson cuffed his hands in front of him and attached the ankle restraints.

The guards marched him down the cell block. None of the inmates taunted Dexter, as was typical when an inmate departed. There were a few softly uttered words of support—"Peace, brother," "Take care of yourself, man"—but mostly, a widespread silence that approached reverence.

"These guys are really gonna miss you, Bates," Steele said.

"They can always write me," Dexter said.

They took him to inmate processing, where the final transfer paperwork was completed. He was being sent to Centralia Correctional Center, another medium security prison, to serve out the balance of his sentence. He had put in for the transfer purportedly to take advantage of the inmate work programs offered at that facility, and it had taken almost two years for the approval to come through.

The administrator, a frizzy haired lady with a wart on her nose, expressed surprise that Dexter was not taking any personal items with him. Most transferring inmates left with boxes of belongings in tow, as if they were kids going away to summer camp. Dexter assured Wart Nose that he would get everything he needed once he was settled in his new home.

Paperwork complete, they walked Dexter outside to the boarding area, where an idling white van was parked, exhaust fumes billowing from the pipe. "Illinois Department of Corrections" was painted on the side in large black letters. Steel bars protected the frosted windows.

It was a cold, overcast December morning, a fresh layer of snow covering the flat countryside. An icy gust shrieked across the parking lot and sliced at Dexter's face.

He wondered about the weather in Chicago, and felt a warm tingle in his chest.

Steele slid open the van's side door, and Dexter climbed in, air pluming from his lips. Two beefy correctional officers from Centralia waited inside, both sitting in the front seat. A wire mesh screen separated the front from the rear bench rows.

"Sit your ass down so we can get moving," the guard in the passenger seat said. "It's cold as fuck out here."

Steele lifted the heavy chain off the vehicle's floor and clamped it to Dexter's ankle restraints. He nodded at Dexter, his blue-eyed gaze communicating a subtle message, and then he slammed the door.

As in police vehicles, there were no interior door handles. Packed inside and bolted in place, a prisoner bound for another concrete home could only sit still and enjoy the ride.

"Headed to our home in Centralia, eh?" the driver asked. He glanced in the rearview mirror at Dexter. "Just so you know brother man, whoever you were outside won't mean shit there, got it? You'll be everyone's bitch, especially ours."

"Spoken like a man who's always wanted to be a cop," Dexter said. "Did you fail the exam? Or wash out of the academy?"

"What a piece of work," the passenger guard said, shaking his head. "You must want deluxe 'commodations in the hole soon as you get there."

At the manned booth, a guard waved the van through the tall prison gates. Dexter looked out the window. The snowy plains surrounded them, so vast and featureless they nearly blended into the overcast horizon.

By design, many state correctional centers had been erected in barren wastelands, to make it almost impossible for an escaping inmate to progress far before recapture. Dexter had heard rumors of inmates who managed to get away being tracked down within three miles of the joint, upon which they were brought back, weeping like babies, to an increased sentence and a long stay in solitary.

The two-lane road was crusted with dirty slush and riddled with potholes. It wound through nothingness for close to five miles before it fed into a major artery, which eventually intersected the highway.

At that time of morning, there was no traffic, and there wouldn't be much at all, anyway. The road dead ended at the prison, a place most normal people preferred to avoid.

The guards switched on the radio to a country-western station. The singer crooned about seeing his lady again after being away for so long.

Dexter wasn't a fan of country western, but he could dig the song's message.

"What time is it?" Dexter asked.

"You got somewhere to be, asshole?" the driver said.

"I want to make sure we're on time. I've got a hot date with my new warden."

"Whatever. It's a quarter after nine, numb nuts."

Nodding to the music, Dexter dug his bound hands into the right front pocket of the parka.

A key was secreted inside, courtesy of his good man Steele. Correctional officers were even more receptive to bribes than cops, and that was saying something.

"I'm really feeling this song," Dexter said. "Turn it up, will you, man?"

"That's the smartest thing you've said yet," the passenger guard said, and cranked up the volume.

Dexter used the key to disengage the handcuffs, the loud music drowning out the tinkle of the chains. Leaning forward slightly, he stretched his long arm downward and unlocked the ankle restraints, too.

Then he sat back in the seat, and waited. He crooned along with the song, his intentionally bad voice making the guards laugh.

"You sure ain't got no future in music," the driver said. "Jesus Christ, you're terrible." Dexter shrugged. "A man's got to know his limitations, I guess."

After they had driven for about three miles, they came around a bend. There was a gray Dodge Charger stalled on the shoulder of the road. A blond woman in a shearling coat and jeans was at the trunk, apparently trying to lift out a spare tire. Her long hair flowed from underneath a yellow cap, blowing like a siren's mane in the chill wind.

"Would ya lookit that?" The passenger guard leered at the woman. "Pull over, Max. Let's help her out."

A green Chevy Tahoe approached from the opposite direction.

"You know we're not supposed to stop, Cade," Max said.

"You better not stop," Dexter said. "You're going to screw up my schedule."

"Shut up," Cade said. He turned to Max. "Look, it'll take ten minutes. That young broad can't change the goddamn tire by herself."

"You just wanna get laid," Max said.

"Hey, I'm a Good Samaritan. I gotta do my charitable deed for the day."

"To get laid," Max said. But he slowed the van and nosed behind the Dodge. "You got ten minutes. No word of this to anyone."

"I'll snitch on you," Dexter said.

"The hell you will," Cade said. He licked his fingers, patted down his eyebrows, and then climbed out of the van. Strutting like a rooster, he approached the blonde.

The oncoming Tahoe suddenly slashed across the road, snow spraying from the tires, and blocked off the van. Tinted windows concealed the occupants.

"Holy shit," Max said. "What the hell's this?"

On the shoulder of the road, the other guard noticed the Tahoe, and froze.

Dexter dug his hand in the coat's left front pocket and clutched the grip of the loaded .38, also compliments of Steele.

A gunman wearing a ski mask and a black jacket sprang out of the Dodge's trunk. The masked man shot Cade twice in the head with a pistol, and the guard dropped to the pavement like a discarded puppet.

Cursing, Max fumbled for his radio.

"Hey, Max," Dexter said. "Look, buddy, no chains."

When Max spun around, Dexter had the gun pressed to the wire mesh screen. He shot the guard at the base of the throat, just below the collar.

The guard's eyes widened with surprise, and he slid against the seat, a bloody hole unfurling like a blooming flower in his windpipe.

The passenger side door of the Tahoe swung open. A refrigerator-wide black man attired like a correctional officer scrambled out and ran to the driver's side of the van.

The ski-masked shooter bounded out of the trunk. The blonde took the ring of keys from Cade's belt, and unlocked the van's side door.

"Morning, Dex." She smiled brightly.

"Hey, Christy."

Moving fast, Dexter and the ski-masked man lifted the

guard's corpse off the ground and laid it across the floor of the van. In front, the guy dressed like a guard had gotten behind the wheel and was propping up the wounded guard in the seat to look like a passenger if one gave him a casual glance.

The dying guard was moaning entreaties to God in a blood-choked gurgle.

"Someone shut him up." Dexter slammed the side panel door. "Fuck it, I'll do it myself."

Opening the passenger door, Dexter shot the guard twice in the chest, permanently dousing the struggling light in the man's eyes. Except for the splash of blood on his coat, he appeared to be sleeping off a hangover.

"Good to see you, man," the new driver said.

"Same here." Dexter nodded, closed the door. "Let's roll out."

The ski-masked gunner scrambled behind the wheel of the Dodge, the blonde got in on the passenger side, and Dexter hustled in the back.

Beside them, the Tahoe backed up and executed a swift U-turn, maneuvering behind the prison van, which had begun to rumble forward.

Both the SUV and the van were driven by longtime colleagues, upstanding members of the Windy City's finest.

"How long?" Dexter asked.

"Two minutes and fourteen seconds," Javier, his former partner said. He had peeled away his ski mask. A native of the Dominican Republic who had moved to the States when he was five, Javier was a lean, bronze-skinned man with dark, wavy hair and a pencil-thin mustache.

Javier flashed a lopsided grin that reminded Dexter of their wild days working together.

"We kicked ass, Dex."

"Like old times," Dexter said.

"How's it feel to be out?" Christy asked. Unlike every other member of the operation, she wasn't a cop—she was Javier's wife, and as trustworthy as any brother of the badge.

"Like being born again," Dexter said. "Hallelujah."

Christy passed him a brown paper bag that contained a bottle of iced tea and two roast beef-and-cheddar sandwiches wrapped in plastic. Dexter ate greedily. After four years of bland prison food, the simple meal was like a spread at a four-star restaurant.

A bag from Target lay on the seat beside him. He opened it, found a pair of overalls and a plaid shirt.

"The rest of the stuff?" Dexter asked.

"The duffel with all your things is in the trunk," Javier said. "But you need to get out of that ape suit pronto, man. Who would I look like giving a prisoner a taxi ride?"

Dexter peeled out of the prison jumpsuit and dressed in the civilian clothes.

When they reached the main artery that ran through town, Javier made a turn that would take them to the highway. The prison van, followed by the Tahoe, went in the opposite direction.

They would drive the van over a hundred miles away and abandon it, and its cargo of dead guards, in a pond. With luck, it would be at least several days before the cops would discover it.

Dexter settled back in the seat and dozed. He dreamed, as usual, of her. She was weeping, screaming, and pleading for her life.

It was a good dream.

When he awoke over two hours later, they were bumping across a long, narrow lane, freshly plowed of snow. Tall pines and oaks lined the road, ice clinging to their boughs.

Javier turned into a long driveway that led to a small A-frame house surrounded by dense forest.

"My mother's crib," Javier said, and Christy laughed.

Dexter laughed, too. The house was no more inhabited by Javier's mother than it was by the Queen of England. Javier had bought it in his mother's name to conceal his ownership, a ploy that many of them had used at one time or another to hide their connection to various properties and valuables they purchased—things decidedly *not* paid for with their regular cop salaries.

A car, covered by a gray tarp, sat beside the house.

"What's that?" Dexter asked.

"Something special for you," Javier said.

They parked. Dexter got out of the car and walked to the covered vehicle, snow and ice crunching under his shoes. He peeked under the tarp.

It was a ten-year-old black Chevy Caprice, a model that was once the ubiquitous police cruiser.

Dexter laughed. "You kill me."

"Glad the joint hasn't taken away your sense of humor," Javier said. He opened the Dodge's trunk and handed a big, olive green duffel bag to Dexter. *"Feliz Navidad, amigo."*

Dexter placed the bag on the ground and unzipped it. It contained a Glock 9mm, five magazines of ammo, a switch-blade, a concealable body armor vest, a prepaid cell phone, clothing, keys to the Chevy and the house, a manila envelope, and five thick, bundled packets of cash in denominations of twenties, fifties and hundreds, totaling approximately ten thousand dollars.

It wasn't a lot of money, but more waited in Chicago. Substantially more.

"Santa brought you everything on your wish list," Javier said. "In spite of how naughty you've been."

Dexter grinned. In the manila envelope, he found an Illinois driver's license, U.S. passport, and a Social Security card, all listed under the alias of Alonzo Washington.

"Alonzo Washington?" Dexter asked.

Javier smiled. "Sound familiar?"

"The flick about the narc—*Training Day,* right? Denzel's character was named Alonzo something."

"I thought you'd appreciate it."

"You're a regular fucking comedian, aren't you?" Dexter tapped the IDs. "These solid?"

"As a rock," Javier said. "The finest money could buy."

In the ID snapshots, Dexter's face had been digitally altered to depict him as clean shaven. Dexter rubbed the thick, woolen beard he had grown in prison.

"We threw some Magic Shave and a couple razors in the bag, too," Javier said.

"I've had hair on my chin since I was fifteen. I'll hardly recognize myself."

He turned to the house. Although it offered perhaps fifteen hundred square feet, a decent amount of space but nothing spectacular, to a man who had lived in a seven-by-twelve cell it would be like having the run of the Biltmore Estate all to himself.

"Utilities are on," Javier said. "Christy went grocery shopping this morning, packed the refrigerator with everything a growing boy needs."

"Your loyalty," Dexter said. "That means more to me than anything. Thanks."

"Speaking of loyalty, we tried to track down your ex-wife," Christy said.

"Wife," Dexter said.

"Right. Anyway, she's dropped off the grid, like you thought. We got nothing."

"That's good," Dexter said.

"How the hell is that good, after how she screwed you?" Javier asked.

"Because," Dexter said, a grin curving across his face. "I get to find her myself."

PART ONE

What's Done in the Dark . . .

1

The night that changed Joshua Moore's life began, ironically, with a party.

On Sunday, December 16, Joshua and his wife, Rachel, hosted a holiday get-together at their home in south metro Atlanta. Over twenty people, a lively blend of family and friends, crowded into the four-bedroom house. It was their first time holding an event at their home since they had moved in five months ago, and Joshua's head was spinning from all the activity.

People gathered in the family room, dining room, kitchen, living room, and hallway, eating, drinking, talking, and laughing. The dining room had been turned into a buffet, featuring a full spread of appetizers, desserts, and beverages such as crab cakes, hot wings, egg rolls, meatballs, pasta salad, peel-and-eat shrimp, cheeses, cookies, cakes, fruit punch, soda, wine, and a glass bowl brimming with rum-spiced eggnog. Holiday music played over the in-house stereo system, loud enough to enliven the mood but low enough to encourage conversation.

"You look dazed," Eddie Barnes said. Standing in the living room beside a seven-foot high Christmas tree that dwarfed his slight frame, Eddie nursed a glass of eggnog. "Take a load off and chill for a sec."

"Good idea." Careful not to spill his soda, Joshua sat on one of the new microfiber sofas they had purchased upon moving in. He stretched his legs in front of him—which, at his height of six feet five, was a considerable length. "I can't remember the last time I threw a party."

"I do," Eddie said. "Sixteenth birthday. In your parents' basement. I was the deejay, remember? Mixmaster E?"

"Man, that was a long time ago. Sixteen years?"

Eddie bobbed his clean-shaven head. "We're getting old, dawg. Married with kids and shit."

"Speak for yourself. I don't have any kids."

"They're on the way. See how much Rachel's been talking to Ariel? She's getting child-rearing tips, trust me. Look at 'em." Eddie motioned with his glass.

Joshua looked over his shoulder. Dressed in a red sweater, green slacks, and a cute Santa cap, Rachel was in the hallway speaking to Ariel, Eddie's wife. Ariel bounced their three-year-old son on her hip with practiced ease, while their six-year-old daughter pranced around them. Tanisha May, Rachel's business partner, was also part of the group. The two as-yet childless women resembled chicks taking lessons from a mother hen.

Joshua shrugged. "We're in no rush to have kids. We only got married six months ago. We're planning to just enjoy being married, do some traveling, you know."

"What's that saying? Man plans—God laughs. You never know what life'll hit you with. Be ready."

"You must've tipped some extra rum into that glass. You're talking crazy."

"I joke, but fatherhood is cool, Josh." Eddie gazed at his

young children with a proud smile. "Makes you grow up real quick. Can you honestly say, right now, that you would die for someone else?"

Joshua looked at Rachel again. As sometimes happened when he regarded her, his heart kicked, an almost painfully poignant feeling.

"I'd die for my wife," he said.

"Most definitely. Now take that same feeling that you'd sacrifice it all for her, and multiply it by ten—*that's* how you'll feel when you have children."

"How'd you feel when Ariel was pregnant?"

"Tired as hell. She'd be snoring so loud and rolling around in the bed so much I got maybe two hours of sleep a night. Sometimes I had to sleep in the guest room."

"Seriously? What else?"

"When she was walking around with my babies growing in her? Dude, if you had looked at her the wrong way, I might have jacked you. Some superman, protective thing kicks in. I didn't want her to go anywhere alone. Didn't want her to drive or lift anything. I was sort of tripping out for a minute."

"Sounds like it. Anyway, like I said, it'll be a while before Rachel and I get to that point."

"Do some traveling, yeah. Get your money right. Spend some more time getting to know each other."

"We already know each other pretty well, or else we wouldn't have gotten married."

"Nah, dawg. You're only six months in—you don't know each other yet. Talk to me after ten years."

"There you go." Joshua shook his head. "Newlyweds don't get any respect."

"It's all relative. My folks have been married damn near forty years, and they look at me and Ariel like we just met yesterday."

"I hear you. Hey, be back in a minute—I'm gonna grab another crab cake before they're all gone."

Joshua started to rise off the couch—and spilled his soda. Cola splashed onto the beige carpet. He swore under his breath and looked around for a napkin.

"I'll take care of that," Rachel said, suddenly beside him with a delicate hand on his arm.

"Sorry. You know how clumsy I can be."

"Don't say that, baby." She took a wadded napkin and pressed it against the darkening damp spot on the carpet. "Can you get some more ice out of the garage, please? Tanisha wants to make some strawberry daiquiris."

"Sure."

"Thanks, love."

Joshua glanced at Eddie, who had followed their interaction with amusement, and headed to the garage to fetch a bag of ice from the freezer. Eddie, he knew, could remember a time when his spilling a drink at a party would have provoked a hurtful remark from whoever happened to be his girlfriend at the moment. He had been dating since he was a teenager, but Rachel was the first woman who truly loved him for who he was, clumsiness and all.

Sometimes, he honestly wondered how she had fallen in love with him in the first place. He was no one special. He wasn't rich—he was a freelance graphic designer, and earned a reasonable but unremarkable income. He wasn't particularly handsome—though he was tall and husky, he wore thick glasses to correct a bad case of astigmatism, which back in the day his classmates had teasingly called "Coke bottles." And he sure as hell wasn't suave—no man with a knack for knocking over drinks, bumping into people, or dropping dishes could be considered smooth by any stretch of the imagination.

Further mystifying him was the fact that she, by comparison, was perfect. Sweet-hearted. Intelligent. Successful in her chosen profession as a hair salon owner and stylist. Supportive of his goals, and pursuing goals of her own. And not to overlook, she was absolutely fine—five feet six, with big pretty brown eyes, smooth skin the color of honey, and a body that would have roused the pulse of a dead man. Although he had often dreamed of finding a woman like Rachel, it had seemed one of those farfetched fantasies, like one might have of hitting the lottery some day.

But somehow, he had found her—and when he had told Eddie that he would die for her, he meant it.

Around nine, the last guest departed, and blessed calm took over the house. Joshua collapsed on the love seat in the family room, legs too tired to stand any more.

A minute later, Rachel entered from the kitchen. She eased onto his lap, languidly stretched her arms above her head, and released a deep sigh.

"Finally, we can relax," she said.

Coco, the three-year-old Chihuahua that Rachel had brought to their relationship, scampered across the room and leaped onto Joshua's lap, too. Restless from being caged upstairs during the party, the dog whined and tried to kiss Joshua on the mouth, and he gently nudged her away.

"Daddy doesn't want to give you smooches now, sweetie," Rachel said. She plucked Coco off his chest and tucked the dog against her breast like a purse. "Daddy's saving his kisses for Mommy."

Tail wagging, the dog looked at Joshua longingly.

"I think she needs a boyfriend," he said. "Anyway, what do you think about the party? I thought it was a hit."

"Me, too. It was a lot of work, but everyone seemed to have a good time."

He studied her face. Although she had channeled her energies into hosting the party, he'd had the nagging sense that she was distracted by something. A couple of times during the event, he'd noticed her off to herself, not speaking to anyone, her gaze clouded, as if she were deeply immersed in thought.

Now, however, her eyes only looked tired.

"Are you feeling okay?" he asked.

She nodded.

"Just wrung out."

"Too bad tomorrow's Monday. I'd love to sleep in."

"Oh, you're funny. You can sleep in, Mr. I Work from Home. I have to get up at the ass crack of dawn and open a salon."

"I meant I'd love to sleep in *together."* He touched her leg.

"Oh?" Mischief sparkled in her eyes.

"I'd like one of those long, lazy mornings. Hugging, cuddling."

"Hugging, cuddling, and other bedroom activities."

"Something like that."

"I can tell Tanisha I'll be in late and have someone cover my appointments." She set Coco on the floor. Then she placed her hand on his groin, and slowly began to massage.

"But why wait until tomorrow morning to get started?" she asked.

"You're not too tired?"

"Are you?" She squeezed him.

He groaned.

"Let's go upstairs."

"Let's not."

She began to pull her sweater over her head.

Although he thought he had a healthy sex drive, she was often insatiable. He knew she had been with men before him—though he didn't know how many and didn't care to ask—but he often got the sense that with him, she felt free to express herself in ways that she never had before. As if with him, she was free for the first time in her life.

Weird, but that was the impression he had.

At some point, they made their way upstairs to the master bedroom. Exhausted, they fell asleep, lying against each other like spoons in a drawer.

Later that night, he awoke to Rachel screaming.

2

"No . . . no!"

Snatched to alertness by her cries, Joshua bolted upright in bed. He'd never heard Rachel scream like that, and he was half-convinced that he was dreaming. He quickly realized that he wasn't—his heart was knocking too hard.

He grabbed his glasses from the nightstand, fumbled them on.

The dark bedroom came into sharp focus. They were alone. Rachel was having a bad dream.

Bed covers pulled up to her chin, face concealed in darkness, Rachel whipped her head back and forth, bed springs creaking as she screeched at her dream assailant.

"*No, please . . .*"

He'd never seen Rachel suffer a nightmare; she normally slept as soundly as the dead. But she was in such a state of turmoil that he was afraid to touch her, worried that any physical contact might drive her into an uncontrollable frenzy.

Maybe he *was* dreaming.

Rachel shrieked again. "You bastard!"

He flinched at the fury in her voice. Who was she fighting? She rarely swore like that, and he'd never heard her address anyone with such rage and terror.

But it had to be a man. A woman would call only a man a bastard.

Although part of him wanted to wake her and put an end to her torment, another part of him was curious, and out of that curiosity, didn't want to intervene. He wanted to wait and see if she would say something else that would clue him in on her relationship with this guy who, whoever he was, frightened her terribly.

She'd never mentioned a prior relationship with an abusive man. Actually, she never said much at all about her previous relationships. "What's in the past is over and done with," she would say with a shrug. "All that matters is that today, we're together." And with that, she would change the subject.

He never pushed her for more details. Was the past really that important? He hated talking about old flames, too, because it was embarrassing to remember how women had used to treat him like a human doormat.

Rachel flung away the covers. She flailed her arms and kicked, as though trying to keep someone from climbing on top of her.

"Get off me, damn it!"

Beside the bed, Coco let loose a high-pitched bark. At night, the dog slumbered in a pet kennel atop the nightstand on Rachel's side of the bed. Like most Chihuahuas, Coco was protective of the person she regarded as her master. She scratched at the bars of her cage, big eyes flashing in the darkness, four pounds of righteous fury.

The little dog shamed him into action. He clicked on the bedside lamp.

Rachel's face was contorted with her efforts to fight off

her attacker, her dark, curly hair disheveled, hands clenched as she shoved at an invisible body.

He touched her shoulder. Her skin was clammy, but she didn't respond to him.

"Rachel, wake up." He shook her gently. "It's only a dream."

But she was oblivious to him. She gagged, as if being choked, and her hands went to her neck, trying to pry away an imaginary stranglehold.

A cold finger tapped his spine. This had gone far enough.

Choking, Rachel kicked wildly, hands grasping at her neck. A thick vein pulsed in stark relief on her throat.

Coco was barking as if she were one of the hounds of hell.

He grabbed Rachel's wrists and pulled them away from her neck. It wasn't easy—she had the desperate strength of someone fighting for her life.

"Rachel, wake up."

"Get off!" Spittle sprayed his face. She thrashed like an angry snake.

He pressed her hands down to her sides. He braced his knee across her legs, to keep her from kicking him.

"Rachel, listen to me! It's only a dream. Wake up!"

She turned to his voice, and finally, her eyes opened.

She had the most beautiful eyes he had ever seen, a light shade of brown flecked with gold that reminded him of autumn days, but at that moment, her eyes glistened with fear and confusion.

"It's me, Josh. Everything's okay. You were having a bad dream."

She blinked, comprehension sinking into her face. She stopped her struggle, and sucked in sharp breaths. Perspiration shone on her brow.

"Only a bad dream," he said.

"A dream?" Her voice, normally musical and confident, was as soft as a frightened child's.

"Only a dream."

A sob burst out of her. She came into his arms. "Hold me."

He held her and whispered words of comfort. She squeezed against him, fingernails dug into his back.

Soon, her sobs subsided. Her breaths grew deeper, and within a few minutes, she had drifted back to sleep. Coco, too, settled down to slumber again.

He laid Rachel on the bed, pulled the covers up to her chin. Although she had fallen back to sleep, sleep eluded him.

In the year that they had known each other, he thought he'd come to know Rachel well—certainly, well enough to want to spend the rest of his life with her. He knew all the basics, of course: she was thirty years old, two years younger than him, had never been married or had children, drank alcohol socially but didn't smoke, had grown up in Illinois the only child of parents who'd died when she was only five and been raised by her aunt, and had built a lucrative career as a hair stylist. She loved Mexican food, white wine, novels by Alice Walker, museums, comedy films, vacations to the beach, and dogs.

But mysteries remained. He'd never met any of her family, or any of her friends that she'd known before she moved to Atlanta. At their wedding, the guest list was composed mostly of his own friends and family, the only people on her side being coworkers and friends from her hair salon.

By way of explanation, she said that her family was small, scattered across the country, and didn't keep in touch, and that she'd never been the kind of woman who'd had a large roster of friends. She was a loner, she said, a symptom of growing up an only child.

He had accepted her explanations about her past. There

was no reason for her to lie. He loved her, she loved him, and he took what she told him at face value.

But as he gazed at her closed eyes, a question hung over him like sour smoke.

Who had she been fighting in her dream?

3

Joshua awoke at five-thirty, much earlier than usual. Beside him, Rachel was still dozing.

Last night, they had spoken of sleeping in together, enjoying another leisurely lovemaking session and going off to their respective jobs later in the morning, but he was too wound up to lie in bed any longer.

He put on a T-shirt and sweatpants, padded downstairs, and brewed a pot of coffee.

They'd moved into the house five months ago, but he was still getting used to the place. It was far more spacious than the one-bedroom apartment he'd lived in for the past few years, and far more luxurious than anything he'd ever aspired to own. At times he felt as if his life there was temporary, as if he were only house-sitting until the rightful owner returned to reclaim it.

It was the same way he sometimes felt about Rachel—as if his time with her was doomed to be short-lived. At such moments of doubt, he was convinced that something was going to happen that would take her away from him. She was going to get bored with him, like his ex-girlfriends always did, and file for divorce. She was going to get diagnosed with terminal cancer. She was going to die in a car wreck. Something tragic was fated to occur that would tear them apart.

He had to learn how to let go of his baseless worries, and live in the moment. Carpe diem, as Rachel liked to say.

He poured a cup of coffee. He slid open a large counter drawer, where he'd stored one of his notebook computers, set it on the counter, and switched it on.

As the computer booted-up, he sipped coffee and looked around, feeling an odd yet compulsive need to reassure himself of the realness of his life.

Rachel had plunged into decorating their home with a passion. She'd had some rooms painted bold colors, deep reds and bright yellows; other areas were soothing shades of beige and green. Framed artwork adorned the walls, striking prints of ebony-hued men and women, photographs of beaches and oceans, and hand-carved, wooden figurines from Ghana decorated the end tables.

In celebration of the holiday season, a lush, lighted wreath garlanded the fireplace. A seven-foot high artificial Douglas fir towered in the family room, boughs bedecked with glittering ornaments and twinkling lights; an equally tall, similarly decorated tree stood in the living room near the bay window. Collectibles of honey-skinned Santa Clauses, angels, and elves stood here and there, spreading holiday cheer.

Virtually every room featured photos of them. Romantic snapshots of their honeymoon in Hawaii. Pictures of them at various restaurants, or attending parties with friends. Tons of photos from their wedding.

Although it was a large home, it was cozy, rich with the warmth of the life they had created together. Looking around took the edge off his anxiety. Turning back to the computer, he opened Microsoft Outlook to check his business e-mail.

Four months ago, he had left the graphic design firm where he'd been employed for several years and started a freelance graphic design business. He had long aspired to branch out on his own, but self-doubt had always prevented him from making the move.

Rachel had encouraged him to pursue his dream. She did very well with the hair salon, she said, and she could afford to keep up their household while he got his business up and running. "You're going to be successful," she had told him. "You're talented and hardworking. I know it's going to work for you."

Her confidence in him was all the push he needed. He launched Moore Designs with a few thousand dollars in start-up capital, a computer loaded with design software, and an iron determination to prove that his wife's faith in him was justified.

Business had been going well, better than he had expected. He specialized in book cover designs for small and large publishers, corporate identity packages, brochures, posters, and Web site design. Although he'd begun as a one-man shop and hadn't planned on hiring employees anytime soon, due to demand he'd begun farming out certain projects to independent contractors.

His e-mail client was unable to connect with the mail server. He tried to open Internet Explorer to browse the Web, and that didn't work either. Sporadic Internet connectivity was an issue he'd experienced frequently as of late. As much as he loved doing business online, it seemed to bring as many headaches as it did benefits.

While he was attempting to connect to the Web again, Rachel came downstairs, Coco trailing on her heels.

Rachel wore an oversized pink T-shirt, house slippers,

and glasses with thin designer frames. Her short hair puffed out in a curly halo. Watching her stroll toward him, the T-shirt clinging to her body, he felt a delicious heaviness in his center that almost made him forget about last night's brush with terror. Almost.

"Morning, baby," she said. "I thought we were going to sleep in?"

"Oh, well, I realized I needed to wrap up some pressing projects before the holidays," he said, which was partly true. "Coffee?"

"Of course."

He opened the cabinet and grabbed a coffee mug. He fumbled the cup. It clanged onto the Corian countertop, the impact chipping the mug's rim.

"Sorry," he said.

"You don't have to apologize." There was no harsh judgment in her eyes; there never was. "Happens to the best of us."

He carefully took out another cup and poured coffee for her. She took it from him, and then set it aside and came into his arms.

The top of her head barely reached the middle of his chest. Standing on her tiptoes, she tilted her head backward to look up at him.

"I love you," she said.

"Love you, too."

"You're the best thing that's ever happened to me. Ever."

"Okay." He smiled, a little taken aback by her affection. "Ditto."

"All right, Patrick Swayze."

She snuggled against him. Her body felt good against his, a perfect fit, as if this was exactly where both of them were supposed to be, enveloped in a gentle embrace.

At such moments, it was easy to believe in soul mates. In destiny. He was probably just a hopeless romantic, but sometimes he believed God had created Rachel just for him, and him for her.

But the memory of last night was a thorn pricking his thoughts.

"How'd you sleep?" he asked.

He felt her body tense.

"Fine." She moved out of his arms and picked up her coffee.

"Remember any bad dreams?"

She shook her head. She added cream and sugar to her coffee, stirred it with a spoon.

"Who were you fighting?"

The spoon slipped out of her fingers and clattered onto the countertop.

"What?" She picked up the spoon, frowning.

"You had a nightmare. You were kicking and swinging like you were fighting someone—you even started choking at one point. The whole time, you were screaming at a man. I know it was a man, because you called him a bastard."

The crease in her brow deepened. "I don't remember that at all."

"Not at all?"

She dropped her gaze, shook her head. "I have no idea who I could've been screaming at, either."

"Whoever it was, you were terrified of him."

Cupping the coffee mug in both hands, she shrugged.

"Dreams are just . . . well, dreams," she said. "They don't always hold a meaning—sometimes they do, I admit, but not always. How many times have you had a dream about something that was totally make-believe?"

"Pretty often. But you should've seen yourself, Rachel. I mean, you were really fighting."

"Did I kick the guy's ass?" She smiled mischievously.

"I don't know. I woke you up. I was getting worried."

"You should've let me sleep through it. I would've finished kicking this mystery guy's ass and then our conversation this morning would be, 'Baby, you were beating the hell out of somebody in your sleep last night. Hope it wasn't me.' "

She was trying to make him laugh, and it usually worked. But he pursed his lips tightly.

"I don't know," he said. "Thinking about how you were acting . . . it wasn't funny at all. Even Coco was upset."

Sitting between them, Coco glanced from him, to Rachel, as if corroborating his story.

"I'm sorry, but I don't know what else to tell you," she said. "As far as I'm concerned, it was just a meaningless nightmare that I can't remember. That happens to everyone sometimes."

From her tone, he could tell she didn't want to discuss the subject further.

"Sure, okay," he said.

Coco whined to be picked up. Rachel plucked the little dog off the floor and cradled her in her arms, cooed to her softly.

"Since we're not sleeping in, I'll get ready for work," she said.

"We can go back to bed. I can work later, no biggie."

"Nah, I better go." She stood on her tiptoes and gave him a quick kiss. "Busy time of year, baby. Sistas are beating our doors down with the holidays coming up."

He watched her return upstairs. The room was dull in her absence.

His thoughts doubled back to their conversation about her

nightmare, and the dream assailant. He didn't know who the nightmarish figure might have been—but he knew one thing for certain.

She had lied to him.

4

Rachel had lied to Joshua. Again.

As quickly as possible, she left home. The longer she stayed in Joshua's presence, the worse she felt about what she'd done.

She backed her silver Acura TL out of the garage and drove away from the house, winding through the subdivision of spacious homes and winter-browned lawns. It was a quarter to seven, but the December sun was still in hiding. Although she loved the holiday season, she disliked the late sunrises at that time of year. A shower of sun rays as she drove to work might have lifted her spirits.

Or perhaps not. She was burdened with such heavy thoughts that nothing might have improved her mood.

Why had she lied to Joshua—again? He was kind, honest, and loyal, the kind of man she'd longed to meet and had doubted she would ever find. He deserved the best she could give him of herself. He deserved the truth.

But the truth would break his heart.

Last night's dream was fresh in her mind. After she'd

awakened, Joshua believed she had fallen back to sleep, but when he shut off the lights she'd lain awake for almost an hour, worrying.

Worrying about *him*—the man whose name she dared not voice, not even internally, out of an almost superstitious fear that doing so would conjure him out of the ether like an evil spirit.

But she'd received very disturbing news about him yesterday. News that had almost certainly brought about her nightmare.

Don't think about it, girl. Worrying never solves anything, does it?

In typical Atlanta fashion, traffic was already heavy on Camp Creek Parkway, the four-lane road that snaked past their neighborhood all the way to the marketplace where her salon was located. Cars poured onto Camp Creek from intersecting streets that supported an ever-increasing number of residential communities.

In her three years living in Atlanta, she had watched the south side transformed from vast acres of silent fields and undisturbed forests of pine and elm into the metro area's hottest slice of real estate. Some people complained about the rapid pace of growth, but she welcomed it.

It was easier to stay hidden in a heavily populated area.

Stopping at a traffic light, she flipped down the sun visor and examined her face in the mirror. She wasn't looking for flaws, and she wasn't planning to apply makeup. She had been blessed with a blemish-free complexion that required only a light touch of cosmetics.

Instead, she was inspecting her new look.

Before moving to Atlanta, she'd worn contact lenses, instead of the thin frame glasses she now sported. Auburn was her natural hair color, and her lush mane had previously hung to the middle of her back. Upon relocating, she'd dyed her hair black and trimmed it to a cute, curly 'do.

If someone who'd known her before she came to Atlanta saw her today, they wouldn't recognize her. She hoped.

Ten minutes later, she parked in front of her salon, Belle Coiffure. The name was French for "beautiful hairstyle." She and Tanisha, her business partner, had opened the salon two years ago, and business had been booming from day one.

Certain individuals from her past had doubted her abilities, had told her she'd never amount to anything on her own. As the saying went, living well was the best revenge.

The Open sign was already aglow, the interior track lights shining brightly. When she pushed through the glass double-doors, she heard a gospel song by Mary, Mary rocking on the radio. Tanisha was organizing magazines in the waiting area—copies of *Essence, Hype Hair*, *Gospel Music Today*, *Ebony,* and other glossy periodicals.

"Morning, Tee," Rachel said. "I didn't expect you to be here already."

"Hey, girl," Tanisha said. "I've got a seven-fifteen. Otherwise, you know a sista wouldn't be rollin' in till eight."

Tanisha was a tall, light-skinned sister in her mid-thirties, with a sprinkle of chocolate freckles across her cheeks and a hairdo that changed weekly. This week, her brown hair was styled in a twisted up-do with highlights that accentuated her hazel eyes. It looked fabulous, of course. Tanisha believed that each stylist's own hair was her best form of advertising, and Rachel tended to agree.

Tanisha was the first friend Rachel had made when she'd moved to Atlanta. They had worked side-by-side at a shop in College Park. Both of them were driven, talented at their craft, and ambitious. It was only natural that they would decide to step out on faith and open their own salon together.

"You enjoy the party last night?" Rachel asked.

"It was real nice," Tanisha said. "Y'all had everything there—except single, fine men with good jobs."

"You know if I knew any single men, I'd hook you up."

"Single, fine men with good jobs, girl. Not single, buck-toothed, cross-eyed, broke-ass men."

In spite of her weariness, Rachel laughed.

"Girl, you just don't know," Tanisha said. "It's rough out there."

Tanisha had never been married, but she wanted to be. She'd wasted five years of her life playing house with a man who believed marriage was only a piece of paper. A year ago, she'd finally gotten fed up with his refusal to commit to a permanent arrangement. She had moved out, bought her own town house and a show-quality Pomeranian she'd named Mr. Bixby, and jumped back into the dating pool.

"You'll find someone," Rachel said.

"Easy for you to say. You're married."

"The man for you might not look exactly like you think he will, Tee. You've got to look at a man's character. Would you want a pretty boy with a good job—who beats you?"

"Hell, no. I wouldn't let any man touch me. Shit."

"You get my point. It's all about character."

"All I know is, you should thank God that you aren't out there any more. Josh is a sweetie."

Thinking of Joshua laid a leaden heaviness on her shoulders.

"I thank God every day," Rachel said, and sighed.

Tanisha frowned. "Hey, you feeling okay? You look exhausted."

She would never share anything about her dream—or what had produced it—with Tanisha. Although Tanisha was a good friend, Rachel had drawn a firm line between what she would share with friends such as Tanisha and what she would never share with anyone.

"Putting on the party was a lot of work," Rachel said. "I'm still kinda tired."

"When's your first appointment? Maybe you can catch a catnap."

"I've got an eight-thirty, so I may just do that."

Swinging her purse from over her shoulder, Rachel went down the center aisle of the salon, automatically surveying the sixteen stylist stations as she walked, to ensure that each would be ready for business when their stylists arrived. For most of the day, every chair would be occupied with a mix of walk-ins and appointments. If women believed in one thing, it was keeping their hair done. It was no surprise that Madame C. J. Walker, the inventor of the hot comb, had become America's first black woman millionaire.

In the back, behind a door marked STAFF ONLY, there was a supply closet, a staff lounge furnished with comfortable chairs, a sofa, a coffee table, and a TV, a restroom, and an enclosed office. The office contained a bank of filing cabinets and two desks, one for Rachel, the other for Tanisha.

She plopped into the swivel chair in front of her desk. The sofa in the lounge did look inviting . . . but she was afraid to go to sleep, for she might have another nightmare about *him*.

Besides, there was something else she needed to do first.

She unlocked the bottom drawer of her desk. Inside, there was a plastic bag from Walgreen's Pharmacy, sitting atop a black metal case.

She took the bag inside the restroom.

It contained an early pregnancy test kit.

She spoke a prayer, and tore open the box.

5

On Monday morning, after spending the weekend at the hideout in central Illinois, Dexter finally returned to Chicago.

Before leaving, he thoroughly wiped down the house for fingerprints, and he vacuumed for hairs, too. It was highly unlikely that the law would trace him to the place, but taking such precautions was second nature. Once a cop, always a cop.

The story of the missing prison transport van, guards, and inmate had been circulating on the news since Saturday. The reports featured a penitentiary mug shot in which he wore his beard. Although the cops had not formally announced a manhunt, the machinery would be revving up, and within a few more days—sooner if they discovered the sunken vehicle and its gruesome cargo—the machine would be rolling at full steam across the entire region.

It didn't concern him. When the subject of escape inevitably came up in bullshit conversations with fellow inmates—inmates jawed about what they'd do if they broke free like regular folk talked about what they'd do with lottery jackpot winnings—he'd always said that if he got away, he would go to Brazil. He had no more intentions to flee to Brazil than he did the moon, but the gossipy inmates would do the job of spreading disinformation and muddling the cops' search.

It was a clear, crisp morning. The Chevy Caprice, though ten years old, was in good condition, outfitted with a new set of tires.

He slipped on a cheap pair of sunglasses that he found clipped to the sun visor, and started the engine.

He tuned to a radio station that played music from the seventies, when music was music—unlike the bullshit that dominated radio airwaves today. He motored down the highway to the tunes of Earth, Wind, and Fire, Sly and the Family Stone, The Ohio Players, Parliament-Funkadelic, and other classic sounds. He sang along loudly to just about every song, sometimes flubbing the lyrics but pushing on anyway.

At a gas station, he refilled the tank. He had to go inside to pay with cash. A potbellied, hayseed cop was at the food counter getting his daily fix of free coffee and donuts. He glanced at Dexter, but it was the bland, appraising look that cops tended to give everyone.

Shortly before noon, the downtown Chicago skyline came into view on the horizon. Warm tears unexpectedly pushed at his eyes.

Goddamn, it felt good to be going home.

A half-hour later, he took the exit for Ninety-fifth Street, the major east-west road on the South Side. It wasn't a direct route to his destination, but he wanted to drive around for a little while, immerse himself again in the city that had been his home for thirty-four of his thirty-eight years.

In spite of the cold weather—it was in the mid-thirties and the infamous hawk was out in full force—people were hanging out on street corners. They were most of them young brothers, in their late teens or twenties, clad in parkas and skully caps, talking shit and looking hard at everyone driving or walking past. They reminded him of inmates milling in the yard: grown men who had nothing productive to do with their time. The jagged skyline of downtown was visible in the hazy distance, but the business that took place within those towers was as meaningless to these men as constellations in the night sky, light years' distant.

At one time or another, he had probably rousted a few of those brothers, or someone they knew. Good times.

He hit Forty-seventh Street, which took him to Bronzeville, an area once known as the "Black Metropolis" because of all the black movers and shakers who'd once lived in the neighborhood. By the time he had been born, the only movers and shakers around were the thugs who controlled the high-rise slums. The inevitable wave of gentrification had eventually demolished the projects, though, and single family homes and condos had been erected in their place.

The home in which he had lived before his bid in the joint was a one-story, brick, with three bedrooms, built in 1905. It stood along a row of similarly old, elegant properties flanked by skeletal, ice-encrusted trees.

He slowly cruised past the house. It was in good condition, the front yard mantled with snow.

In his so-called divorce, the judge had allowed him to keep the place, since he'd lived there long before he had married the bitch and she displayed no interest in taking the house anyway. As if she were so eager to sever her ties with him. It compounded the insult of her betrayal.

The home had long been paid off, and stood vacant. Javier had paid the property taxes each year and hired a lawn service to cut the grass during the summer months. He was a loyal partner.

Dexter circled around the block, checking for surveillance vehicles. He found none, which meant either that the manhunt had not yet progressed to the city—or, more likely, someone was off taking a lunch break.

He parked around the corner, under a gigantic oak. He rummaged in the duffel bag on the passenger seat, found the hammer he had taken from Javier's hideout, and stuffed it inside his parka.

He also pocketed the Glock.

He went back to the house on foot. Snow and ice crackled under his boots. There was light traffic, no police cruisers.

He crossed the walkway that led to the front door and marched around the side of the house, to the back. A brown, two-car garage stood behind the house, bracketed by snow.

A thermometer was affixed beside the garage door, in the same position where he'd mounted it several years ago. He peeled off his gloves and opened the concealed slot at the base.

A key dropped into his palm.

The key fit the back door. He pushed open the door and stepped into the kitchen.

It was like going back in time. All the furniture was still there, though cobwebs draped the lights and dust covered the counters. Amazingly, the bitch had left with nothing but the clothes on her back.

Most important, the Turkish travertine floor tiles he'd installed were still in place, as was the refrigerator. It was unplugged, but occupied the wall niche for which it was intended.

Uncharacteristically, his pulse had begun to race.

Before going farther, however, he drew his Glock and searched the house. Squatters were always a potential problem in vacant properties.

The house was clear. It was tempting to linger in the various rooms and reflect on old times, but he quickly went back to the kitchen.

He grabbed the sides of the refrigerator and dragged it out of its wall slot, until he had hauled it completely clear of the space. A black oil drip mat lay on the floor where the refrigerator had stood, ostensibly to protect the tiles.

The presence of the mat was an encouraging sign. But his pulse still raced.

He knelt, peeled away the mat, and tossed it aside. He withdrew the hammer from his coat and used the hooked end to loosen the stone tile in the upper right corner.

Once that piece was free, he began to remove the tiles surrounding it, gradually exposing the concrete slab on which the house had been constructed.

A gray, fireproof safe had been sunk in the concrete. It was about two feet long, twenty inches wide, and one foot deep.

At the sight of it, he smiled.

He wiped sweat from his brow with the back of his gloved hand, and carefully spun through the combination. He turned the lever and raised the heavy hinged lid.

"No," he said, breathless.

The box was empty.

One point seven million dollars, in rubber-banded denominations of twenties, fifties, and hundreds, had been stored in the safe, and now it was gone.

6

Price Electronics operated out of a brick storefront on Main Street in Fairburn, sitting alongside a row of businesses that included a pizzeria, an antiques shop, a hardware store, and an Internet café. Part of a historic commercial district, the one- to three-story buildings had been constructed in a range of styles, from Italianate to Neoclassical, and most included awnings that contributed to the downtown street's nostalgic vibe.

Joshua pulled his Ford Explorer into a parking slot in front of the electronics shop, grabbed his laptop off the seat, and headed inside. A bell above the door chimed at his entrance.

The shelves were packed with electronics from almost floor to ceiling. Except for the computers, the items for sale were mostly cutting-edge gadgets and arcane parts, the purposes of which eluded Joshua. Heavy metal played on the in-store stereo.

Tim Price, the proprietor of the business and a friend of

Joshua's since high school, sat behind the long glass counter typing furiously on a BlackBerry, a messy mop of brown hair obscuring his face. Tattoos webbed his gangly arms—colorful renderings of dragons, griffins, and more otherworldly imagery.

Tim drove a custom-painted purple Chrysler PT Cruiser that continued the fantastical theme, sword-bearing warriors, gruesome orcs, long-bearded wizards, and slavering giant monsters adorning the body, like a mobile advertisement for *Dungeons & Dragons.* During their high school days, Tim had been a hardcore role-player and probably would have spent his days playing as a grown man if not for the shop.

Tim looked up, rose from his chair. He was nearly as tall as Joshua. He wore a white T-shirt with the slogan, ANIMALS TASTE GOOD, beneath which were shapes of fish, chicken, cattle, and pigs.

"Big Jay," Tim said. They slapped hands.

"Nice shirt," Joshua said.

"I've already offended one customer today. Some vegan guy."

"Don't you ever worry that wearing shirts like that might cost you business?"

He shrugged. "Screw 'em if they can't take a joke."

Although Tim had earned an electrical engineering degree from Georgia Tech, he'd worked in the shop all his life. His grandfather had launched the store in the seventies and passed it down to his father, who had then given it to Tim about five years ago. They specialized in the sort of obscure consumer electronics that only tech junkies cared about, and a large part of their business was doing repairs.

Joshua placed his notebook computer on the counter.

"I've been having issues getting connected to the Internet," he said. "Rachel's laptop works fine, so I know the problem is with my machine."

Tim raised the laptop's lid.

"Wireless connection?"

"Yeah, you set it up at my house, remember."

"That's right." Tim snapped his fingers. "I'll run some diagnostics. You might've inadvertently downloaded spyware or a virus, corrupted some files. That crap's all over the Web these days, dude."

"I can't do much work until it's fixed. When can you get to it?"

Tim checked his watch. There was an image of Mickey Mouse on the watch face.

"Mickey Mouse?" Joshua asked.

"He kicks ass." Tim's face was serious.

"Mickey Mouse?" Joshua asked again.

Tim broke into a grin. "You got me. Conversation piece. You noticed, didn't you?"

"You're a weirdo."

"So? I know my shit. You can be as weird as you want if you're good at your job. Einstein was eccentric, but we celebrate his genius."

"The only one who celebrates your genius is you."

Tim gave him the finger.

"Anyway, dude, I'll have an answer for you on this by four. How's that?"

"That's cool. I'm about to go have lunch with Eddie."

"You didn't invite me. Is it a black thing or something?"

Joshua laughed. "We've invited you to lunch plenty of times, but we can't ever get you out of this shop."

"In case you haven't noticed, Josh, I'm the only employee. I can't leave."

"Hire some help then."

"I don't trust anyone else to know what they're doing. I've got a family legacy to live up to here."

"Sounds like a personal problem to me."

"Man, get out of here before I decide to start charging you for all the work I do."

7

Joshua and Eddie met for lunch at the Busy Bee Café in the West End, an older area of Atlanta that included the Atlanta University Center—colleges such as Spelman, Morehouse, Morris Brown, and Clark Atlanta. Eddie was an assistant football coach at Clark, and lived in the neighborhood. When he and Joshua met for lunch, the popular soul food joint was usually the chosen spot.

Around half-past noon, the restaurant was packed with college students, school faculty, cops, and business people. The air was redolent with the savory aromas of fried chicken, pork chops, mac-and-cheese, and other southern specialties that guaranteed a coronary if you weren't careful to exercise moderation.

The décor was simple: brown vinyl booths, narrow tables, a long counter, and walls plastered with dining awards and signed photos of celebrities and politicians. You didn't go there for the ambience. The food was the main draw.

A waitress with a short, neatly trimmed Afro took their orders: fried chicken, collard greens, and candied yams for

Eddie; a fried catfish sandwich and fries for Joshua. Both of them requested glasses of sweet tea.

"I don't know how you can eat here every week and stay so thin," Joshua said. "I have to watch myself."

"It's genetic." Eddie patted his flat stomach. "Like my pops. That man's been eating fried chicken and pork chops three times a week for his whole life and he still only weighs a buck fifty. Blood pressure's getting too damn high, though."

"Nothing that tastes good is ever good for you, seems like."

The waitress delivered their iced teas. Eddie picked up the glass and took a long sip.

"So, has something happened since I saw you last night, man?" Eddie asked. "Or did you just want the pleasure of my company?"

Joshua smiled wryly. He couldn't fool Eddie with small talk. They had been friends for far too long.

"I don't know how to put this," Joshua said. "But do you ever get the feeling that you never truly know someone?"

"All the time. Ariel shocks the hell outta me with something at least once a week." Eddie grinned with evident satisfaction. "Welcome to married life—finally."

"I know, you think I've been living in some wedded-bliss dream world for the past six months—and maybe I have," Joshua said. "But I think this is something different."

"What do you mean?"

Joshua pushed up his glasses on the bridge of his nose. "You can't tell anyone what I'm going to tell you. This stays between me and you."

" 'Course."

"I think Rachel's got some secrets. About her past. Stuff she's never told me about and doesn't want to tell me about."

"Don't we all?" Eddie shrugged. "Damn, I thought you were gonna say something serious."

"This is serious. It all started when she had a nightmare last night. She was fighting some guy in her dream. When I asked her about it this morning, she said she didn't remember any of it, had no idea who she might've been struggling with."

"Maybe she doesn't. Do you always remember your dreams? I sure don't."

"I know but . . ." Joshua sighed. "I thought she was lying, that's all."

"She could've been. She might not have wanted to talk about it, 'cause it would dredge up bad memories."

"I guess so."

"All I know is, everyone has secrets, some of 'em good, some of 'em bad," Eddie said. "You haven't told Rachel *everything* about yourself, right?"

"I've told her the most important stuff about me."

"All of it?" Eddie's gaze was keen. "Every deep, dark secret?"

"I don't have any deep, dark secrets."

"Maybe you don't. But some folks do, dawg. Some people have been through some rough shit in their lives—shit they don't want to tell anyone, including a spouse. You've gotta respect that."

"You think I'm overreacting?"

"Nah, I think you're just starting to learn what being married is all about. You can't sweat every little detail about your wife. She's not gonna be perfect, just like you aren't perfect. But you've gotta love her anyway for who she is, overall."

"I guess I'll let it go."

"Rachel's a great woman. You two have a good thing going. You'll hit a rough patch every now and then, like most married folk do . . . but there's no sense in rocking the boat without having a good reason."

"Let's hope I never have a reason, then," Joshua said.

"Nah, man," Eddie said sagely, shaking his head. "You're gonna have a reason one day, trust me. But you better hope that when you have one, that boat doesn't sink."

8

Sitting in the ice-box cold Chevy around the corner from the house, Dexter used his prepaid cell to call Javier at an agreed-upon number. He answered on the second ring.

"Yo," Javier said. "Wassup, boss?"

"It's gone."

"Huh? What's gone?"

"My money."

"What?" Javier nearly shouted.

"All of it. Gone."

"Jesus fucking Christ. Where'd you put it, man?"

Javier sounded genuinely shocked. He would be. He hadn't stolen the cash. He was loyal.

"It was in the house," Dexter said. "In a floor safe in the kitchen. It's all gone."

"Fuck." Javier made a grunt of disgust.

When Dexter had gotten convicted, Javier had offered to store the money for him until he either was released, or broke out. *I've got it under control,* Dexter had told him. Besides, if IAD had opened an investigation into their narc squad activities—always a possibility—not even Javier, as trustworthy and cunning as he was, could have guaranteed the safety of Dexter's savings. The floor safe had served perfectly for a decade.

"She took it," Dexter said. "Probably hired a locksmith to crack the lock, paid him by sucking his dick."

"You told her about it?"

"Use your motherfuckin' head, man. I didn't tell her shit."

"I didn't think you did. She musta peeped it some kinda way, took it when you got sent downstate. How fucked up. Jesus."

Dexter clenched his gloved hand into a fist. It was worse than fucked up. It was, as the saying went, FUBAR—fucked up beyond all recognition.

The secret stash that he'd built represented ten years of backbreaking, dirty police work. Bribes from suspects. Under-the-table payments from hip-hop stars who toured in the city and wanted dependable security from an off-duty cop. Loot he and the other narc cops scored from shaking down drug dealers. Money they earned from stealing cocaine from evidence rooms, replacing it with Bisquick, and reselling the product on the street to the highest bidder.

His rationale for accumulating the money was simple: The system was rife with corruption, from the courts all the way down to the beat cop on the corner, and he was going to get his, by any means necessary. His long-dead dad, a small-time hustler and pimp in his day, had lectured him about how to acquire anything you desired. You couldn't just do your job and expect that because you were a nice, honest guy, you'd get the raise you deserved. No, if you wanted something—money, women, power, anything—you had to do what real men had been doing since time immemorial.

You had to take it.

It was why he'd become a cop, and not a hood like his old

man. Dad had always been running from the law, always coughing up payments to cops so he could stay in business. Dexter didn't want to be the guy on the run paying bribes. He wanted to be on the receiving end of all those sweet fringe benefits—using his badge and any amount of force necessary to take whatever he wanted.

Turned out he was damned good at it. Thanks to his leadership, Javier and the other members of the old team would retire from the CPD with a helluva lot more to fall back on than a cop's pension. With incarceration jamming up his own retirement plans, he'd intended, upon his escape, to use the money to fund his exodus overseas. Many African nations lacked an extradition treaty with the United States, and in such a country, the sum he had earned would have allowed him to live like a sultan.

But once again, the bitch was going to try to rob him of his freedom. He didn't doubt that she, and not someone else, had discovered the money. She'd never been loyal to him, and where there was smoke, there was fire.

"I was going to track her down anyway before I left," Dexter said. "Now she's given me all the more reason to find her ass."

"Explains how she vanished into thin air like she did," Javier said. "She had your loot backing her."

"With one point seven mil, I'd say the bitch could go just about anywhere she fucking well pleases."

"One point seven? That much?" Javier whistled. "You need any funds in the interim, man? Something to tide you over?"

"No more favors. I'll handle it."

"What's your plan then?"

"Everyone who helped her get away . . . everyone she loves," Dexter said, "I'm going to fucking kill them. It's a simple matter of respect, wouldn't you say?"

"Yeah, man." Javier paused. "But what about her?"

"What do you think I'm going to do to her?" Dexter said.

"I . . . I guess I don't wanna know, boss."

"The bitch better have my money—down to the last dollar. After she gives it to me, I'm gonna make her wish her mama had used the fucking coat hanger."

9

That evening at home, Rachel cooked dinner. She was an excellent cook, and Joshua loved to observe her at work. As he sat at the dinette table, skimming the newspaper, he watched her.

Dressed in a flannel shirt, lounge pants, and slippers, she flitted around the kitchen like a hummingbird around a flower garden, adding a sprinkle of spices here, tasting the sauce there, all the while singing in a soft, soothing voice. Under normal circumstances, she derived great pleasure from cooking, and that night, she seemed to be in an especially buoyant mood.

It puzzled him. Earlier, he'd been convinced that she was keeping something important from him, and he'd planned to watch her closely at dinner, just to be sure nothing was wrong. Eddie had advised him to let it go, and he wanted to—but he couldn't. Not while the uneasiness lingered in his gut like an undigested meal.

"Dinner's ready," Rachel said, taking silverware out of the drawer. "Go wash up, baby."

He pushed away from the table. He nearly knocked over the chair, and caught it before it hit the floor. Coco, who'd been resting nearby, scurried away and hid between Rachel's legs.

"Sorry, Coco," he said. "Scared you half to death, didn't I?"

He glanced at Rachel, habitually expecting a rebuke for his clumsiness, but she only smiled—a smile of unconditional love and infinite patience. Not the smile of a woman who nursed deception in her heart.

Maybe his suspicions were totally off-base. There was a pleasant evening ahead—good food, lively conversation, perhaps tender lovemaking—and it seemed foolish to spoil it by dwelling on theories of how she might be deceiving him.

Eddie was right. He needed to let it go.

When he returned to the kitchen after washing his hands, Rachel was setting dinner on the table: shrimp scampi over linguine, sautéed zucchini, and garlic bread. Coco followed at her heels, waiting for a morsel to drop.

"Need any help?" he asked.

"You could turn on some music, light a few candles."

"Special occasion?"

"Maybe."

He turned on the satellite radio system and tuned it to one of their favorite R&B channels. Then he got two candles out of a cabinet, placed them inside the frosted glass hurricane lamps on the table, and carefully lit them.

They often drank wine with dinner. But after Rachel dimmed the recessed lights, she took a bottle of sparkling white grape juice out of the refrigerator.

"You mind doing the honors?" She handed the bottle to him. "I would've gotten champagne, but . . ."

"We *are* celebrating something." Sitting, he twisted off the cap and filled the two wine goblets on the table.

"We're celebrating us," she said.

"Us?"

"Us finding each other. Falling in love. Getting married. Being happy. Do we need a special occasion to celebrate those things?"

"Not at all."

They bowed their heads and said grace. Then they heaped their plates with food and began to eat.

"This looks delicious." He spun linguine around his fork and speared a shrimp. "My mom's a good cook, but she can't touch you."

"Please, don't ever say that around her. She hates me enough as it is."

He winced. His mom had been nasty toward Rachel from the beginning, considered her a corrupting influence on him. He had never understood why his mother felt that way toward her, but there was much that he would never understand about his mom.

"Hate is a pretty strong word," he said.

"How about 'intense dislike'? She has an intense dislike for me. She thinks I stole her precious little baby away from her, to corrupt him."

"She's a little overly protective, that's all."

"A little?"

He laughed. "Okay, she gets out of control, sometimes, I admit. But she means well. She'll grow to love you in time."

"I'm not holding my breath." She chewed a piece of garlic toast. "But maybe she was right about the corrupting part. If she only knew what we did in the bedroom . . ."

He felt her foot slide under the cuff of his jeans and tease his calf. A warm, delicious rush of desire spread through his center.

"You must not want me to finish dinner," he said.

"Sorry, I'm a bad girl." She pulled her foot away, winked. "That's how we messed around and got the first one."

He was bringing the fork to his lips, but her remark made him pause.

"The first one?" he asked.

"When I said we were celebrating us, I meant it." She set down her fork, drew in a deep breath. She blinked, and he saw tears welling in her eyes.

His heart whammed.

"Are you about to tell me . . ."

"I'm pregnant," she said.

"Pregnant?"

"Yes, *pregnant.*" She was nodding, tears spilling down her cheeks. "I took an early pregnancy test this morning—twice to be sure—and it was positive. I'm pregnant with our baby, Josh. You're going to be a daddy."

10

Rachel's announcement left Joshua buzzing for the rest of the evening. She was pregnant. *Pregnant.* He was going to be a father. *A father.*

They had not exactly been trying to conceive, but they hadn't been trying to prevent it, either. Their attitude was that when the time was right, the baby would come. A child was a blessing from God. No one could entirely control the granting of a blessing.

He had an almost irrepressible urge to call everyone he knew and share the good news, but Rachel promised him to silence. She wanted to visit her OB-GYN and confirm the pregnancy with another test, to be absolutely sure. She also advised him that until she passed the first trimester, it would be unwise to tell the whole world about the baby, because in the early stages there was always the possibility of a miscarriage.

In the meantime, she wanted him to keep the news under wraps. He reluctantly agreed to her request, though walking around with the secret was going to drive him nuts. There was so much to think about, so much to plan . . . he felt as if he were going to pop like a balloon.

I'm going to be a dad. I can't believe it.

Although he and Eddie had talked about fatherhood often, it seemed incredible that he would soon join the club. He still felt like a big kid himself. To imagine being responsible for a child's welfare, offering guidance, serving as an example of manhood. It was impossible to wrap his mind around the thought.

He had assumed he would be awake all night, riding high on excitement, but he wound up falling asleep shortly before midnight, exhausted, like a kid who'd eaten too much candy crashing after the sugar rush faded. Rachel climbed in bed, found a comfortable spot in his arms, and drifted asleep, too.

When he awoke sometime later that night, she was gone.

He glanced toward the bathroom. The door was shut, but blackness framed the doorway. She wasn't in there.

He thought about the nightmare she'd had last night. What if she was sleepwalking this time, fleeing her mysterious dream villain?

It was a melodramatic idea—Rachel might have padded downstairs only to get a glass of water—but he couldn't discount it. With her announcement of her pregnancy, he felt an instinctual drive to protect her from all harm. That included Rachel accidentally hurting herself while in the throes of a bad dream.

He put on his glasses. The clock read a quarter past three.

He shuffled into the hallway. It was dark. No light filtered up there from downstairs, which it would have if she were in the kitchen.

He was about to call her name, when he heard a clicking sound coming from the room at the end of the hallway. Rachel's office.

Quietly, he moved down the hall. The door was cracked open about an inch, giving him a narrow view.

Rachel sat before her desk, typing on her laptop. The silvery glow from the display was the only light source in the study, imbuing her face with a ghostly pallor.

What was she doing in here at a quarter past three o'clock in the morning?

He gazed at the screen. He could make out a few words. He leaned forward—and accidentally bumped against the door.

She whirled with a gasp.

"It's only me," he said.

She put her hand to her chest, sighed.

"You scared me."

"I saw you'd gotten out of bed." He stepped inside the room. "What are you doing up?"

"Oh, only reading about pregnancy and newborns." She hit a button on the keyboard, closing the programs she had opened. "I'm so excited I can't sleep. I figured as long as I was awake, I'd do some research."

He wished there was sufficient light in the room to reveal her eyes, because he was positive that she was lying to him. He knew what he'd seen on the screen, and it had nothing to do with pregnancies and babies.

"When are you coming back to bed?" he asked.

"Right now, actually." She switched off the computer. Within seconds, the display went black, and darkness fell over the room.

She brushed past him as she left the office. "Coming?"

He glanced at the blackened screen once more.

"Coming," he finally said, and followed her to the bedroom.

11

Lying in bed together, Rachel cuddled against him. He stared at the dark ceiling, but didn't close his eyes.

"Thinking about our baby?" she said.

"Yeah." *And other things.*

"Justin Anthony Moore," she said.

Shortly after their marriage, they had picked out possible baby names for a boy, or a girl. Rachel had approached the task with an intensity that approached obsession, as if determining a name in advance somehow secured their child's future.

"What if we have a girl?" he asked.

"We're going to have a boy."

"It's way too early to tell, Rachel."

"I don't care about what the ultrasound might tell us. I know what I feel."

"I only want a healthy baby. Boy or girl, it doesn't matter to me."

"A healthy baby . . . that's what I want, too." She was silent for a minute. "Love, do you ever think of going away?"

"Going away?"

"You know, like having a sanctuary . . . from the world. Somewhere you could be totally safe . . . without a care at all."

"Like a getaway or something?"

"Hmmm . . . like that."

"To get away from who?"

"No one in particular. Life . . . the world. Just the four of us—you, me, Justin . . . the dog."

"A secluded getaway would be nice," he said. "Maybe we can buy one if we start playing the lottery."

"Maybe . . ." Her voice had softened to a whisper.

"Where would you want it to be?"

"Somewhere that . . . no one . . . knows about . . ."

"Such as?"

She didn't answer. Her breathing had deepened. She was drifting asleep.

He lay awake a while longer, mulling over their strange conversation and what he had seen on her computer screen, and eventually, he drifted to sleep, too.

12

He awoke at seven-thirty to find that Rachel had already left for work.

There was a note on the dresser, written in her elegant script: *Hey, sleepyhead. Will call with time for OB-GYN appt. Love, R.*

At the mention of the doctor, giddiness bubbled through him all over again. But the memory of how Rachel had lied about her late-night Web research quickly put a damper on his excitement.

On his way downstairs to brew coffee, he paused at the threshold of her study. He pushed open the door.

The answers to his questions might reside on her computer. If he looked, Rachel would never know.

But he hesitated. He wasn't one of those rude individuals who took malicious pleasure in digging through another's belongings. His mother was nosy like that. He harbored bad memories of her rooting through his drawers and closets, looking for anything she could use to make his life miserable.

He turned away from the study and went downstairs. He brewed a pot of coffee. Tim had repaired his computer yesterday afternoon as promised, so he took the laptop to his office and started to work on some initial design ideas for a new client.

His office was located directly beneath Rachel's study. Although it was surely his vivid graphic artist's imagination at work, he thought he could sense her computer up there, tempting him to uncover its secrets.

Finally, he pushed out of the chair and strode upstairs, walking so fast that Coco, sleeping on the sofa in the family room, stirred awake and chased after him, curious about his urgent mission.

He rushed into Rachel's study and punched the laptop's power button.

The machine whirred, proceeding through the boot-up cycle. He sat in the desk chair, started to adjust the height to accommodate his legs, and stopped himself. If he neglected to readjust the chair, she would know he'd been in there.

Sweat coated his forehead. By doing this, he was crossing a line in their marriage, admitting to himself that he no longer trusted her, and there would be consequences to pay for his actions, if not to Rachel, then to his own conscience.

Coco had not entered the room. The little dog sat on her haunches on the threshold, and he swore that her bubble-eyed gaze was accusatory.

"I don't have any choice," he said to the dog, as if the animal would tattle on him. "I have to know what's going on."

The computer reached the Welcome screen. In a log-on box, the username field was populated by his wife's first name, but the cursor blinked in the password field—which was empty.

He clicked the OK button, hoping that the system would grant him access without a password.

It beeped and flashed a pop-up message: *Please enter a password.*

"Shit," he said.

He drummed a tattoo on the desk. He glanced at Coco, typed the dog's name, and hit Enter.

Incorrect password.

He typed his own name.

Incorrect password.

Rachel's salon.

Incorrect password.

"Damn it, what is it then?"

He leaned backward, the chair springs squeaking. He looked around the study. Gazed at her collection of dog figurines sitting on a shelf, the novels and business texts that packed the bookcase, the photograph of a sun-splashed beach standing on the corner of the desk.

Hunched forward, he began to type in anything that came to mind, combinations of numbers and letters, her birth date, their anniversary, his own birth date, the name of her favorite restaurant. . . .

None of them worked.

He spun away from the computer. His knee bumped against the desk and set a ballpoint pen rolling across the desktop. It dropped into a small trash can.

He reached inside the can to retrieve the pen. His fingers brushed across a crumpled piece of paper.

He pulled out the pen, and the paper. He unfurled the paper on his lap.

It was a print-out of a Web page. Unfortunately, the ink cartridge had run dry while printing the document; the text was so faint it was virtually unreadable.

He raised the page to the overhead light.

He could make out four words: *Illinois Department of Corrections.*

There was other text, but it was too pale for him to decipher.

He checked the trash can again. It contained only a discarded wrapper from a black ink cartridge. Nothing else.

Apparently, Rachel had printed this document, seen the low-quality of the text, and had then replaced the cartridge. After which, she presumably reprinted the page.

There was a two-drawer filing cabinet on the other side of the room. He opened the drawers, found the expected files: documents for their home, insurance, tax returns, marriage certificate, financial investments. Nothing suspicious.

He examined the page again.

He'd at least learned why he'd seen the term "correctional center" on her laptop last night—not something that would have been found on a Web site about childbirth and babies. She'd been researching the Illinois prison system.

But why?

On the screen, the pulsing cursor mocked him.

A painful idea occurred to him: if he knew his wife better, he would know her password. If they were truly soul mates, as he believed, he would understand how her mind worked, would be able to figure out the secret pass code she would create.

The realization brought an even more hurtful truth: if their marriage was stronger, she wouldn't be hiding anything like this from him in the first place.

The phone on the desk rang. According to Caller ID, the call was coming from Rachel's salon.

He grabbed the phone and left her study for the hallway.

"Hey, love," she said. "Whatcha up to?"

"Just working."

"You okay? You sound kinda weird."

"I'm fine. Just been busy this morning."

"I won't keep you then. I wanted to let you know that my

appointment with the OB-GYN is for two o'clock. Still want to come?"

"Definitely. Where's the doctor's office?"

She gave him the address, and told him to call her if he didn't think he'd be able to make it. He assured her that he would be there.

"You sure everything's okay, love?" she asked again.

"Everything's fine. I'll see you soon."

He hung up.

Now, both of them were lying to each other.

13

After spending the night in a seedy South Side motel that rented rooms by the hour, Dexter left the city for the northern suburbs.

It was an overcast morning, the gray clouds shedding snowflakes. In the slippery snow, he was careful to keep the Chevy under the speed limit. He couldn't afford an accident, or any incident that would attract the attention of law enforcement.

Around ten o'clock, he arrived in the city of Zion.

Although he had grown up in Chicago, forty-five minutes south, until he'd met his wife he'd never visited the tiny burb. The downtown strip was a conglomeration of mom-and-pop stores and mainstream establishments. Old split-level homes and ranches dominated the neighborhoods. There was a church on almost every corner, and most of the streets had biblical names: Enoch, Bethel, Ezekiel, Gabriel, and the like, harking back to the town's founding as a religious community.

His wife had told him that, until a few years ago, they

hadn't even allowed the sale of alcohol within city limits. It was little wonder that she had left for Chi-town, where he'd met her working in his cousin's hair salon.

His wife's aunt, her closest surviving relative, lived in Zion. While he was incarcerated, and the letters that he mailed to her at their house came back as undeliverable, and his attempts to call her revealed a disconnected number, he became positive that his wife had moved back to Zion to be near her aunt.

Several times, he'd attempted to collect call her aunt from prison. Predictably, the old bitch had refused to accept the calls.

Her aunt lived on the west side of town, in a neighborhood of brick ranches with large yards, winter-stripped elms, and ice-mantled pines. He slowly crawled past her house.

Like the other homes in the neighborhood, hers was a brick ranch, accessible via a long, snow-covered walkway. A Christmas tree stood in the front window, merry lights twinkling.

He wondered if the old bitch might have moved—perhaps into a nursing home or a grave. Then he saw the wooden plate on the mailbox that stated *The Leonards* in scrolling script.

She still lived there.

There were no newspapers piled on the porch or driveway. She'd been a stickler for following the daily news. The lack of a paper lying outside meant that she'd already plucked it off the ground, which probably meant that she was home.

He parked a couple of doors down, shut off the engine, and waited. He watched, patiently.

Occasionally, a car grumbled past, tires spitting up snow. A few houses down, a kid came outdoors with a golden retriever, and the child and dog tumbled through the snow until a woman yelled at them to come back inside.

Two hours later, no one had emerged from the house. It was another freezing day, however, and old folks tended to stay indoors in such weather, their brittle bones unable to withstand the low temperatures.

He pulled his knit cap low over his head.

He already had the Glock and the switchblade stashed inside his jacket.

He climbed out of the Chevy and crunched through the slush. A white delivery van rumbled down the road, and he waited for it to pass before he crossed the street.

He trudged toward the house. Thick, hard snow carpeted the walkway. She probably paid a neighborhood kid to shovel the walk, and hadn't gotten around to having it done yet for the most recent snowfall.

A short set of concrete steps, caked with ice, led to the front door. A half-full bag of salt stood nearby, next to an aluminum snow shovel.

He reached inside the bag and got a handful of salt. He tossed the granules across the steps.

Then he picked up the shovel. Returning to the end of the walkway, he began to scrape snow and ice off the pavement, tossing it aside into the yard.

When he had gotten deep into his work and had cleared off half the path, the front door finally creaked open.

Back turned to the house, he continued to shovel, as if he were only a good neighbor concerned about the snow piling up on an elderly lady's property. Slowly he worked his way backward along the path, drawing closer to the doorway.

"Excuse me," she said. Her cultured voice retained some of the authority of the elementary school teacher she'd been before her retirement. "Excuse me, sir?"

He kept his back to her, kept shoveling, kept inching backward.

He heard the door creak open wider.

"Excuse me, *sir,*" she said. "I appreciate your shoveling off my walkway, but do I know you?"

Only a couple of feet from the porch, he spun around.

Betty stood in the doorway, bifocals perched on the edge of her nose. She wore a white sweatshirt and matching pants and held a tea cup.

When she saw his face, the cup slipped out of her fingers and shattered on the porch steps.

"I'm a little offended, Betty," he said. "How could you ever forget me?"

"Dexter . . . oh, Jesus . . ."

"Long time no see, bitch," he said, and slammed the shovel against her head.

14

The office of Rachel's OB-GYN was located in College Park, just off Old National Highway. Joshua's parents lived less than ten minutes away, so he decided to visit them before he met Rachel for her appointment.

Old National Highway, the city's main drag, was a winding, four-lane road of strip malls, fast-food joints, nightclubs, pawn shops, currency exchanges, barber shops, hair salons, and liquor stores. The dome of a mega-church rose in the distance, resembling a pro sports arena.

Farther along the highway, retail gave way to residential development. Builders had recently discovered the area and were busy erecting the same sprawl of cookie-cutter subdivisions that consumed much of metro Atlanta.

His parents lived in an older section of town, in a neighborhood of Craftsman bungalows, ranches, and old Colonials. Oaks, elms, and maples stretched bare branches into the cloudy afternoon sky.

He parked in the driveway of their ranch house. Although it was midday, his parents were retired, and usually home.

The garage door was open, so he went in via that way. His father had his head stuck under the hood of a yellow Oldsmobile Ninety-Eight that looked as if it hadn't burned gas in a decade.

"Hey, Dad," Joshua said.

His father slid from under the hood like a man extricating himself from the maw of a whale. With skin the color of aged oak, he was a small, compact man, standing about five-six; Joshua had inherited his size from his mother's branch of the family.

A dirty cotton towel peeked from a pocket of his dad's jumpsuit, and he grabbed it and wiped off his hands. He had worked as a mechanic at the local Ford plant before it closed, and though he had retired, he wore the oil-stained gray jumpsuit almost every day. It was a family joke that he would one day be buried in the uniform.

"What you know good, boy?" Dad asked in his gruff voice. A toothpick dangled from the corner of his mouth, dipping up and down when he spoke.

"I was in the area and wanted to stop by to say hello."

Dad grunted, used the same soiled towel to blot sweat off his face. He nodded at Joshua's Ford Explorer, brown eyes shining. "How that truck holdin' up? 'Bout time for an oil change, ain't it?"

He visited his parents every couple of weeks, and every time he saw them, his dad suggested that it was time for an oil change. The mechanic in his father couldn't resist the compulsion to fix every car he encountered; Joshua was certain that the Oldsmobile his father was currently diagnosing belonged to someone in the neighborhood.

"I'll bring it by soon for you to work on," Joshua said.

Dad grunted, and his eyes dimmed. "Mama's inside," he said, turning back to the car.

It was an ordinary exchange with his father. Beyond the subject of automobiles, they never had much to talk about.

He went inside the kitchen. A gigantic pot seethed on the stove, filling the house with the delicious aromas of chicken, broth, dumplings, and vegetables.

Curious, he lifted the lid off the pot—and hissed when the heat stung his fingers. The lid slipped out of his grasp and clanged onto the floor.

"That must be my baby in there," Mom said, coming around the corner. "Clumsy as ever."

"Hi, Mom."

He kissed her on the cheek, which required him to barely bend at all. His mother was a shade less than six feet, her body as thick as a tree trunk. Gray-haired, she wore a shapeless blue house dress, an apron, and threadbare slippers. A pair of bifocals suspended from a lanyard rested on her broad bosom.

Without the glasses, though, her dark eyes were as sharp as ever. They cut into Joshua with the precision of surgical scalpels, and he felt himself weakening under her gaze, swiftly regressing in age from thirty-two to twelve.

"Pick that lid up off the floor, boy," she said. "And don't be a dummy—use a mitt this time."

He grabbed the oven mitt off the counter and used it to pluck the lid off the tile.

"Now wash it off 'fore you put it back on my pot."

He took the lid to the sink, rinsed it under cold water, and carefully placed it over the pot.

"Come in my kitchen snoopin' and messin' up," Mom said. "Shoot, if you kept in touch with me like a good son should, you'd know I was cookin' chicken and dumplins. Sit down."

He sat at the end of the kitchen table. Mom shuffled to the stove, lifted the lid off the pot, and stirred the soup with a big spoon.

"I was in the area and wanted to stop by to say hi," he said.

"Wanted to stop by to say hi? Like we just acquaintances or somethin'. You ain't been by here in a month."

"It hasn't been that long, Mom. I visited last week."

"Maybe *you* did. But I ain't seen that heifer you married since Thanksgiving. That's plain disrespectful. You come to see us, but she can't?"

"She's been busy with the salon."

"Wouldn't trust that heifer as far as I could throw her," Mom said, hands on her wide hips. "What kinda wife talks her husband into quittin' a *good* job so he could go out there and be unemployed and strugglin'?"

His mother had been against him leaving his job to start his business. Although he was earning more money and was happier being his own boss, in his mother's mind, he was jobless and broke. She blamed Rachel for it, of course.

"She ain't an honorable woman," Mom said.

"Why do you say that?"

"She just ain't. I feels it right here." Mom touched her breast. "But you ain't listen to what I think, oh no. Mama done lived sixty-some years but don't know nothin'!"

He was quiet. Eventually, her tirade would run its course.

She ladled some soup into a bowl and plinked a spoon inside. "Come here and take this."

He got up, took the bowl, and returned to the table.

"Blow on it, first, boy, that's hot," she said.

He blew on a spoonful, and then tasted it. "It's delicious, Mom."

Mom nodded, and shuffled to the garage door. She

opened it and yelled at his father: "Earl, get from up under that car and come in here and eat!"

He swallowed another spoonful of soup. His mom usually had to yell three or four times before his father gave up the joys of automobiles for the company of his family. Theirs was an odd marriage, seemingly devoid of tenderness, but his parents had been together for thirty-five years, a milestone that few members of Joshua's generation would ever reach.

Although if he was trapped in a marriage like the one his parents had, who would want to stay?

Mom poured a glass of sweet tea and plopped it on the table. "Drink that."

He took a sip. "Wow, that's really sweet."

"That's how I always make it, boy. You done forgot? What that heifer been givin' you to drink—wine?"

If he ever disclosed to his mom that they often drank wine with dinner, she would have branded him an alcoholic and said she was going to pray for him.

"Uh, no, Mom. No wine."

"Hmph." Mom sat next to him, the chair squeaking under her weight. She smiled, showing new dentures. "Chaquita came by here yesterday."

He almost choked on a dumpling. "She did? Why?"

" 'Cause she *respects* me. Unlike your wife."

Chaquita was his ex-girlfriend. She and Joshua had dated for two boisterous years before she dumped him, declaring him too dull and soft for her tastes.

Puzzlingly, Chaquita and his mother stayed in touch. They sometimes went shopping together or out for lunch, like mother and daughter.

"She asked after you," Mom said. "That girl still loves you, you know."

"She broke up with *me,* Mom. Anyway, I'm married now. Whatever feelings she thinks she has for me, she needs to let them go. I'm going to be with Rachel for the rest of my life, hopefully."

"Hopefully? You sound kinda doubtful to me. Sound like the bloom is off the rose. What kinda problems you havin' with that heifer?"

"No problems." He lowered his gaze to the bowl, shoved another spoonful of soup in his mouth.

"What's done in the dark will come to light," Mom said, with obvious pleasure.

"Excuse me?"

"You know what I mean! I'm talkin' 'bout *dirt,* boy. Skeletons in the closet. Deep, dark sinful secrets. All that mess—it's gonna come out."

"Well, everyone has secrets, Mom. You never . . . you never know everything about anyone."

"I know everythang 'bout your daddy!" She pointed to the garage, shaking her long finger. "You know everythang 'bout your wife?"

He glanced at his watch. "Mom, I've gotta go. I've got an appointment at two."

"What? You just got here!"

"I know, and I'm sorry. I'll be back soon, promise."

His mother followed him to the door, muttering.

"Remember what I said, boy. What's done in the dark . . ."

"Will come to light, I know," he said.

He gave his mother a kiss, and went to his truck. As he pulled away, she yelled at his father again to come inside and eat. A normal day in the Moore household.

Driving to the doctor's office, he realized why he had visited his mother. He'd wanted to talk to someone whose doubts about Rachel's honesty exceeded his own. He'd wanted to talk to someone who would fan the flames of his discontent, someone who would whip his emotions into an uncontainable storm.

Because he'd decided that he was going to confront Rachel, and demand the truth.

15

Whacking Betty upside the head with the shovel had knocked her out cold. She slumped in the doorway, resembling a drunk who hadn't quite made it through the door after a long night of boozing.

Dexter hooked his hands underneath her armpits and dragged her inside. She was a slender woman, easy to move. He kicked the door shut behind him.

The small foyer opened into the living room. It was furnished with a burgundy sofa and chairs, an oak coffee table, a television broadcasting a soap opera, and the tall Christmas tree he had seen from the street.

Photographs were everywhere. Pictures of Betty and her dead husband. Pictures of his wife. However, none of the shots of his wife were recent; he'd seen all of them before.

But that meant nothing.

He propped Betty against the sofa. Her bosom rose and fell slowly, and her lips were parted, drool spilling over them, but her eyelids didn't flutter. She would be unconscious for a few moments yet.

He locked the front door and cinched the curtains shut. Shadows sprang from the corners of the room, like old friends.

Brandishing the Glock, he swept the house, boots knocking across the floor. To his knowledge, Betty was spending her golden years living alone. But securing the scene was an old habit.

He also was seeking signs of his wife. He doubted that she lived with Betty, but she surely would've visited the old bitch often, and she might've left behind personal effects that would give him proof that she was in the area.

There was no one else in the house. He found nothing of his wife, either. *Strange.*

In a drawer in the kitchen, he found a thick roll of duct tape. Returning to the living room, he found Betty unconscious, but breathing at a faster rate. About to awaken.

He bound her thin wrists in her lap with a swath of tape, and wrapped up her bony ankles, too. He lifted her off the floor and placed her in a La-Z-Boy recliner.

He slid the coffee table across the carpet and sat on it, so he could look her directly in the face and analyze every nuance of her expressions when he spoke to her.

Her face in repose, Betty was a striking woman for her age. A thick, full head of gray hair. Healthy cinnamon complexion. High, sculpted cheekbones. Full lips. Based on the photos he'd seen of her in her youth, Betty had been quite the fox. She bore a strong, family resemblance to his wife.

"Oh, Betty," he said, softly. "Wake up, old girl. I want to talk to you."

Her eyelids fluttered. She was playing possum.

He popped open the switchblade and whisked the tip across the back of her hand, drawing a narrow line of blood.

Betty's eyes flew open, and she let out a bleat of pain.

Violence had always been the most persuasive tool in a

police man's arsenal. The most effective means to get to the desired result. Betty was going to be dead before he left the house, of course—he owed that to his wife for her blistering betrayal—but the old broad might have some useful information to share with him.

"We need to chat," he said.

Her honey-brown eyes glistened. She had eyes like his wife, too.

"I read in the paper that you might have escaped from prison," she said. "You're a fool to come back here, but then you never were very smart."

He smiled—and sliced the blade across her other hand, carving a crescent moon-shaped wound. She issued a satisfying wail.

"Where's my wife?" he asked.

"She's not your wife any more, you idiot. She divorced you while you were incarcerated. Surely you know that."

He waved the knife before her eyes like a hypnotist's pendulum. She stared at it, gnawing her lip.

"Let's be clear on one thing," he said. "There was no divorce. I never consented to it."

"It doesn't matter whether you consented to it or not. In the eyes of the law, you're divorced."

"I am the law, Betty. Or have you forgotten?"

"Okay, Dexter," she said. "You're correct. I'd like to help you, I genuinely would. But can you first put away the knife, and free my arms and legs, please?"

"Don't patronize me. It's transparent and, frankly, coming from you, ridiculous."

She lifted her chin defiantly. She was a proud woman and hated to be put in her place.

"Back to my first question." He spun the knife around his fingers like a stage magician. "Where is she?"

"I don't know."

He lowered the blade to her slender forearm. Punctured the skin with the knife's tip.

"Please." Breathing harder. "*I don't know.* I haven't seen her in three years."

"When did she leave?"

"About a year after you went to prison."

"Why?"

"She wanted a fresh start."

"A fresh start." *With my goddamn money.*

"I truly don't know where she's gone," Betty said. "She said . . . it wouldn't be safe for me to know. Because of you."

"Have you talked to her on the phone since she's left?"

"No," Betty said quickly. Too quickly.

He drew the blade down her forearm, opening another thin cut.

"It was earlier this year!" she cried. "On my seventieth birthday. She called me."

"From where?"

"There was no number on Caller ID, and she knew better than to tell me where she was calling from, or to give me her number."

"What did she say?"

"She said she was doing fine." Betty sniffled. "She said that she loved me . . . and missed me something terrible."

"I'm touched. But I'm not sure I believe you have no clue whatsoever about where she's gone, or how to get in touch with her. No, I don't believe that at all."

Betty blinked away tears. "But I've told you the truth."

"I know my wife. She adores you. She would never sever her ties with you and call only once a year."

He surveyed the living room, the hallway, and the kitchen beyond.

"There has to be something," he said.

"There's nothing, I promise you."

He detected an undercurrent of anxiety in her voice. He'd interrogated enough suspects to know the tone of a lie.

"Where's your little black book?"

"Pardon?"

"Your address book, you old bitch. It's a black, leather-bound book. I've seen it here before."

"It's in the study. Look on the desk, near the telephone."

In the study, he found the book where she'd said it would be. It lay near a cordless phone and a stack of envelopes.

He flipped through the address book. Underneath his wife's name, the last address listed was of their house in Chicago. The phone number was their old number, too.

He noticed the pile of envelopes beside the phone. Most of them were recent utility bills and bank statements, but one of the letters had been sent from Thad Harris, in St. Louis, Missouri. It had a postmark of December 11, one week ago.

The envelope had already been opened. Inside, he found a personal check written from Thad to Betty, in the amount of one thousand dollars.

He scrutinized the check like a bank teller suspicious of fraud. He found an entry for Thad in Betty's address book. The phone number and address were the same as the information printed on the check.

Beside the stack of envelopes lay a faded checkbook. He paged to the registry. In her careful handwriting, Betty had entered a series of deposits, each in the amount of one thousand dollars, which she had notated every month for the past year.

He returned to the living room and waved the check in Betty's face.

"What's this?" he asked.

"What is it? I can't read without my glasses. Since you're so smart you must remember that about me."

"It's a payment from Thad Harris to you, for one grand," he said. "I remember Thad. He worked with my wife at the salon in Chicago. He was a fag, but a good friend of hers. Why is he sending money to you every month?"

Betty's gaze slipped away from him.

"He's . . . he's paying me back for a . . . for a loan I once gave him."

He cut her—a quick, clean slash down the side of her face. She shrieked, and blood began to flow in bright rivulets.

"I appreciate honesty," he said. "It's a simple matter of respect, Betty."

Betty's lips worked, but no words came out. Blood trickled from the cut and into the corner of her mouth.

He picked up the cordless phone off the nearby end table. He settled on the coffee table in front of Betty again.

Betty watched him like a cornered animal.

"Listen up," he said. "My wife has money that belongs to me, and I intend to get it by any means necessary. You're going to help me."

Betty spat out a stream of blood. Glared at him. Stubborn old broad.

"You're going to call Thad," he said. "You're going to speak very calmly. You're going to tell him that it's urgent for you to get my wife's address. Make up a story."

"But he . . . he won't have it. No one does."

"She's sending him money to give to you—he'll have it. By the way, I'm quite sure it's *my* money that she's been forwarding to you. She ever told you where she gets it from?"

"I . . . I assume she works . . ."

"Doing hair? Or fucking? Those were about the only two things she could do with any skill at all." He barked a laugh.

"Whatever she's doing, she's not earning enough to give you a grand every month. She's too goddamn stupid."

Betty sobbed quietly, the tears tracking down her cheeks mingling with the blood.

He punched the number from the check into the handset. When the line rang, he placed the phone against Betty's ear.

"Start talking," he said.

Eyes burning, Betty waited. "It's gone to voice mail."

"Leave him a message. We'll sit here together and wait for a call back."

Glaring at him, Betty spoke into the handset: "Thad, it's Aunt Betty. Tell Joy that I'll always love her, dear . . . and please, *tell her to run for her life,* because Dexter is out of prison and he's here—"

He tore the phone away from her ear and killed the connection.

"You fucking bitch," he said. "And I was thinking of letting you go easy."

"I wouldn't give you the pleasure." She grinned at him, blood smearing her cheek and chin like war paint.

He pressed the blade against her throat. But the old woman, her frail body shaking, only looked up at him—and spat in his face.

He wiped the spittle off his jaw.

And then he started cutting in earnest.

16

Dexter is really out.

Thad Harris, a trusted friend from the life she had left behind, had called Rachel's cell phone while she was cutting a client's hair. He'd been hysterical. She had hurried to the back office to take the call.

Oh, my God, Joy, your Aunt Betty left me a message, I got it like a half hour ago and I'm calling you right away . . . Dexter is really out! He's out of prison, and he's with her, and she said she loves you and you've gotta run, Joy, you've gotta run . . .

Speaking with a calmness that masked her true emotions, she had urged Thad to be careful, thanked him for the call, and said she had to go. She stared at the cell phone in her palm, chewing her bottom lip.

That past weekend, Thad had called her and said Aunt Betty had discovered a story in the newspaper: a van transporting Dexter to another prison had mysteriously gone missing. She wanted to believe that the van had crashed somewhere—hopefully leaving Dexter mortally injured—

but fear had nonetheless set in, nibbling away at her thoughts, invading her dreams.

His escape was the worst thing that ever could have happened, for all of them.

Fingers trembling, she called Aunt Betty's house, first punching in a code to conceal her number from Caller ID.

The phone rang once . . . twice . . . and before the third ring there was a click and a pause, as if the call had been forwarded.

She swallowed. Something about this didn't feel right.

On the fourth ring, someone picked up the line, but did not speak. A car engine grumbled in the background.

She licked her dry lips and softly said, "Hello?"

"I knew you would call," Dexter said in his distinctive gravelly baritone. "You sound as sexy as ever, frightened, though. Why would that be?"

A lump as big as a lemon seemed to have gotten stuck in her throat, keeping her from speaking, making it almost impossible for her to even draw breath.

"I'm your husband, after all," he said. "Till death do us part. In sickness and health. For richer or poorer. Locked down or free."

She was gripping the phone so tightly that her knuckles were bleached of color.

"You'd have no reason to be afraid of me," he said, "unless you've done something that you knew would make me angry, now would you?"

She wanted to hang up, but her fingers were locked around the handset, and wouldn't obey.

"Everyone who helped you get away, everyone you love—I'm taking them away, and I think you know I don't sell no wolf tickets, baby."

She opened her mouth, whether to scream or curse at him she didn't know, and it didn't matter, for no sound came out.

"And I think you know exactly why I'm doing it."

Tears tracked down her cheeks, curved along her chin, plopped onto the desk.

"When I find you—and I will, and you know it—you better have my money, every last fucking dollar."

Click.

She sat still, phone mashed to her ear as if glued, the dial tone drilling through her skull.

Gripped by a sudden wave of nausea that broke her paralysis, she bolted out of the chair, raced to the bathroom, flipped up the toilet lid, and vomited so violently into the bowl it felt as though her stomach lining had torn loose.

None of the other stylists came to check on her. The music playing out front, and the chattering women hard at work on hair would have drowned out any noises from back there.

Breathing hard, she straightened. At the sink, she removed her glasses and washed her face with cold water, rinsed out her mouth, and then blotted her skin dry with a paper towel.

Her eyes were red and puffy. She hadn't realized she was crying.

Aunt Betty, oh God . . .

She choked down the bitter grief that surged up her throat, and forced herself to return to the computer at her desk. She accessed the Internet, found the number for the Zion Police Department, and called from her cell.

In a slow, but steady, voice, she resisted giving the dispatcher her name, but informed them that Dexter Bates had broken into her aunt's house and committed a violent crime. She supplied a detailed physical description of Dexter. She even gave them his inmate number, reading it from the profile she'd printed off the Illinois Department of Corrections Web site—a step she'd taken last night just in case her deepest fears came true.

The dispatcher promised to send officers to her aunt's

house immediately. She hung up and rocked in her chair, hugging herself tightly, as if to keep grief from blowing her to pieces.

God, why Aunt Betty?

She tossed her glasses onto the desk and pressed her fingertips against her eyelids, to block the flow of tears.

Her cell phone rang, playing the ring tone she had assigned to Joshua: "Always Be My Baby" by Mariah Carey.

The doctor's appointment. He was probably calling her to confirm that she was meeting him.

She paused . . . and then let the call go to voice mail.

I'm so sorry, Josh.

She touched her abdomen. She imagined the as-yet-unformed heart of their child beating softly inside of her. Justin.

I'm sorry, but I've got to protect our baby.

Sniffling, she wiped her eyes and rose from the chair.

It was time for her contingency plan.

17

Parked outside the doctor's office, Joshua attempted again to reach Rachel on her cell. It was a quarter past two, and not only was she late for her appointment, she wasn't answering her phone, either.

Was she stuck in traffic and having cell issues? Or had she lied to him again?

Until lately, he never would have considered the latter possibility, and it disturbed him to harbor such doubts about her. But he couldn't help it. Her recent behavior had been suspect.

He passed the next few minutes tapping the steering wheel and listening to Christmas music on the radio. Stevie Wonder was singing, "Someday at Christmas," one of Joshua's favorite holiday tunes, but the song failed to cheer him.

Something was wrong.

He called Rachel's cell again. Again, he got her voice mail.

Finally he called the salon. One of the stylists told him

that Rachel had left a short while ago for a personal appointment.

He twisted the radio knob to a station that continuously broadcasted traffic news. In a city such as Atlanta where people drove like bandits, you never could discount the possibility that someone running late hadn't gotten delayed in a ten-car pileup somewhere.

But there were no traffic snarls on the south side.

He went inside the doctor's office, identified himself to the receptionist, and asked if Rachel had called to say she was going to be late, or had requested to reschedule. The receptionist was a young black woman with a dried-out Jheri-curl. She eyed him up and down in that appraising manner that black women often did, shook her head, and told him to advise his wife that she would have to pay a twenty-five dollar fee for missing her appointment without giving twenty-four-hours' advance notice.

"Right, I'll be sure to let her know."

Back in his Explorer, he called their house, on the remote chance that Rachel would be home. Surprisingly, she picked up on the third ring.

"Hey, baby." Her voice was subdued, as if she had been asleep.

"Rachel, I've been here at the doctor's office for almost half an hour waiting for you. What happened?"

There was a long pause.

"Please . . . come home," she said. "I need to see you."

"You don't sound good. Is everything okay?"

"Come home. Please." Her voice nearly broke on the word, "please."

"I'm on my way."

18

At home, he found Rachel on the sofa in the family room. Coco lay curled on her lap, slumbering.

Rachel smiled wanly. She wore a red terry cloth bathrobe, her legs folded beneath her, Indian style. A box of Kleenex stood on an end table; crumpled tissues lay on the table, and one was bunched in her lap.

"You've been crying," he said. "What's wrong?"

She gently placed Coco on the floor, rose off the couch, and came to him.

"Hold me," she said.

He held her. She was freshly bathed, the lemony fragrance of her body wash filling his nostrils. Her still-moist skin dampened the front of his shirt.

But when he felt her trembling, and heard her stifled sob, he realized that her tears, not bath water, were saturating him.

"Baby, what is it?" he asked. "Please, tell me."

She tilted her head backward, looked up at him. Tears shimmered in her eyes—eyes that held secrets and pain.

A horrifying thought came to him, something so awful he was afraid to put it into words. But he needed to know. "Is there something wrong with . . . our baby?"

She shook her head. Wiped her eyes.

Some of the tension drained out of him. "What is it then?"

"Upstairs." She slipped out of his embrace and went to the staircase, her robe billowing around her legs. Coco scampered after her.

"Rachel? Come back and talk to me. Please."

She disappeared upstairs.

He followed her. She was in their bedroom, standing at the double-windows that overlooked the dense, winter-peeled woodlands beyond the back of their house.

She had dropped her robe to the carpet; she was nude. In the blend of gray afternoon light and shadows, her rear profile was like a luscious illusion.

He felt a stirring in his jeans. With all of the questions circling his thoughts, this was hardly the right time for sex, but his body apparently had other ideas.

"Do you love me?" she whispered, her back to him.

"Of course, I love you. I'll always love you."

"Will you?" She looked over her shoulder.

"Come on, girl." He sat on the bed, almost squashing Coco; the tiny dog scrambled off the mattress and darted into her pet kennel on the nightstand. "I don't understand why you're acting like this. What brought all this on?"

"I love you, too." She moved away from the windows and in front of him. He felt heat radiating from her body, as if she was burning up with some inner flame. "I'll always love you . . . no matter what happens."

No matter what happens.

The words, ominous and mysterious, made him open his mouth to ask what she meant. But she put a hold on his questions by pressing her fingers to his lips, buttoning them shut.

Then she took one of his hands and placed it on her hip, as though offering her body to him.

His fingers lay against a long, faded scar that curved from her lower abdomen to her hip. She bore similar scars across her shoulders, and on her back. They looked as if they had been made with a sharp blade.

When he'd once asked her about them, she told him she had gotten them from an old accident, and then promptly changed the subject.

As if aware of his inspection, she cupped the back of his head and pulled him forward. His lips brushed against her stomach.

She grasped his shirt, began to pull it off.

Although he wanted to learn the reason for her sadness, he understood on an intuitive level that she *needed* this intimacy with him, that it would salve her wounded spirit better than any words he might possibly speak. He would ask her questions about what had happened and many other things later. For now, he would do only what he had vowed to do on the day they married: love her.

19

Afterward, they lay together, tangled in bed sheets. The room was submerged in shadows, their slow breaths the only sound in the room.

Lying on her side as he lay on his back, Rachel placed her hand on his chest and playfully walked her fingers upward to his chin. He took her fingers and kissed them.

"We need to get together more often in the afternoons," he said. "This is much better than taking a nap after lunch. Although I could use a nap now—you wore me out."

"We won't be able to do this when the baby comes along. Hard to be spontaneous when you've got a newborn that needs constant attention."

Her sadness, whatever its cause, seemed to have faded, for the most part, as though their bodies had burned it away during their lovemaking.

"Why you were so upset earlier?" he asked.

She looked away to the shadowed ceiling. "I don't want to ruin the mood, baby. We'll discuss it at dinner."

"Fair enough."

But an internal voice immediately rebuked him: *You're too soft, man. What was all that crap you talked about putting Rachel on the spot and asking tough questions about how she's been acting lately?*

It was true, of course. There was much that he needed to speak to Rachel about, from her behavior that afternoon to her recent lies, but as much as those things upset him, he didn't necessarily want to talk about them.

His tendency to avoid conflict had long been a character flaw of his. Sometimes he was convinced that was partly why Rachel was drawn to him. She loved him; he believed that. But it was reasonable to assume that she also loved how he never pushed her for answers to hard questions. Someone like her, whom he suspected had never been completely forthcoming about her past, would be attracted to a spouse who never probed too deep.

He'd thought his parents had a dysfunctional marriage, but in a way, his own marriage was equally screwy. That he was aware of it and was reluctant to force changes, however, made him question how solid the foundation of their relationship really was. Was it built on firm ground, or sand? And did he really want a truthful answer to that question?

She bent her arm and propped her hand against her head. "Speaking of dinner, what would you like me to cook?"

He yawned. "I can eat anything. Whatever you want to make is cool with me."

"I think I'll go to the grocery store, then." She sat up.

"Right now?"

"It's almost four. I want to beat the after-work hordes."

"I'll wait here. I'm going to take a nap."

"These hips worked you over, huh?" She rolled off the bed and tapped her bare backside. "Respect the booty, baby."

He laughed. "True dat."

He watched her dress in a powder blue jogging suit, Atlanta Braves cap, and sneakers. She came to the bed and kissed him.

"I love you." She squeezed his hand. "Always."

"Always."

She left the room. He turned over in bed, closed his eyes, and fell asleep almost instantly.

When he awoke, it was half-past six. Coco sat on her haunches at the closed bedroom door. She was shivering in the distinctive way that Chihuahuas did when they were anxious.

"What's wrong, kid?" he asked.

The dog whimpered. Frowning, he got out of bed and opened the door.

"Rachel? Are you here?"

There was no answer. The house was dark and silent.

She'd been gone for over two hours. He couldn't imagine that a routine trip to the grocery store would take so long.

He hurried downstairs.

On the kitchen table, he found a letter.

20

The letter lay on the table, framed by the hurricane lamps they'd burned at dinner last night. A small silver key rested at the foot of the paper; it resembled one of those keys you might use to open a padlock.

He began reading.

Dear Joshua,

It is with deep regret that I'm writing this letter to you. I've prayed that things would never come to this. But one lesson I've learned, unfortunately, is that prayers sometimes go unanswered.

There's a lot about me that you don't know, baby. I've lied to you about many things in my past. I never lied with the intention of hurting you. I lied because I was ashamed of my past. I lied to protect myself. Most of all, I lied because I was afraid of losing you.

But it looks like my past has finally caught up with me. So I'm going to be leaving, for a while. This is for your safety, mine, and most of all, the safety of our baby. (Yes, I truly am pregnant with your child. I would never lie about that.)

As terrible as it will be for us to be apart, this is the best decision for our family. You must trust me on this. It is for our protection.

I can't tell you where I'm going, and I can't say when I will be able to come home. I wish I could tell you these things, but I can't.

Please don't try to find me, or to contact me. I will get in touch with you when it's safe. Again, this is for our protection. Please, trust me on this.

I've left you a key. It will unlock something that I pray you won't need.

I may have lied about many things, to my everlasting shame, but I never lied about how much I love you. Please know that. You are the only man I've ever truly loved.

Your wife,
Rachel

P.S. Please take good care of Coco. I've left her with you as proof that I'm going to come home soon.

He read the letter again. Then once more. Numbness traveled through him, starting from his fingers that grasped the letter and traveling in an icy current up through his wrist, into his arm and shoulder, through his chest, and then spreading through the rest of his body. Like an overdose of anesthetic.

His legs became deadened tree stumps. Swaying, his knees folding under him, he slid down the cabinet doors and dropped to the floor on his butt, barely registering the pain that stung his tailbone.

My wife's left me.

He couldn't believe it. Wouldn't.

He rose on quivering legs and wandered around the house, dazed.

None of what she'd said in her letter made any sense. He was going to get to the bottom of this and prove that she was bluffing, playing a sick joke, suffering from a mental illness of some kind . . . anything other than what she'd claimed in her note. This could not be happening to him, to them.

He lurched into the garage. Her Acura was gone. He'd figured it would be missing, but he'd needed to see the vacant space, to believe what she'd written.

He tried to call her on her cell phone. She didn't answer; her voice mail picked up immediately, indicating that her phone was shut off.

He left her a message anyway: "Rachel, it's me. I got this letter. Listen, baby . . . I don't understand this. I can't believe it. Whatever's going on . . . I need you. Please, call me. *Please . . .*"

He couldn't go any further; a sob was boiling up his throat. He hung up.

He turned around and around in the family room, as if lost in his own home. The Christmas decorations, the holiday cards clustered on the fireplace mantelpiece, the photographs of their wedding day and their happy times together, seemed to be exhibits of someone else's life, not his.

Coco was perched on the sofa she'd shared with Rachel only a few hours ago. She watched him, her big eyes apprehensive.

The little dog was as anxious as he was. Coco had probably seen Rachel write her letter, had stood nearby as Rachel had prepared to leave, had watched Rachel leave her behind in the house as she entered the garage and got in her car and sped away to an unknown destination.

Rachel had, in a real sense, abandoned both of them.

His erratic behavior had probably thoroughly unsettled

Coco. Seeing the dog forced him to realize that he had to get himself together, because he was on the verge of coming unglued.

He made another phone call, this one to Rachel's salon. Tanisha told him that she hadn't spoken to Rachel since she'd left for her appointment earlier that afternoon.

"If she gets in touch with you, call me right away," he said. "It's very important."

"Sure, honey," Tanisha said. "Is everything okay?"

"It's fine." He was in no shape to answer a barrage of questions. "Remember, call me, okay?"

In the master bedroom, he checked the walk-in closet. It was a large chamber—the walk-in closet was one of the areas that had sold Rachel on the house—and half of it was dedicated to her belongings.

Rachel was fastidiously neat. Her clothes hung inside, arranged by color, season, and occasion. Her shoes were tucked away in a stackable shoe organizer, and her purses and other accessories sat on built-in shelving. Nothing was out of place.

Would she have run away with only the clothes on her back?

He rushed out of the closet, entered the guest bedroom. Flung open the closet door.

They kept their luggage stored in this closet; his aunt and uncle had given them a set of luggage as a wedding gift. One of the large suitcases was missing.

The vacant garage space could have meant only that she was out running errands. The missing luggage was proof of her serious intent to go away.

Although she apparently hadn't taken any of her clothes, she could easily purchase clothing on her way to wherever she was going. It seemed like the kind of thing she would do—start fresh.

His heart banging, he went into her study. She'd left behind the laptop, but the computer was off, and he remembered the password lock from that morning.

He searched her desk, seeking a Post-it or some other note of where she might have gone. He found nothing. Her desk was clean, and even the trash can was empty.

Back in the kitchen, a laminated list of emergency telephone numbers was pinned to the refrigerator by a magnet for Coco's veterinarian. He picked up the phone, to dial the police, and then he paused to reconsider.

What could he possibly tell the cops? That his wife had left him a letter? He'd watched enough TV police dramas to understand that it wasn't illegal to leave your spouse.

Further, there was no evidence that someone had forced her to leave—though it was obvious that her *fear* of someone had sent her on the run.

As terrible as it will be for us to be apart, this is the best decision for our family. You must trust me on this. It is for our protection.

Who was she running from? The man in her nightmare? Someone who had been in prison in Illinois?

And what was the key for?

He just didn't know.

But he could predict what the police would think of her cryptic letter. They would be suspicious, not merely of Rachel, but possibly of him, too. They might suspect foul play, might think that he had done something to Rachel and written a phony letter to hide the evidence. Everybody knew that whenever something awful happened to a married person, conventional cop wisdom assumed that the spouse, especially when the spouse was a man, was always the prime suspect.

Although he could avoid mentioning the letter at all and could report her as a missing person, he was pretty sure that she had to be missing for at least forty-eight hours before the cops would even talk to him about it.

No, he couldn't call the cops. Not yet. Maybe not at all.

He started to put down the phone, but then, out of vain hope, he dialed Rachel's cell again. Voice mail picked up right away.

He hung up without leaving a message, his hand shaking.

A vibrating noise came from a darkened corner of the kitchen. He hurried over there, nearly tripping over his feet.

The noise came from the side counter, where they stored mail, a glass bowl that held their keys, an erasable task list, and their respective cell phone chargers. His BlackBerry lay on the counter, vibrating rhythmically.

Rachel's cell phone stood there, too, nestled in the recharging cradle.

His calls to her had been pointless. Not only had she left him behind—she'd left him no means to get in touch with her, either.

A check of his BlackBerry confirmed that he'd received only a stupid text message advertisement from the phone service provider. Nothing from Rachel.

He stumbled into the family room and collapsed on the sofa.

A photo sat on the coffee table. It was a wedding shot of them walking down the aisle at his family church, arms interlinked, the pastor having recently declared them husband and wife.

He cradled the photo in his hands. And wept.

Drawn by his wracking sobs, Coco wandered into the room and hopped onto the couch. She crawled into his lap.

He set aside the picture and held the dog close. He rarely

cried, but the tears poured out of him from a deep chasm in his heart, scalding his cheeks like a purifying fire . . . and soon, concentrating his thoughts as sharply as a freshly smelted iron sword.

Wherever she had gone, whatever this was all about, he vowed that he was going to get to the truth, no matter what.

PART TWO

...Will Come to Light

21

Like a manta ray gliding through deep sea waters, Dexter plied the night-darkened streets of St. Louis, Missouri.

At a Wal-Mart outside Chicago, he'd purchased several items, including a StreetPilot GPS navigation system. With the technology available these days, it made no sense to pore over an unwieldy paper map, and there was a strong likelihood that he had a lot of driving ahead of him.

He also bought another pay-as-you-go cell phone. After speaking with his wife on the other cell, he discarded it in the flatbed of a pick-up truck bound in the opposite direction. The law could use cell signals to trace his location.

He'd taken care to avoid toll booths, too. Cops loved to nab felons who blithely passed through toll plazas and let surveillance cameras snap their photos and tags.

The GPS system directed him to a subdivision on the outer limits of St. Louis. A tall, wrought iron fence ran along the perimeter of the community, festooned with holiday lights. Shrubbery garlanded with more lights flanked a large sign that read HAWTHORN ESTATES.

There was no gate; he drove through the wide entrance. The community's grandiloquent title was misleading. The residences were hardly estates. They were modest ranches and two-story homes with partial brick fronts and Hardiplank siding.

He followed a gently curving road. The houses and lawns were dusted with snow that resembled cake frosting. Most properties boasted light displays; some of them had representations of little baby Jesus in the manger, reindeer, Santas, and snowmen.

The home he sought was ahead, on the left. It was a two-story model with an attached garage, and neatly maintained shrubbery entwined with Christmas lights, which happened to be shut off.

The rest of the house was dark, too.

Thanks to Betty's message, Thad knew he was on the prowl. Had he gone somewhere else to spend the night? Perhaps in the arms of a lover?

It was only half-past eight, however. Thad could have been out to dinner, or working.

He parked around the block and shut off the engine.

An hour ago, using a tool kit he'd picked up from the store, he had removed the Illinois license plates and replaced them with a set of Missouri tags that he had stolen off a car parked at a strip mall. The Chevy had the further advantage of being so nondescript, it was virtually invisible.

He loaded his pockets with items he anticipated he would need, and got out of the car. Pulling his knit cap low over his head, he walked briskly back to Thad's house, wisps of breath puffing in front of him in the frosty night air.

None of the neighbors were out. It was dark, and too damn cold.

Arriving at Thad's property, he headed straight to the

backyard. Pine trees bordered the rear perimeter, shielding him from view of the homes on the other side of the lot.

The patio was a snow-mantled slab. It was accessed via a basic, sliding glass door.

He tore away several strips of duct tape and affixed them to the glass. Then he banged a hammer into the center of the taped-over section, punching through the window without the accompanying sound of broken glass raining to the floor.

He stuck his gloved hand through the hole and unlocked the door.

It was a lavishly decorated home, which he would have expected of a man of Thad's orientation. The rooms were painted bright colors. The furniture had soft edges, smooth lines, fluffy decorative pillows on the sofas and chairs. Lots of photos of Thad and another brother. An abundance of live plants. Colorful artwork, many pieces featuring depictions of chiseled, bare-chested black men.

No one was home.

Leaving the lights off and making use of a utility flashlight, he rummaged through a bedroom set up as a home office. He searched through the file cabinet and the stack of paperwork on the desk. Nothing.

But there was a paper shredder in the corner, the bin bristling with destroyed documents. His wife would have urged Thad to shred the record of each payment she sent him. He appeared to have been dutifully following her instructions.

He went to the kitchen. In the refrigerator, he found bacon, eggs, butter, orange juice. He located a couple of pans and a bottle of Crisco, and fired up the gas burners on the stainless steel cook top.

Cooking by the bluish glow of the flames and a soft light above the range, he prepared eight strips of bacon, four fried eggs, and two slices of buttered wheat toast with grape jelly. He sat at the pine dinette table and ate, drinking the juice directly from the carton.

He loved breakfast food, especially at night. It reminded him of his old man, who would stumble in after a long night of hustling and boozing and drag his mother out of bed to cook for him, always breakfast stuff. As a man, he had taught his own wife to do the same thing.

He was chewing the last piece of toast when he heard the garage door grumble open. He had placed the Glock beside his plate. He picked it up and rose from the table.

The garage door clambered shut. He heard two voices outside, both men. One was deep, authoritative; the other was lighter, and quasi-feminine—Thad's. Apparently Thad wanted his partner to search the house before he entered.

Dexter moved into the hallway that led to the garage entry door, standing beside the light switch.

"You smell bacon?" the deep-voiced lover boy asked.

Dexter didn't hear Thad's response.

A key jiggled into the keyhole. The knob twisted, and the door creaked open.

Dexter flicked on the light. The guy from the pictures—a tall, athletically built, dark-skinned brother with dreadlocks—stood in the doorway. He wore jeans, a leather bomber jacket, and Timberlands. He had gray eyes.

When he saw Dexter, his eyes opened wide with surprise. "Who the hell . . ."

Dexter shot him twice in the head. The guy tumbled back into the doorway.

From the garage: "Malik!"

Dexter stepped over the dead man and moved through the door. There was a Honda Civic parked on the left. Thad sat on the passenger side of a Toyota SUV on the right, his mouth gaping in terror.

Stepping closer to the truck, Dexter aimed the gun at him.

"Step out of the vehicle. Put your hands up where I can see them."

Crying, Thad opened the door. He was brown-skinned guy, about five-nine, thin-boned, with a clean-shaven face, a fade haircut, and diamond stud earrings in both ear lobes. He wore a pink sweater and jeans.

"Please don't kill me," Thad said. Tears slid down his cheeks.

"Move away from the vehicle. Keep those hands up."

Hands in the air, Thad edged away from the Toyota. He glanced at his lover sprawled on the floor, and choked back a sob.

"Please . . . Dexter . . ."

Grunting, Dexter roughly grabbed him by the scruff of his neck.

"Let's go talk inside, Thad," he said. "Malik's nose wasn't fooling him, by way. I did cook bacon, and that's one of the things I'd like to talk to you about."

22

That night, Joshua went to his parents' house.

He couldn't bear to stay home. Unavoidable reminders of Rachel filled the house, from the largest elements to the minutest details: from the colors she had elected to paint each room to the silk flower arrangement on the dining room table; from the wedding photographs on the fireplace mantelpiece to the selection of food in the refrigerator.

Even his office, the only room that was exclusively his, was a testament to her influence. She had selected the furniture, her framed bridal portrait stood on the edge of the desk, and when he switched on his computer, the screen saver was a stunning photo of a volcanic mountain in Hawaii, where they'd honeymooned.

He needed to get away from his wife, away from *it*—*it* being the home they had created together. It felt like a giant, living creature to him, in much the same way that houses were often supernaturally alive in haunted house movies; the place was suffocating him, walls pressing in on him from all sides, until his only recourse was to throw some clothes and toiletries into an overnight bag, pack up Coco in her pet carrier, and flee to his parents' house.

He considered going to Eddie's, but only for a moment. Eddie would be sympathetic to his troubles, but seeing Eddie, his wife, and their young children in their comfortable home, enjoying familial bliss, would be another poignant reminder of everything he seemed to be losing. Going to his parents was the least upsetting choice.

His mother answered the door. Although it was only nine o'clock, she was dressed for bed in her bathrobe and nightgown, and multicolored rollers bounced in her hair.

Over her shoulder, he saw his dad. As expected, the old man, clad in his pajamas and thick white socks, was dozing in the recliner, ragged snores rumbling from his chest.

He went inside and settled on the sofa, placing Coco's pet carrier beside him.

"What you doin' here, boy?" Mom asked. "Somethin' wrong?"

"It's like this, Mom." He cleared his throat and started to fabricate a story of how Rachel had gone out of town for a business trip. But his mother stopped him with one declarative sentence.

"You been cryin'."

Before leaving the house, he had squeezed a few drops of Visine into his eyes, and during the drive over, he'd repeatedly checked his eyes in the rearview mirror to make sure they looked clear and normal.

"What are you talking about, Mom? I'm fine."

"You don't look fine." Standing in front of him, she bunched her fists on her wide waist. "I'm your mama, boy. I know you, and you been cryin'. What's wrong?"

"Nothing." Shrugging, he turned toward the television.

"You can talk to me, baby." She sat beside him on the sofa. "It's trouble with your wife, ain't it?"

He couldn't look at her. Tears hung like lead weights in his eyes. Why did his mother have to be so damn perceptive?

"I know it is." Gently, she rubbed his broad back. "Let it out, baby. Let it all out. Mama's here for you."

He sucked in a hitching breath—and then he told her what had happened, leaving out the part about Rachel's pregnancy. Rachel had sworn him to secrecy, and though she was gone, he wanted to keep his word.

"That bitch!" Mom rocketed off the sofa and stormed across the living room. "No, she didn't!"

His dad, who normally slept so soundly an atomic bomb blast couldn't rouse him, cocked an eyebrow.

"This is why I didn't want to tell you," Joshua said. "I didn't want you to overreact."

"That low-down, lyin', dirty bitch!" Eyes blazing, Mom tilted her head back to the ceiling, shrieking so loudly it was as if she wanted Rachel to hear her, wherever she might be on the planet. "Bitch! No-good harlot! How dare she leave my son? *How dare she?*"

His dad's eyelids slid shut. It was typical—once he confirmed that the uproar had nothing to do with him, he tuned out.

Mom paced heavily across the room. In her rage, the belt of her robe had come unloosened, her nightgown flapping like a sail as she moved back and forth.

"I *told* you that woman was low-down, boy, I been tellin' you from the beginning that she was no good. Black-hearted heifer!"

"Mom, please calm down."

"What kinda woman leaves a good husband behind? You're a good man." Mom snatched a tissue from a box of Kleenex on the cocktail table and honked into it.

"I'm going to work this out," he said. "It's going to be fine, Mom. Trust me."

"Trust you?" Mom crumpled the tissue in her meaty fist. "I trusted you not to marry that bitch heifer in the first place. Now look what happened. She done run off with another man!"

"Another man?"

Mom glared at him with fanatical conviction.

"She ain't runnin' scared from somebody like she want you to believe. She's runnin' off *with* somebody. The same dog she's been sleepin' around with from the very beginning—dogs run in packs, baby. They run in *packs."*

"Mom, that's crazy. Rachel isn't cheating on me. I know her better than that."

Mom sneered. "Hmph. Just like you knew you and her would always be together, huh?"

"I know she's not cheating on me."

"Did I raise you to be a fool? You need to find her man's dirty draws 'fore you'll believe it? Use your damn head, boy!"

He bowed his head. Hot blood pounded in his ears, and he was beginning to develop a headache.

Mom sat beside him again. She patted his hand.

"It's gonna be all right, baby. You with Mama now."

"I just need some time to think about things, Mom. Clear my thoughts."

"You ain't gonna want to hear this." She clenched his hand tightly. "But you need to let her go."

"What?"

She leveled her thick finger at him. "Get this straight. She walked away from *you.* And let me tell you—ain't no judge in divorce court gonna give a damn thing to a woman that's done run out on her husband to be with another man. You'll get to keep the house, if you want it."

"I'm not even thinking about divorce."

"You better start thinkin' 'bout it—'cause she probably ain't comin' back."

"This situation is . . . it's not like you think it is at all, Mom. It's complicated."

Mom shook her head sadly, as if embarrassed for him.

"Baby, you deserve a woman who appreciates you." She glanced at Coco in the pet carrier, and her mouth twisted. "Not some heifer who'll leave you high and dry, and then expect you to take care of her pissy little rat dog."

In the kennel, Coco whimpered. His mother had always despised the dog, probably because she belonged to Rachel.

"I'm going to take things one day at a time," he said. "That's about all I can do right now."

"You welcome to stay here long as you want. You eat dinner?"

Although he hadn't eaten anything since earlier that afternoon, stress had stolen his appetite.

"Not hungry, thanks."

"You need to eat somethin'." She shuffled toward the kitchen. "I'm gonna heat up them chicken and dumplins. Go on and put your stuff in your bedroom. I'll get the bed ready in a bit."

He sighed. When she was in full mothering mode, there was no stopping her.

"And take that little rat dog outside to pee 'fore you let it out that cage. If it pisses on my carpet, we gonna have us a problem."

"All right, Mom."

From the kitchen doorway, she smiled at him. "In spite of what's done happened, it's real good to have you home again, baby. I hope you stay a while."

Don't count on it, he thought.

23

Dexter turned on the track lights in the kitchen. He spun a chair away from the table and pushed Thad, still weeping, into it. He bound Thad's hands behind him with duct tape, and taped his ankles together.

Dexter set the roll of tape on the counter and headed to the living room, Thad's fearful gaze following him. An entertainment center housed a wide-screen TV, DVD player, stereo system, receiver, speakers, and a collection of DVDs and CDs.

The CD library included many of Dexter's favorite artists from the seventies and eighties. Scanning the album titles brought back good memories.

"You can't decorate worth shit, but you've got great taste in music, my brother," Dexter called into the kitchen.

Thad mumbled an incoherent reply.

Dexter selected a classic Stevie Wonder album, *Songs in the Key of Life*, and placed it in the CD player. "Love's in Need of Love Today" kicked out of the Bose speakers. He turned up the volume higher.

Snapping his fingers, he strolled back to the kitchen. Glistening sweat saturated Thad's face.

"You know one of the things I enjoyed most about being a cop?" Dexter said over the music.

Teary-eyed, Thad shook his head.

"Interrogating suspects," Dexter said. "I had a real knack for it, if I do say so myself. When my partner and I played the old good cop, bad cop routine, guess who played the bad cop?"

Thad shook his head again. Sniffled.

"I did, of course. But the thing was, even though I really knew how to make a guy spill his guts, I was still bound by departmental policy, for the most part. I would sometimes think to myself—the *things* I would do to this asshole if I wasn't a cop and he was hiding vital information from me."

"But I don't know anything!" Thad shouted.

Dexter gave him a patient smile. "I know, Thad, I know. At first, you guys never do."

Dexter had left the frying pan full of bacon grease on the cook top. He switched on the burner underneath to the highest setting.

The grease began to sizzle and pop.

"Nothing like bacon grease," Dexter said. "Back in the day, my mother used to fry chicken and catfish in it. Damn, that was some good eating."

Thad had stopped crying. His reddened eyes were almost comically huge, and he was panting.

He struggled to break his bonds, but to no avail.

"What . . . what do you want from me?" Thad asked in a fragile voice. "I'll do anything. Please . . ."

"You've been in communication with my wife, Thad."

"I don't know where she is, I swear, I don't."

Sighing, Dexter gripped the handle of the frying pan and lifted it off the burner. Tiny spatters of grease jumped onto his hand, stinging him, but it was nothing compared to the hot, thick oil bubbling in the depths of the pan.

He brought the pan across the kitchen toward Thad. Thad reared back in the chair, lips peeled back from his teeth in terror.

"Oh, God, no . . . please . . ."

Dexter tipped the pan, dribbling some of the oil onto Thad's leg. Thad screamed and rocked wildly in the chair. The grease sank into the denim of his jeans, smoking and searing, and Thad's thigh quivered as if gripped by seizure.

"You jumped ahead in our discussion," Dexter said. "I haven't asked you where she is. I only said you've been in communication with her."

"Yes!" The thick veins on Thad's neck stood out like cables. "Yes . . . I've talked to her . . . oh sweet Jesus . . ."

"Stick to the order of the questions." Dexter returned the pan to the burner and lowered the heat to prevent excessive smoking. He wiped off his grease-spattered hand with a kitchen towel.

Head lowered, Thad was muttering weepy prayers and rocking. The oil had eaten through the denim and scorched his flesh. A sweet, meaty aroma flavored the air, and it wasn't bacon.

"Next question, Thad," Dexter said.

Thad's head snapped up, sweat flying.

"Why have you been sending money to Betty?" Dexter asked.

"Joy . . . she wanted me to do it."

"Why you? She has a handful of other relatives. She could have sent the money to them to give to Betty."

"I . . . I don't know. She trusts me, I guess."

"Probably true. I also think the fact that you aren't in her family was a factor. She thought I would be less likely to track down someone like you than I would one of her relatives."

"I don't know. I . . . I guess so." He hissed in pain.

"You talked to Joy today?"

"No." Thad whipped his head back and forth. "I haven't talked to her in a long time . . . months."

Dexter returned to the stove and picked up the frying pan.

"Okay, okay, it was . . . it was today!" Thad yelled.

Dexter brought the pan near Thad's face. Frantic, Thad actually tried to blow on the bubbling grease, as if that would cool it off.

Dexter walked behind him. Thad craned his head around, watching, whimpering.

"God . . . no . . ."

Tilting Thad's head forward with one hand, Dexter poured a generous measure of oil down the back of Thad's neck.

"Aaaaahhhhh!" Thad thrashed so frantically that he tipped the chair sideways. Man and chair crashed against the tile. Thad knocked his head against the floor, but didn't pass out. He probably wished he had—the flesh at the nape of his neck was bubbling like a slab of fatback, and the air was thick with the noxious fumes.

Dexter placed the pan on the burner again. About a quarter inch of grease remained.

"Tell the truth, that's all I ask," Dexter said. "It's a simple matter of respect, Thad."

Sobbing, face mashed against the floor, Thad said, "I talked to her today."

"Of course. You know how I know? Because she called Betty, not long after Betty left you her lovely message. I talked to Joy, myself, I sure did."

"Then why . . . why are you doing this to me . . ."

"We'll get to that." Hands on his knees, Dexter knelt so

that he could gaze into Thad's anguished eyes. "Listen to my next question very carefully. Don't fix your lips to tell me another lie, because if you do, I'm going to pour some sizzling bacon drippings into your ear canal, which I think would be pretty damn excruciating and might even kill you."

"Oh, Jesus . . ."

"Where does Joy call you from?"

"Atlanta! God, forgive me . . . she calls me from Atlanta . . ."

"Atlanta."

"Yes!"

Dexter turned over the answer in his mind, like a jeweler examining the quality of a diamond with a loupe. Atlanta. The so-called Black Mecca. It was such a popular city for black folks that she probably figured she could blend in there, get lost in the chocolate masses, and start her life anew.

"Do you have a record of her address?" Dexter asked. "An envelope from a recent payment?"

"Shredded . . . all of them . . . like she tells me to do . . ."

"Can you remember if she lives in Atlanta proper, or a suburb?"

Thad squeezed his eyes shut. Gasped. "Not sure . . ."

Dexter pursed his lips. "She using a different name now?"

"Rachel . . ."

Rachel was his wife's middle name.

"Last name?" Dexter asked.

"Hall . . ."

Rachel Hall. Clever. Hall was her mother's maiden name, a fact that she probably didn't realize that he remembered. He eventually would have figured it out, but he would have lost precious time in the interim.

"Thank you for your cooperation, Thad." Dexter stood.

Chest heaving, Thad kept his eyes squeezed closed, as if

he were wishing this entire experience were a nightmare from which he would soon awaken. Mild shock was likely beginning to set in.

"We're not done," Dexter said.

Thad's eyes opened. His gaze was dim, but held a trace of terror.

"But . . . told you . . . everything . . . I know . . ."

"My wife robbed me—did you know that, too?'

Thad blinked fuzzily. "I . . . uh . . ."

"You knew, motherfucker. Where'd you think she got all the money she was sending you? Don't fix your mouth to tell me that she happens to have a good job."

"But . . ."

"She robbed me, and you've been helping her. I wouldn't be the man I am if I let you go. Fuck me over, and I'll fuck you ten times worse and every stupid bastard who helped you—that's the kind of man I am, Thad. I believe in reckoning."

"Please . . ." Thad was crying again, but hoarsely, as if his vocal chords were giving out.

Dexter picked up the frying pan. Bending, he balanced it over Thad's head.

Whimpering, Thad attempted to turn his head away. He succeeded only in smearing his face in the blood, saliva, and liquefied flesh that had pooled on the floor.

Dexter dumped the remaining oil into Thad's ear. It was that last serving that pushed Thad over the edge, because regretfully, the guy almost immediately blacked out. Blood, seething oil, and other unidentified substances spilled out of his ear canal and sautéed his neck.

Dexter replaced the pan on the cooktop and switched off the burner. He checked Thad's pulse, and found what he had expected. The brain was the body's engine—and the boiling grease had traveled through Thad's ear canal and fried his brain like tempura.

Dexter let the man's lifeless arm drop to the floor.

Time to clean up. Then he would be on the road again, with Georgia on his mind.

24

Asleep in his old bedroom, Joshua had the most vivid dream of his life.

He and Rachel were strolling barefoot along a pristine white beach, hand-in-hand. A summer sun smiled down on them, and a cool, salty breeze ruffled the comfortable white shirts and shorts that both of them wore. They were alone on the shore, the vast sun-spangled ocean on their right, stretching to a hazy horizon.

Something warm clung to his shoulder. He turned his head and looked into the innocent eyes of a child who was perhaps a year old. A boy. With soft skin the color of nutmeg, the child had Rachel's eyes and nose, Joshua's lips and cheekbones, a full head of dark, curly hair.

Justin, he thought. *Our son.*

Rachel looked at their child, then at him, and smiled—an expression of the purest joy, free of worry and fear. Her curly hair was auburn, not black, and she wasn't wearing her customary glasses.

He brought Rachel's hand to his lips and kissed her fingers.

Let's go to the house, she said. She winked, seductively. *Justin looks like he needs a nap.*

A house was ahead, on the left. It was a two-story Cape Cod, with lots of sun-silvered windows. A stone footpath, shaded by a palm tree, led from the shore to the house's broad patio and a balcony staircase.

Justin tugged at his ear, drawing his attention away from the house. His son pointed excitedly at something in the distance: a ferry that bobbed on the ocean waves like a child's bath toy.

That's the ferry, little man, Joshua said. *You've been on the ferry before, remember?*

Justin only giggled, and tugged his ear again.

Rachel had walked ahead; she was waiting at the patio door, Coco at her ankles, tail wagging. He kissed his son on the forehead, and followed Rachel inside. . . .

He awoke in darkness, breathing hard. His face was wet, and he realized that perspiration wasn't the culprit. He had been crying in his sleep.

He wiped his eyes with the heels of his hands.

The dream had been so *real*. He touched his earlobe; he felt the soft flesh throbbing from when his son had tugged at it during the dream.

Justin. It was the name he and Rachel had agreed upon, if they were blessed with a male child. His memory of the child's innocent face, the smooth texture of his skin, and the sweet, baby-fresh scent of him was imprinted on his mind as powerfully as the recollection of a recent experience.

And what about Rachel? He'd never seen her with auburn hair, and she always wore her thin-frame designer glasses.

A small shape shifted at the foot of the bed, reining his mind back into the darkened bedroom. Coco was sleeping with him on the king-size bed, and was having a dream of her own.

He'd tried to put the little dog in her kennel, where she slept at their house, but she had whined incessantly. Mom had banged on the door and yelled at him to make the dog shut up, or she was going to throw her outside and chain her to a tree in the backyard. When he brought Coco out of the kennel and put her in the bed with him, she had fallen into a restful slumber.

He could comfort the dog. But who could comfort him? The dream had left him with an almost paralyzing sense of loss, for it might never come true.

Would he ever see Rachel again? If she did return some day, would he ever be able to trust her? How could he trust someone who would leave him?

How could he trust someone who had lied about so much?

25

When she would look back, she would realize that everything that terrified her about Dexter Bates—everything that would make her regret the day they had met—was apparent on their very first date.

At exactly seven o'clock on a sultry July evening, Dexter rang the bell at her apartment in Hyde Park, a two-bedroom unit that she shared with a coworker. She was twenty-two years old and had lived in Chicago for only four months, and the excitement of the Windy City was a welcome change from the sleepy suburb in which she had grown up.

After checking herself in the mirror one last time, she went downstairs and met Dexter in the lobby. He was six feet tall, with the broad-shouldered build of a college athlete. Dressed in a navy-blue button-down shirt and gray slacks, hair neatly cut and mustache precisely trimmed, he resembled a young Denzel Washington.

She wore a light green sundress that flattered her figure, and open-toe heels that showed off her new pedicure. Her thick auburn hair, freshly styled by her roommate, spilled over her shoulders.

Whistling, Dexter scanned her from head to toe.

"You're so fine you should be against the law," he said.

She smiled shyly. "Are you going to arrest me, officer?"

"You keep looking like this and I just might."

He was a veteran of the Chicago Police Department, a detective in the narcotics division. When he walked—chin raised, shoulders squared as if marching to a silent cadence—he looked as though he had the entire city on a choke chain.

She immediately felt safe around him, protected.

She'd met him only a week ago. He'd strutted into the hair salon where she worked to chat with his cousin, the owner of the shop, and the gaze of every woman in there had been automatically drawn to him. In a sharp gray suit and Italian loafers, he radiated virile manly energy and cool authority.

Growing up, the only strong male presences in her life had lived on the television screen—watching Bill Cosby play Cliff Huxtable in The Cosby Show *was like seeing the father she wished she could remember. Both her parents had died when she was a child, and her aunt had raised her, her uncle having passed, too.*

Dexter must have possessed a sixth sense that drew him toward women like her, women who craved a powerful man, because before leaving the salon, he had walked by her station and introduced himself. He was polite, yet smoothly confident. In her peripheral vision, she saw the eyes of the other women narrow with envy when he asked for her phone number.

On their first phone conversation, he asked her on a date. Of course she wanted to go out with him. What woman wouldn't have?

"Shall we?" Dexter said, and offered his arm.

She put her arm through his, and he escorted her to his car. It was a white Corvette convertible, shimmering like a pearl in the waning evening sunlight. The polished chrome wheels gleamed.

"You're wondering how I can afford a ride like this on a cop's salary," he said.

"Actually, I hadn't thought about it. I assume that you're good with your money."

"Right answer."

He opened the passenger door for her. She settled onto the buttery leather. The interior was immaculate, and it held a new-car scent.

He got behind the wheel.

"I'm a neat freak. Guess it's obvious."

"I try to keep the apartment neat, too, but my roommate is messy. She leaves her clothes everywhere."

"Slobs should be shot."

His bluntness caused her to do a double-take.

He merely shrugged. "Better buckle up, baby."

He exploded out of the parking lot, shifting the manual transmission almost violently. She braced herself as he veered around a corner.

"A powerful machine like this needs a powerful man," he said, and winked.

She laughed uneasily, her stomach churning.

He drove with reckless abandon, as if he didn't care about being pulled over by a traffic cop, and he probably didn't. She didn't know much about police officers, but she knew they protected one another, like members of an elite fraternity.

He took her downtown to a popular, expensive steak-house. She was going to place her own order with the server, but Dexter took charge and ordered for the both of them.

"When you're with me, I'll take care of everything," he said.

"Thank you. I'm not really used to that."

"You've never dated a real man, sweetheart, that's why."

But she had dated authoritative men before, though none quite as electrifying as Dexter. In them, she saw, perhaps, the father she had never known. It was an unsettling idea—dating a man because he represented the father you had lacked as a child—but over time, she would come to seriously question if it might explain why she had allowed herself to be with him.

Dinner—a petite filet for her, a porterhouse for him—was delicious. But halfway through their meal, as they were chatting about sports—well, mostly she listened to him talk about the Bears—Dexter shouted at the server so suddenly that she dropped her fork against the plate.

"Hey, you, waiter!" He snapped his fingers and thrust his wineglass in the air. "Look here—my glass is empty. What the hell's the matter with you? I'm paying all this money for our goddamn dinner and you can't keep my glass full?"

The red-faced server offered an apology and scrambled to retrieve more wine.

"You spit in it, and I'll arrest you," Dexter called after him.

Dexter caught her watching the exchange.

"It's a simple matter of respect," he said.

"Could the server have only made a mistake?" she asked.

"Sure—and I'll make a mistake when it's time for the tip."

He changed the subject, but the incident lingered in the back of her mind.

After dinner, they went to see a movie. Although she expressed interest in seeing a Julia Roberts romantic comedy, when they reached the box office Dexter bought tickets for an action film.

During the movie, he put his arm around her shoulder and pulled her close. Her pulse raced, and she let herself melt into him. He smelled good, of woodsy spice and soap. And he was so sturdy and strong, unafraid to speak his mind.

Perhaps his outburst at the server had somehow been justified. After all, he had paid a lot of money for the meal and deserved good service. She would not have demanded a wine refill in the same tone as he, but he was a man, not only a man, but a cop, and clearly had little time for foolishness.

He moved his hand from her shoulder to her bare leg. He stroked gently, insistently, and she shivered as ripples of pleasure passed through her.

"You're so beautiful, you drive me crazy," he whispered in her ear. "After this, we should go back to my house and chill for a while."

"I'd like that," she said softly.

Although she was not a virgin, she had never slept with a man on the first date. But then, she had never been on a date with a man as compelling as Dexter. Being with him was like being swept along on a strong, fast-moving river; his energy was so primal and magnetic he seemed impossible to resist.

After the film, walking back to his car, they were talking about the movie, strolling casually along the sidewalk—when a man burst like a jack-in-the-box from the shadows of the alley.

Snarling, he seized her arm.

She screamed, but the man slapped a grubby hand over her mouth and jammed a knife against her side. Pain pierced her, and she cried out against his dirty palm.

"Shut up, bitch, or I'll cut your guts out," he said. His eyes were savage.

She bit back a scream. He dragged her into the dimly lit

alley and pinned her against the cold brick wall. Her purse strap rolled down her shoulder, and he grabbed the strap, snatched the purse away.

Dexter stood still on the sidewalk, his dark eyes like bullets.

Help me, please, *she thought.* Don't just stand there! You're a cop for God's sake!

"Give up your wallet," the guy spat at Dexter.

"Do you know who I am?" Dexter asked. His voice was low, almost a hiss.

"You're the one who's gonna pay me tonight."

He drove the knife deeper into her side, slitting her dress, puncturing her skin. Kicking futilely, she shrieked against the man's hand.

A gun suddenly appeared in Dexter's grip, so quickly it was as if he had produced it from his sleeve like a magician conjuring a card. She hadn't been aware that he was carrying a gun.

"Let her go," he said. "Or you'll be the one whose brains are gonna be hosed off the concrete tonight."

She wanted to shout with glee.

Staring at Dexter, the man swallowed. He eased the knife off her. He took a step back, dropping her purse to the ground.

"My . . . my bad," he said. "Stupid-ass mistake, man."

Tears of gratitude flooded her eyes. Dizzy, she leaned against the wall.

Her only clear thought was that Dexter had saved her.

The guy turned to run, but Dexter charged forward and slammed the butt of the pistol against his face. There was a yelp of pain, and the ugly sound of cracking bone and cartilage.

The man folded over, went down.

Hugging herself, she slid along the wall, moving away. She was so stunned she barely felt her legs underneath her.

Dexter moved over the robber. He kicked him sharply in the ribs. The man let out a choked gasp and curled into a ball.

"You disrespected me," Dexter said in a cool tone, as if kicking a man already down was as normal as strolling through a park.

"I'm . . . sorry . . ." the guy wheezed. "Please . . ."

"Not good enough."

She saw a glint of metal. Blinking fuzzily, she realized that Dexter had put on a set of brass knuckles. He flexed his hand eagerly.

Her gut churned.

"Dexter . . . please, let him go," she said. "I'm okay now. Let's go, okay?"

Dexter glared at her as if she had interrupted a private party.

"Go back to the sidewalk and wait," he said. "This is police business now."

His tone was cold—and final.

She bent on wobbly knees, grabbed her purse, and backpedaled down the alley.

Dexter grabbed the guy by his collar and hauled him to his feet. The man pleaded, but Dexter cut his cries short with a hard punch to the stomach that undoubtedly busted several blood vessels.

"You don't know who you're fucking with, do you?" Dexter asked.

He began to hammer the robber's face and body with steady, workmanlike punches, brass shattering bone, the man's drooping head knocking like a dummy's against the brick wall.

Dexter chanted repeatedly with each blow: "Take my woman? Huh? It's a simple matter of respect . . . need to learn respect . . . don't you know who I am . . ."

She stumbled out of the alley and rounded the corner. Her stomach convulsed. She drew deep inhalations of the humid night air to halt the wave of nausea.

Run, girl. *The voice was as clear and bright in her head as the stars above.* Run, girl, go home, and don't ever speak to him again.

But she didn't go anywhere. She thought, perhaps crazily, that it was too late to get away, that he had already decided to make her the one, and if she tried to run away, he would make her sorry. Just like he was making that would-be robber in the alley sorry for what he'd done.

Several long minutes later, Dexter marched around the corner. His eyes shone. He looked strangely invigorated, and there was not a single drop of blood on his person.

It was as if the violent episode had never happened. She didn't ask what had come of the robber. She was too afraid to ask, or to look.

"Come here." Dexter pulled her to him and kissed her lustily, placing his palm possessively on her butt.

She sighed, let her body open against his . . . and felt something deep inside her surrender to his strength, his iron will. This man would take care of her. He would defend her, he would fight for her, and if his flash of sudden violence frightened her, maybe it was because she'd spent her entire life in ignorance of how true men of authority behaved.

That was what she believed back then.

He took her hand. "Let's get out of here and go to my place."

She went home with him.

And stayed for three terrifying years.

26

The next morning, Joshua left his parents' house early. He had much to do, and he had to get home to start.

The day was overcast and chilly, with a knife-sharp wind that reminded him that it was the middle of December. Christmas was less than a week away. This would have been his and Rachel's first Christmas together as a married couple.

His heart clutched painfully. He had to stop thinking about stuff like that.

He pulled into the garage, and found Rachel's spot empty. He'd imagined that her Acura would be sitting there, that everything would be back to normal and yesterday would prove to have been only a bad dream.

He walked Coco around the yard for a few minutes to let her potty, and then he went inside.

The house was as he had left it last night. Although everything looked the same, it all seemed vacant and cold to him, as if it were a museum displaying relics of a life that he had once lived.

He checked voice mail on the landline, and e-mail on his computer. There were no messages from anyone, not even potential or current clients. It was as if the whole world had abandoned him.

He was in no shape to work, anyway. Graphic design demanded concentration and imagination, and every time he closed his eyes, he saw Rachel's face and felt a sick fluttering in his stomach.

He ate a breakfast of cereal, fruit, and orange juice that tasted like cardboard. He tried to follow the morning news on TV as he ate, but found it difficult to concentrate.

After putting away the dishes, he entered Rachel's study. The room smelled of her: sweet, clean, feminine. It was almost too much to bear.

He sat in the spring-backed chair, adjusting the height to keep his knees from bumping against the edge of the desk.

He tried to view the room as if he were seeing it for the first time, in the hope that a clue would jump out at him. He looked at the colorful wall hanging that read, *Too Anointed to Be Disappointed.* Her collection of novels shelved in the bookcase: Alice Walker was a favorite author of hers. Her assortment of ceramic dog figurines. Photos from their wedding. A picture of an unnamed, white-sand beach.

The beach photograph brought to mind last night's dream. He felt a coiling of emotion in his gut.

Nothing in the room sparked any inspiration. Back to square one: the computer.

He raised the lid of the laptop and powered it on.

An inch-long strand of hair lay on the keyboard, atop the space bar. He plucked it off the key, held it between his thumb and forefinger.

Ever since he'd known her, Rachel had had dark hair. This strand was lighter, closer to auburn.

In his dream, Rachel's hair had been auburn, too.

He'd never seen her color her hair. But she owned a hair salon, and it would have been easy for her to dye her hair at work, and keep her true hair color a secret.

He pulled a Kleenex from a box on the desk, and set the strand of hair on the tissue, for later consideration.

The laptop had finished its boot-up cycle and brought him to the sign-on screen, where he'd been flummoxed yesterday. He stared at the display, big hands resting on the keyboard.

Combing through the files on Rachel's computer seemed a logical step to learning more about what she'd hidden. But again, a password eluded him.

Thinking of what he knew about her background, he typed in a few Chicago-related words—*Chicago, the windy city*, *the sears tower*—and all of them proved fruitless.

There had to be a better way to gain access to the system. This was going nowhere.

He turned off the computer, unplugged it, and wrapped the power cord around the plastic casing. He carried the machine downstairs and slid it inside a canvas satchel.

He remembered Rachel's cell phone. Her address book or call history might also yield valuable information. He took the phone out of its charger on the kitchen counter, and pressed the On button.

The first screen on the tiny LCD display requested a pass code to proceed.

The security precautions seemed extreme. This was her personal cell, and she only used the laptop at home, for the most part.

What have you been hiding from me, Rachel?

He switched off the phone, and dropped it into the bag, too.

27

Tim was watching television behind the counter when Joshua entered the shop. He was smoking a cigarette and sipping a cup of coffee.

"You back already?" Tim asked.

That day, Tim wore a long black T-shirt that read, in giant red and green text, IT'S A BLACK THING—YOU WOULDN'T UNDERSTAND.

"Interesting shirt," Joshua said.

"It's a vintage shirt, dude. From like the eighties. Classic."

Joshua heard a Public Enemy song playing on the stereo at low volume. His memory of the track's title was fuzzy, but he thought it was "Fight the Power."

"Is this Black Pride Day in Price Electronics?" Joshua asked.

"I appreciate all cultures, my brother," Tim said and nodded sagely. He blew out a ring of smoke and grinned.

"Whatever, man. I need your help again."

"With?"

Joshua placed the satchel on the counter and opened it. He withdrew the laptop and the cell phone.

"First, I need access to this computer. When I turn it on, I get stuck at the log on screen when it asks me for a password."

Tim took a puff on his smoke, frowned.

"You don't know your own password? Even when I'm at my *most* stoned, I remember my freakin' passwords, dude."

"This isn't my computer. It's my wife's."

"Then why not ask her the password?"

He was not about to tell Tim what had happened. Although Tim was a friend, they had never shared details of their private lives with each other. Theirs was mostly a friendship that revolved around their work lives.

"She's not around for me to ask," Joshua said.

"Your lady creeping around on you?"

"What?"

"Okay, it's none of my business. But if you want some advice . . ."

"You ever been married, Tim?"

"You crazy? Hell, no, that's like, legalized bondage."

"Exactly. So no, I don't want any advice."

"Suit yourself." Tim shrugged, slid the laptop toward him and raised the lid. "What're you looking for on here?"

"I need to look through some files. I'm not exactly sure which ones yet."

"This is highly unethical, you know," Tim said. "Invading your wife's privacy and all. You one of those ultra-jealous, stalker husbands? Like that guy in that Julia Roberts movie, *Sleeping with the Enemy* or whatever?"

"It's for a good reason, Tim, I promise."

Squinting at Joshua, Tim tapped ashes into a tray that looked like a hollowed-out mouse pad.

"All right, look," he said. "I can probably get in, but it's not gonna help you much if she trashed all the files. She might've covered her tracks or whatever. I can recover deleted files, but that can get a little hairy."

"Let's deal with that later. I just want to get on the system and see what I find."

Tim pointed at the cell phone with his cigarette. "What about that?"

"It has a password, too."

"Damn, your wife is like, super private with her stuff. Who puts a password on a freakin' cell phone?"

"She did."

"What the heck is she hiding, man? Like, government secrets or something?"

"Wish I knew. Can you hack it?"

"Piece of cake, both of 'em. Come back around . . ." Tim studied his watch. It had a 3-D image of Barney on the face.

"Barney?" Joshua asked.

"He was my childhood hero. Don't knock him."

"We were teenagers when Barney came out."

"So? He's always so happy. He makes me laugh."

"To each his own." Joshua shook his head. "What time should I come back?"

"About sevenish. I'd get to it earlier, but I've got a lot of crapola on my plate today."

"No problem. I owe you."

"One of these days, you need to let me come break bread with the brothers."

"There you go."

As Joshua was walking back to his Explorer, his cell rang. It was Tanisha.

"Can you come to the salon, honey?" she asked. "Rachel wants me to give you something."

His heart slammed.

"You talked to her? When?"

"She called me about five minutes ago. I don't understand what's going on, but you need to come to the salon. When can you get here?"

28

Driving all night without sleep, Dexter arrived in Atlanta on Wednesday morning.

He'd visited the city many times. During his early twenties, he'd made the annual sojourn to Freaknic, the now-defunct, legendary spring break party that invariably would degenerate into a sort of Bacchanalian bash: people dancing in the streets, falling down drunk, and fucking with wild abandon.

Needless to say, he had fond memories of the ATL.

It had been several years since he'd been to the city, and it had grown. As he wove through the heart of downtown on Interstate 75/85 South, new, gleaming skyscrapers dominated the skyline, reminding him of Chicago. Giant electronic billboards advertised airlines and athletic events. The day was young, but traffic clogged the roadways, too, crawling at a maddening pace.

In a metro area so vast and populous, tracking down his wife would prove a challenge. Undoubtedly, she had chosen to relocate here because she doubted he could find her in an unfamiliar city.

What she failed to realize was that while he didn't know the city intimately, he knew *her* intimately. Knew her habits, her idiosyncrasies. Her likes and dislikes. Her particular way of viewing the world. It would not have mattered if she'd chartered a boat to sail to the most remote island on the high seas. He possessed the map to her soul, and it would eventually lead him to her.

Exiting the highway past downtown, he found a Waffle House, an inexpensive diner that specialized in artery clogging food. He ordered a huge breakfast. Five scrambled eggs. Two sides of sausage, two sides of bacon. A side of hash browns, scattered, smothered, and covered. A bowl of grits. A pot of coffee.

He didn't plan on slowing down the search, and he had to keep his energy level up.

"You real hungry this morning, huh?" the waitress asked, after delivering the hot plates to his table.

He looked up. She was a chunky sister with streaks of red in her permed hair, a gold tooth, and a tattoo of a rose on her forearm. Her name tag read Vernethia.

"Where's the closest library, sweetheart?" he asked.

"Hmm." Her gaze was fuzzy. "Umm . . . I don't know."

What a travesty. A grown woman didn't know the location of the nearest public library. He hoped she didn't have any children—stupidity was often an inherited trait.

"Do you have a phone book here, Vernethia?" he asked. "In the back office, perhaps?"

Her dumb eyes brightened.

"Lemme check."

She returned with a Yellow Pages directory. He placed it beside his plates and thumbed through it until he found what he was looking for.

An hour later, with the aid of the StreetPilot, he arrived at Southwest Regional Library on Cascade Road.

Inside, a bank of several, free-to-use computers stood against a wall. He settled in front of one of the machines and logged onto the Internet.

As a narcotics detective, being technologically savvy had given him an advantage over his colleagues. Any narc could rough up a suspect or shake down a dealer. But he'd made full use of police technology in chasing down leads, researching, or conducting surveillance, and had amassed an arrest rate that had blown many of his peers in the dust.

Inmates weren't allowed access to the Internet. It would have given them contact with Outside, and restricting exposure to the outside world was one of the primary purposes of imprisoning someone in the first place. But certain correctional officers who appreciated a quality bribe had enabled him to enjoy regular Web access, to stay abreast of the ever-changing realm of cyberspace.

He went to a Web site called Omega Search. Omega Search was a free search engine for people. It pulled data from public records and government sources: court documents, county and state property records, and the like. You could find a person's addresses for the past ten years, their phone numbers during the same period, and date of birth. Another feature allowed you to see an overhead satellite photo of the target's residence.

In the Information Age, nothing was private. Many companies were in the business of compiling, generating, storing, and selling confidential personal data. Even an unlisted phone number, while not accessible in directory assistance or a phone book, could be sold for other uses.

He'd narrowed his wife's location to Atlanta. All he needed was her home address, and the key to finding her address on Omega Search was her name.

He entered "Rachel Hall" in the search field, and restricted results to the state of Georgia.

The site returned eight hits. Five of them were "R. Hall," which could have stood for anyone with a first name that began with the letter "r." Of the remaining three, one of them used the alternate spelling of Rachel, "Rachael." There were two Rachel Halls.

All of the entries included street addresses and phone numbers.

He sent the document to the printer.

As he stood at the printer waiting for the document, a young woman strolled past. He smiled at her, and she smiled back, but then she wrinkled her nose, as if she smelled something putrid.

"The fuck is her problem?" he said, watching her wander away.

He gave his armpit a whiff, and grimaced. He'd been so focused on his work that he'd neglected his personal hygiene.

He took the print-out to the Chevy, and then returned inside the library with his duffel bag. He holed up in the men's restroom, where he washed with soapy water, changed into fresh clothes, brushed his teeth and hair, applied deodorant, and shaved.

Afterward, he checked himself out in the mirror. He looked like a clean-cut, upstanding member of society again.

Back in the car, he entered the address for the first entry into the StreetPilot. When in doubt, start from the beginning.

With only eight possibilities to explore, he would find her by that evening.

29

Driving fast enough to risk a speeding ticket, Joshua arrived at Belle Coiffure.

It was late morning, and almost every chair in the salon was occupied. The air had been filled with the chatter of the stylists and their clients, but at his entrance, the women turned, almost as one, and checked him out, the volume in the room lowering during their impromptu inspection.

He cleared his throat. Entering Rachel's salon—or any place inhabited exclusively by women—had always made him nervous. Because of his height and broad build, he tended to attract a lot of female attention, and their appraising looks brought back his memories of being an ungainly kid, the tallest one in his class, a target of merciless teasing from boys and nervous giggling from girls.

His unanswered questions added to his discomfort. What did these women know about Rachel? Did they know she had left? Did they think she had run away because of him? Did they think she had left him for another man?

He cleared his throat again. “Is Tanisha here?”

“She’s in the back making a call,” a young stylist on his left said. She smiled. “You can go on back there. We know you.”

He felt their gazes on him as he went down the center of the room. He knocked on the STAFF ONLY door.

Tanisha answered. She was talking on the phone, but she said to him, “Hey, honey. Come on in.”

She indicated a sofa for him to sit on, but he remained on his feet. He was too wound up to sit.

He looked around the back office. He’d been in there a few times before when visiting Rachel, but he tried to view the space with fresh eyes.

The area was furnished with a sofa, a handful of chairs, a television, and a coffee table on which were scattered magazines such as *Essence* and *Black Hair*. In an office enclosure, there was a file cabinet and two desks, one for Tanisha, the other for Rachel, a desktop computer sitting on each.

He doubted Rachel would have stored any files of a personal nature on her work computer, since Tanisha probably had access to it. She would have been more cautious.

Photographs also cluttered Rachel’s desk. A couple of their wedding photos, and one of her beloved beach pictures. All shots that he had seen before, in their home.

Rachel’s desk had three drawers. As he wondered whether she had hidden something significant in one of them, Tanisha ended her phone call.

“You got here fast,” she said.

“I’ve been trying to get in touch with Rachel,” he said. “What did she say?”

“Not much.” Tanisha sat in one of the desk chairs, swiveled around to face him. “She said she was going to be away for a while, and asked if I could keep running things here at the salon."

"Did she say how long she'd be gone?"

"I asked her. She wouldn't tell me. I don't think she knew herself, to be honest. She was real vague."

"Where did she call you from?"

"I asked her, but she wouldn't say, and nothing showed up on Caller ID."

He ground his teeth. He sat on Rachel's desk chair, pushed up his glasses on his nose.

"Did she tell you anything useful?" he asked.

"It was a really brief call, Josh. She didn't answer any of my questions. She said she was fine, and she wanted you to know that she was safe—and she wanted me to give you something."

"That was my next question."

Tanisha produced a key from a ring that was clipped to her waist. She unlocked the bottom right drawer of Rachel's desk and removed a black steel box that was about the size of a standard dictionary. A silver padlock secured the lid.

He took it from her. It weighed perhaps five pounds. He shook it, and something shifted inside.

"What is this?" he asked.

She shrugged. "I thought you would know. I didn't know she was keeping it in her desk."

"Do you have a key to open it?"

"No, I looked." She jangled her key ring. "None of these fit, either. I tried." Redness flushed her fair complexion. "Sorry, I know I was out of line for that, but Rachel was talking so weird I was hoping to get some answers for myself, too."

"And I was hoping to get some answers from you. I don't know much more than you do."

"This is probably none of my business," Tanisha said, "but I know you've been treating Rachel well. I know you're a good man. But . . ."

"But what?"

"But Rachel has always been so secretive. She's my girl and all, and we work well together, but our friendship is kind of superficial. She doesn't let people in, if you know what I mean."

He was surprised that Tanisha had such insight into Rachel's personality, but on retrospect, he shouldn't have been surprised at all. Tanisha had known Rachel a couple of years longer than he had, and had worked with her daily. Her opinion of his wife was as valid as his.

"She's very private," he said.

"I could be way off base," Tanisha said, "but in my experience, when someone tries to keep you from getting too close, it's 'cause they have something to hide."

"What do you think she was hiding?"

"I don't know, but let me tell you what happened yesterday, around lunch. Rachel was doing a client's hair, and all of a sudden, she gets a call on her cell and practically runs back here to take it. Like it was an emergency."

"Any idea who called her?"

"I thought it was you, actually. Maybe fifteen minutes later, she left. She said she had to go to an appointment, but she looked to me like she'd been crying her eyes out. Of course, she wouldn't admit it—she was keeping me at arm's length, like she usually does."

He thought about when he'd seen Rachel at home yesterday, and the bizarre bout of tears that she declined to explain. *What the hell had happened?*

"So." Tanisha clasped her hands together in her lap. "I don't know what you can do with that information, but that's what happened here. Whatever went down, it probably had something with her leaving so fast. When was the last time you saw her?"

"Yesterday evening. I think she's in some kind of trouble, but I've no idea from what, or who." He added: "She left me a letter."

She touched his arm. "I'm so sorry."

"She said she's coming back. But she didn't say when."

"Take it from another woman," Tanisha said. "If a woman's in trouble, a man usually has something to do with it."

"Has she ever mentioned another guy, anyone you can remember?"

"No way. In the three years I've known Rachel, you're the only man she'd ever even *dated*. She'd say you were the most special guy she'd ever met."

"Obviously, not special enough to tell the truth," he said, under his breath.

"Come again?"

"Never mind. One more thing: did Rachel dye her hair?"

"Oh, yeah, all the time. Auburn was her natural color, but she liked to keep it dark. Why?"

"It was something I never knew about her," he said softly.

"Between you and me, I get the feeling there's a lot we don't know about Rachel." She smiled bitterly.

He stood, putting the box under his arm. "Thanks for giving this to me, whatever it is. And thanks for talking to me about Rachel. It's helpful."

"I wish I had more answers for you. You love that girl to death. It's all in your eyes."

"Yeah."

"God'll work it out." Tanisha closed her fingers around the gold crucifix that dangled from her necklace. "Stay faithful, honey. Let go, and let God."

He barely heard her last words—a ray of insight had struck him. He thanked Tanisha again and quickly left the salon, oblivious this time to the curious glances from the assembled women, walking as fast as he could without breaking into a run.

He knew where he could find the key to open the box.

30

At home, Coco greeted Joshua excitedly, running in circles and whining to be taken outside for a walk, but the little dog would have to wait.

He switched on the lights in the kitchen and placed the box on the table.

When Rachel had left him the letter yesterday, she'd also left him a key. He'd stored both in a kitchen drawer. Leaving them in clear view was too hurtful a reminder of what had happened.

He dug the key out of the drawer and inserted it into the padlock. It fit. He turned it, and the lock clicked open.

He removed the padlock and raised the lid.

A layer of black velvet concealed the contents. He grasped the edge of the fabric, peeled it away.

His heart beat soared.

A revolver lay inside, in a metal tray fitted to the weapon's contours. The gun had a black rubber grip, and a stainless steel barrel about three inches long. Smith & Wesson was engraved on the side of the barrel.

He didn't know what he had been expecting, but he certainly had not been expecting this.

Slowly and carefully, he lifted the gun out of the tray. The tray shifted at the disturbance, and something moved underneath. He placed the gun on the table, and lifted out the tray, too.

There was a cardboard box of ammunition.

"Jesus," he said.

This latest discovery was another piece in the jigsaw puzzle that was his wife. Why had she kept this gun at the salon? Had she been concerned that she'd have to put down her curling iron and blow someone away?

He tried to imagine Rachel, his sweet-tempered wife, wielding this lethal weapon, and it just didn't fit into what he knew of her.

But as Tanisha had aptly noted, there was a lot that neither of them knew about Rachel.

He gripped the revolver's black handle.

He'd never fired a real gun. His only experience with firearms was of the toy variety: Laser tag, Paintball, video games. When he was a teenager, his dad had been a weekend outdoorsman and would go hunting for white-tail deer and quail, and he would want to bring Joshua along, but his mother had forbid it. She'd been concerned for Joshua's safety.

He cautiously touched the trigger. The thought of handling the revolver and actually using it for self-defense was almost as absurd as the idea of Rachel using the weapon. He was not a combative person by nature, would have rather fled the scene than engage someone in a violent confrontation of any kind—least of all a gunfight.

He opened the box of ammo and dumped a couple of rounds into his palm. They were shiny, silver, deadly.

Was the revolver loaded? He didn't know, and didn't know how to check, either.

He was tempted to pack the revolver in the box, shove it to the rear of a closet, and forget about it. But Rachel's warning from her letter whispered through his thoughts.

I've left you a key. It will unlock something that I pray you won't need.

Did she believe he actually might be in danger, too? If so, from who?

He placed the gun and the ammo back in the box, and locked it. But he didn't store the box in the closet—he left it on the kitchen table.

And then he called Eddie.

31

Eddie lived in the West End, not far from where he worked at the college, in a tree-lined, historic district of Craftsman bungalows, Victorians, and Colonial Revival homes. Like many in-town Atlanta neighborhoods that had once suffered severe urban blight, the West End was in the midst of a revitalization campaign. Less than a mile from the historic area, new condos were being constructed, big box stores were opening for business, and well-heeled residents who wouldn't have dared to visit only a few years ago were purchasing old homes and renovating them.

Eddie's green clapboard-shingled Craftsman stood behind a wrought iron fence, a narrow paved lane leading to the detached garage. A web of holiday lights was spun across the trimmed shrubbery and eaves, and a plastic Frosty the Snowman spread cheer in the front yard.

Eddie greeted Joshua at the door.

"Hey, dawg. Come on in."

Joshua walked inside with his satchel dangling over his

shoulder. Although much of the exterior and interior of their home had been restored to its period detail, the furnishings were completely modern: microfiber sofa and chairs in light earthy colors, glass tables, track lighting, stainless steel appliances. A child safety gate surrounded the home entertainment center, childproof lever locks protected the doorknobs, and cushions softened the edges of the tables.

The house was quiet.

"You here alone?" Joshua asked.

"The wife's at work, the kids are at day care—that's right, they're at day care and I'm home in peace. I'm playing *Madden* and eating Cheetos."

When Joshua had called Eddie, he hadn't told him the reason he wanted to visit. Eddie, an assistant football coach at Clark, was on vacation since the season had recently wrapped up, and probably assumed Joshua wanted to hang out playing video games and eating junk food, as if they were teenagers again.

"Check this out." Joshua placed the satchel on the sofa, removed the box, and set it on the coffee table.

"What's that?" Eddie asked.

Joshua unlocked the case, opened it, and pulled back the swatch of velvet.

Eddie's eyes swelled like balloons.

"Oh, shit. Where'd you get that from, man?"

"Rachel gave it to me."

"Rachel? Your wife?"

"It's a long story."

"Well, tell a brother. Damn."

Joshua related the entire course of events to Eddie, starting from the nightmare Rachel had experienced the other night—which he'd already told Eddie about—and on through his discovery of the handgun that morning.

"I don't believe it," Eddie said. "How the hell could she do this to you, man?"

"I thought I knew her." Joshua shrugged, exhausted from his retelling of the story. "Guess I was wrong."

"I need a drink. You want something?"

"It's kinda early for a drink."

"This ain't the time to be straitlaced. Your wife is gone. You need a damn drink."

While Eddie dashed to the kitchen, Joshua glanced around the room. Photographs of Eddie and his wife and children were everywhere. Colorful snapshots of familial bliss.

Feeling a hard lump forming in his throat, Joshua had to look away.

Eddie returned. He offered Joshua a glass teeming with dark amber liquor and ice cubes.

Joshua sniffed it. "What is this?"

"Cognac. It'll set you right."

Joshua took a small sip. The cognac hit him like a taste of fire, but it immediately loosened the ball of tension that had been knotted in his chest for the past two days. He exhaled a deep breath.

"See?" Eddie sipped his own shot of cognac. "Relaxes the nerves. You were wound up tight as a clock spring, dawg."

"I wouldn't want to make this a habit, but thanks." Joshua tapped the gun case. "What do you make of this?"

Eddie set his liquor aside and plucked the revolver out of the box.

"It's a .38," Eddie said. "Nice piece for home defense."

"So you know guns?"

With an adept flick of his wrist, Eddie swung out the cylinder.

"It's not loaded," Eddie said. "Rule number one: always assume a gun is loaded, until you prove that it isn't."

"That means the answer to my question is yes."

"My pops was an army man. He taught all of us how to handle a piece. Matter of fact, I've got a couple of pieces here, too, under lock and key 'cause of the kids, you know?"

"I never knew that about you."

"You never know everything there is to know about anyone, do you?"

"Tell me about it." Joshua smiled grimly.

Eddie lifted the tray out of the box and located the ammo. He shook one of the rounds into his palm and held it up for inspection.

"Hollow points," Eddie said. "These will get the job done for real."

"All I know about hollow points is what I've heard in a few hip-hop songs. They seem to be the ammo of choice for gangstas."

"Here's the deal. When they hit flesh, they expand." Eddie traced his index finger along the top edge of the round. "It goes from looking like it does now, to a mushroom. Tearing up all kinds of tissue in the process."

Joshua grimaced. "I don't know if I can shoot someone, Eddie. I mean, you know me. I'm not a violent guy."

"Remember our little talk at your party the other night? About protecting your wife and your kids?"

Although he hadn't told Eddie about Rachel's pregnancy, in retrospect, their conversation that night seemed prescient. "I remember."

"If you meant what you said, then you'll do whatever you've gotta do," Eddie said. "I don't agree with what Rachel's done, but she's still your wife, you still love her. She's running scared from somebody, man, and when push comes to shove, you've gotta be ready to protect your own. Are you? If not, you might as well lock this gun in the box and forget about it."

Joshua sat quietly, swirling the cognac around the glass. He took another sip. It was like liquid fire going down his throat, but it felt good, like a fortifying element steeling his spirit.

He reached for the gun.

"Show me how to use this," he said.

32

Dexter had logged over three hundred miles that day, driving from one place to another around metro Atlanta, and he had yet to find his wife's residence.

He'd visited single-family homes, townhouses, and apartment complexes. He'd driven through the hood and upscale subdivisions. He'd been mired in gridlock in various parts of town—this city had the worst traffic he'd ever seen in his life—for a cumulative total of maybe five hours.

But no luck.

He was convinced that he would know intuitively when he arrived at his wife's home. The exterior details of the residence, and the neighborhood in which it was located, would be telltale indicators of whether he was at the right place. He knew his wife.

So he continued to drive, undeterred, crossing an entry off the print-out after each unsuccessful visit. He interrupted his work only to eat, grabbing fast food and wolfing it down in the car, staying on the move.

It reminded him, pleasantly, of detective work. When you

were a cop, success was usually a matter of methodically grinding it out, finding leads, discarding leads, until you finally struck pay dirt and caught your man—or woman.

The cold, gray winter afternoon had darkened into a frigid evening when he began driving to the next-to-last address on his list. It was an apartment in College Park.

The StreetPilot instructed him to hook a right at the next intersection. He made the turn, which plunged him down a stomach-flipping hill. At the foot of the hill, the road banked to the left, wove around a cluster of pine trees, and then unfurled into a long straight-away bordered by winter-ravaged trees and shrubbery.

A large sign came into view ahead on the right: FOREST RIDGE APARTMENT HOMES.

A cool tingle traveled the length of his spine. This was it. This was where she lived. It *felt* right.

Entry to the complex was restricted by a set of electronically activated, wrought-iron gates. Big, red holiday bows adorned the centers of the gates, and a call box, also garlanded in holiday finery, stood in front of the gateway, between the entrance and exit paths.

He drove to the call box and lowered his window. Chilly wind hit him in the face. He squinted against the gust, studying the small lighted display and the accompanying keypad.

Residents were listed by first name initial and last name; a three-digit code was beside each entry, so you could call the person you were visiting and ask them to buzz you inside.

Putting his thumb on an arrow button, he scrolled to the "H"s. He did not find any Halls.

A Honda Civic with a Papa John's placard on its roof had pulled up behind him. The driver tapped his horn, impatiently.

Dexter veered to the right, out of the entryway, and stuck his arm out the window to wave the driver past.

The pizza delivery driver punched a code into the call box, and the gates began to swing inward.

Dexter pulled behind the Honda, only inches from the rear bumper, to fool the sensor system. He followed the car through the gate without incident.

So much for security.

The complex was a maze of four-story buildings with stacked stone foundations and gray siding, accessible via blacktopped, debris-free roadways. The leasing office and a clubhouse stood off to the right, near a large fountain with an angelic sculpture centerpiece. A sign on the clubhouse advertised an upcoming holiday party for community residents.

His survey of the property cemented his belief that his wife lived here, or had, until recently. The gated entry offered the promise of safety that she would desire, and the environment was solidly middle class: upwardly mobile single professionals and young families saving for their first homes would choose to live in such a place.

Most important, besides the complex's appearance, the needle on the compass of his intuition was vibrating as if he stood smack dab on magnetic north.

According to Omega Search, her apartment number was five-seventeen. He followed the signs to building five hundred, and found it located squarely in the middle of the community. Unit five-seventeen was on the third floor, and knowing his wife, likely faced the parking lot so she could look through the window and see who was coming and going.

A handful of late-model cars were parked in front. When he and his wife had lived in Chicago, he hadn't allowed her to own a car; a pretty woman with her own set of wheels was destined to get into trouble. But she had once expressed interest in an Acura sedan, a silver one, and he was sure that she had purchased the vehicle when she'd relocated, using his money. Her way of celebrating her liberation from him and all of that feminist bullshit.

But there were no Acuras parked nearby.

He parked in front of the building, checked his face in the sun visor mirror. Satisfied with what he saw, he got out of the car and climbed the stairs to the third floor.

Apartment five-seventeen, as he'd suspected, was an end unit that overlooked the parking lot. A couple of phone books were stacked on the doorstep, and a trifold menu for a Chinese restaurant bristled between the knob and door jamb.

He rang the bell a couple of times, but predictably, no one answered. The apartment was vacant.

He ought to drop a pointed note to Omega Search. Their database was out of date. How long ago had she moved?

He considered kicking in the door, but there would be little point. Whenever a tenant left, the apartment manager most likely dispatched housekeepers to clean these units from top to bottom. There would be nothing inside that might tell him where she had moved.

He looked at the doors surrounding him. He approached the apartment directly across the corridor from five-seventeen. He placed his ear against the cold door.

He heard a television broadcasting the news, and a woman talking loudly, probably on the phone. She sounded young, which was good.

He straightened his jacket, grateful that he had cleaned up that morning and changed clothes. He rang the doorbell.

The volume of the television dropped. A few seconds later, he felt the woman looking at him through the peephole.

He kept his expression friendly and relaxed, though tense anticipation bubbled in his gut. For a six-month period during his police career, he had worked as an undercover narc. Playing a fictitious character was easy when it was necessary for the job.

"Who's there?" she asked from behind the door.

"I'm sorry to bother you this evening," he said, using a crisp, official voice. "I was wondering if you knew Rachel Hall? She lived in five-seventeen. I'm her cousin Brian, from Chicago."

A pause. Then, "Hold on."

He heard a security chain pop free. The door opened.

He found himself looking at a woman in her mid-twenties. She was about five-seven, mocha-skinned, with shoulder-length dark hair. She had soft, almond-shaped brown eyes that would believe anything a brother with half-decent game would tell her.

She wore a green V-neck sweater that showed off a mound of luscious cleavage, and black slacks that hugged long, shapely legs. She was barefoot, her pedicured toes nestled in the carpet. Her ring finger was bare, and when he glanced over her shoulder, he didn't see anyone straining to find out who had rung the doorbell.

"Hi." He gave her his best, disarming smile.

Automatically, she smiled back at him, showing pretty dimples, and he knew she would give him anything he wanted.

"Hey," she said. "You said you're Rachel's cousin?"

"I flew in from Chicago this morning for a business trip, and thought I'd drop by to visit Ray-Ray. I haven't talked to her in a couple of years—"

"Sweetheart, you're kinda late." She had a syrupy sweet Southern accent. "Rachel moved out like six months ago."

"Are you serious? I asked Aunt Nita a hundred times if

this was the correct address. I think she's going senile in her old age, God bless her."

"Uh huh." The girl giggled. "Rachel moved out when she got married."

He blinked. The phrase—*when she got married*—almost destroyed his act. Married? Was she telling the fucking truth? The bitch had gotten him thrown into prison, stolen his money, come down here, and gotten married?

He had a sudden impulse to grab this young woman by the throat and throttle her, to choke her as if she were his wife, his cheating, thieving wife—

But he caught himself so quickly that the girl didn't appear to notice his temporary lapse.

"And you know, I asked Aunt Nita about that, too," he said. "I said, 'Aunt Nita, are you sure Ray-Ray didn't move after she got married?' She said no." He shrugged. "But it's not as though I was invited to the wedding."

"Chile, who you tellin'?" She rolled her eyes. "I lived next door to her for a year, and *I* didn't get an invitation. Plus, I was going to her salon, too. Ungrateful."

Her off-handed mention of the salon clinched the deal. Although his wife had relocated, changed her name, and supposedly gotten married, she was plying the same trade. Dumb bitch. She couldn't do anything else.

"She didn't invite you, either? Well, Ray-Ray could be a trip sometimes." He sighed, glanced at the parking lot, and then turned back to her. "Where's her salon? I'll try to catch her there."

"It's over in East Point, like ten minutes from here. Hold on a minute. I think I have her card somewhere."

She disappeared inside. He waited in the hallway. He balled his hands into fists, nails digging into his palms and leaving red marks like stigmata.

She got married . . .

When the woman returned to the door, he unclenched his hands and smiled.

She had brushed her hair and applied a fresh coat of burgundy-colored lipstick. He thought he picked up a whiff of perfume, too.

She handed a business card to him. Their fingers touched, briefly.

"I'm Shakira, by the way." She was smiling hard, displaying those dimples.

"Nice to meet you, Shakira."

He studied the card. It was printed on thick, glossy red stock, with embossed white lettering. The name of the salon was Belle Coiffure. It listed the master stylists and owners as Tanisha May and Rachel Hall, and even had a small photo of the two women posed together.

His wife was wearing glasses, and she had cut her hair and dyed it black, but it was her.

"You've been to this place?" he asked.

"Yep. It's real nice. I haven't been in a minute, though. It's kinda hard to get an appointment."

"Ray-Ray always could do some hair, you know." He tapped the card against his wrist. "Thanks for this, Shakira. I'm going to visit the salon right now—I'll be sure to tell Rachel you said hello."

"Okay." Leaning against the doorway, arms folded across her bosom to lift her perky breasts higher, Shakira batted her eyelashes. "How long you gonna be in town?"

"That depends on how long my business keeps me here."

" 'Cause I was gonna say, if you need someone to like, show you the city . . . I'm a native. A luscious Georgia peach." Her gaze was direct.

"What's your number?" he asked, and then chuckled. "Since I already know where you live."

As she told him her number, he programmed it into his cell phone.

"I may call you later tonight," he said. "After I visit Rachel. She and I have some catching up to do . . . yeah, *a whole lot* to talk about."

33

After only three dizzying months of dating, she and Dexter were wed by the Justice of the Peace on the South Side of Chicago.

By then, at his urging, she had already moved in with him. The marriage was only a formality.

Her family and friends thought she was crazy for marrying so quickly. "When love is real, you can't put a time frame on it," she had told them, in the most sincere tone she could muster, and hoped they believed her.

Mostly, she wanted to believe it herself. Since she'd been a little girl, she had entertained fantasies of a fairy-tale wedding: a beautiful bridal dress, a lovely church ceremony, a stretch limousine, a big bridal party and three-tier cake, and most of all, the perfect man, someone gentle and strong and kind, someone she had married because of true love.

Deep down, she knew she didn't marry Dexter out of love.

She married him out of fear.

Although the night of their first date was the only time she had seen him beat someone, she knew, from overhearing his conversations with his cop buddies who came by the house (at all hours, it seemed) that dispensing violence was a regular part of his job. They joked about roughing up suspects. They bragged about who they had shot in the line of duty. Dexter, in particular, boasted about how no one, ever, got away from him, and he apparently had an arrest record a mile long.

She could attest to his persistence, his driving will. While dating, he called her every day, at least three times. They went on dates daily. If she wasn't working at the salon, she was almost always with him, or somewhere he could keep close watch on her—he hated when she went home to Zion to visit her aunt Betty.

Always when she was with him, there was a tangible sense of violence waiting to strike, like the quiet before a thunderstorm. It was in his eyes. In his tone. In his body language and coiled muscles.

Turning down his marriage proposal was never an option.

He didn't unleash his fury on her until after they were married—when they were on their honeymoon in Jamaica.

Lying under an umbrella on a white sand beach at an all-inclusive resort in Negril, wearing a bikini and sunglasses, she was reading an Alice Walker novel while Dexter was off playing beach volleyball with a group of men and women who'd started up a game. She glanced at him from time to time. He was playing aggressively, talking loudly and boastfully, leaping up and spiking the ball hard enough to drive it into the back of the skull of anyone unlucky enough to get in the way.

He seemed absorbed in the match, ignoring her, and she didn't mind at all. She had learned to cherish her alone time. Her Me Time. Since she had met Dexter, the time she spent alone, doing what she wanted to do, had dwindled to virtually nil.

A tall, handsome, dark-skinned native strolled by, bare-chested and in baggy shorts. He smiled at her and uttered a greeting in the distinctive Jamaican patois.

She smiled. "Hello."

She went back to her reading, and the man wandered off down the beach.

Later that afternoon, back in their ocean view room at the hotel, she was luxuriating under the shower when Dexter suddenly ripped aside the shower curtain.

She let out a startled cry.

"Oh, hey," she said. "You scared me."

His dark eyes bore into her. He was nude, sweat glistening on his muscular body. She noticed that he was erect, too.

"Scared you, huh?" he said. "Is it 'cause you was in here daydreaming about fucking that Mandingo motherfucker you were flirting with on the beach?"

She blinked, warm water beating down on her shower-capped head.

"What . . . what're you talking about?"

His voice was low and dangerous.

"Soon as I turn my head, you're giving someone else the eye."

"I . . . I wasn't flirting with anyone. Some guy walked by and said 'hello,' and I said 'hello' back, it was only a friendly exchange—"

"Lying bitch!"

Snarling, he grabbed her by the arms and hauled her out of the shower stall. She screamed and kicked.

He flung her hard to the tile floor, the impact knocking the breath out of her. He jammed a cotton towel deep into her mouth. She gagged, struggled to pull it out.

He twisted her arms behind her back and handcuffed her, as if she were under arrest. The cold cuffs were so tight they bit into her flesh.

"Simple matter of respect, bitch. I put that goddamn ring on your finger, didn't I? You belong to me . . ."

God, this couldn't be happening. Not on her honeymoon, not with the man she had married.

She tried to roll over to get him off, but he was too big, too strong. He flipped her over onto her stomach and sat on her legs.

Then he punched her in her right kidney. The pain was unbelievable—like dynamite exploding in her body. She shrieked hopelessly against the towel, and hot tears blurred her eyes.

"Ungrateful bitch."

She felt his rigidness thrust inside her. Raw, forceful, utterly invasive. He liked rough sex, as she'd learned during the first month they'd dated, but this was something else.

This was rape.

He mashed his hand into the back of her head, nailing her tear-streaked face to the floor, and hammered into her like a machine.

"You belong to me, bitch," he whispered, "don't you ever fucking forget it, bitch, you're mine."

She closed her tear-rimmed eyes and prayed to God for it to end soon.

Mercifully, Dexter climaxed after only a few minutes, spurting his warm fluids onto the back of her neck. He unlocked the handcuffs, and snatched the towel out of her mouth.

Shuddering, she kept her face turned away from him, squeezed her eyes shut.

"Look at me," he said.

She wouldn't. He could go to hell.

"Look at me!"

He grabbed her chin and forced her face toward him. She opened her eyes.

His nostrils flared. "Don't ever think about fucking around on me again. Got that?"

She nodded. Her mouth was dry from the gag, and her throat burned from screaming.

He tossed a bath towel at her.

"Now get your ass back in the shower. We've gotta get ready for dinner."

He walked out of the bathroom, shutting the door behind him.

It took at least a minute for her to drag herself up off the wet floor. Her entire right side throbbed, her wrists were chafed, and she had the painful need to urinate.

She would shower in a moment, but not because he had ordered her to—she would shower because she felt filthy. She wanted to scour her skin under hot water and scrub away his touch, his sweat, his disgusting fluids.

Taking the towel he had thrown onto her, she wiped the semen off the back of her neck, and almost collapsed onto the toilet seat.

When she let her bladder go, she cried out. It felt as if acid were streaming out of her.

She didn't have to look in the toilet bowl to know that it contained blood.

A few minutes later, she flushed the toilet and grabbed the edge of the sink to help her stand. The vanity was cluttered with hotel toiletries, wrapped in glossy designer paper and embossed with the name of the resort.

She stared at herself in the mirror. Her eyes were bulged and blood-red.

With a cry, she swept the toiletries into the sink.

She wasn't on some scenic island resort with the man she loved, no matter the romantic stories she'd fabricated for her friends and family.

She was in hell, and Dexter was its crown prince.

34

That evening, Joshua returned to Tim's shop to pick up Rachel's computer and cell phone.

"Check out what the maestro's done for you, dude," Tim said. He slid the laptop across the counter toward Joshua.

Joshua flipped up the lid and hit the Power button. The computer beeped and launched into the boot-up cycle.

"What's the password?" Joshua asked.

"We're not there yet. Keep watching."

Joshua expected to see the Windows log-on screen. But the computer bypassed it altogether and began to populate the display with familiar program icons: Internet Explorer, Microsoft Word, Excel, and so on.

"Wow," Joshua said.

"Applause, please." Tim grinned and took a bow.

"You're the man," Joshua said. "How'd you do it?"

"Do you really wanna know? It's pretty technical."

"Never mind then." He picked up the cell phone. "You worked the same magic on this?"

"Try it."

Joshua turned on the phone. The small color screen flashed the logo of the cellular provider, and then, instead of prompting him for a pass code, depicted a screen saver of one of Rachel's favorite beach photos. Icons for the Menu and Phone Book filled the bottom of the screen.

"I owe you big time," Joshua said.

"Actually, it was kinda fun. I haven't hacked in a while." Tim nodded at the laptop. "The only files I accessed on the hard drive were the ones I needed to modify in order to get in. Everything else, I've left to you. Happy snooping, dude."

On the drive back home, Joshua stopped by McDonald's to grab dinner. He wasn't actually hungry, but he needed to eat something to keep himself going. He'd been coasting all day on tense expectation.

When he stepped inside the house, the phone was ringing. He raced to it, heart in his throat, and stopped when he saw his parents' number on Caller ID.

His mother had called him on his cell phone at least three times in the past couple of hours. He'd let the calls go to voice mail. He was in no mood to deal with her when he had so much other stuff going on.

But if avoided her any longer, she might show up, unannounced, at his front door. He answered the phone.

"Where you been, boy?" Mom said. "I been callin' you for the last two hours! You was supposed to come over for dinner."

"I never said I'd be over for dinner, Mom."

"Yes, you did! When you rushed out this mornin', you said you'd be back for dinner."

"I don't remember that. But if I said it, I'm sorry. I already picked up something from McDonald's."

"McDonald's? You done had me slavin' in this kitchen all day and you done went and ate some junk food? What's wrong with you?"

Teeth clenched, he closed his eyes. It took every molecule of control in him to resist slamming the phone onto the cradle.

His mother was saying, ". . . fried up some chicken, cooked some macaroni-and-cheese, sweet potatoes, turnip greens . . . peach cobbler."

"Okay, great. Sounds delicious. Make me a plate and I'll pick it up tomorrow."

"Chaquita ain't gonna be here tomorrow!"

"Chaquita?"

"She came over here for dinner. She wanted to see you."

"Why?"

"Why you think? I told her that heifer walked out on you."

"Jesus Christ, Mom, why'd you tell her that? That's none of her business!"

"Don't take the Lord's name in vain. Chaquita ain't never stopped lovin' you. She wants to help you through all your troubles."

"I don't need her help." He looked at his satchel on the kitchen table. "I've gotta go. A . . . a client is calling me with an emergency."

"You better come by here tomorrow. Had me fix all this food for nuthin' . . ."

"I'll stop by, promise. Bye."

He hung up before she launched into another rant.

Someday he would have to deal with his mother's overbearing manner and intrusions into his life. But it was easier to avoid her, or suffer her antics, than it was to confront her. He hated confrontations.

He took the laptop and cell phone out of his satchel, placed them on the table.

He realized that his tendency to avoid confrontations had landed him in this position: studying his wife's possessions for clues as to her whereabouts and past. Early in their relationship, he should have pushed Rachel for full disclosure. He should have demanded the truth.

Because of his weakness, he was left alone to muddle through her life and piece clues together like an amateur sleuth.

Coco wandered into the kitchen. He pulled away a chair and sat, and the dog hopped into his lap, tail wagging.

"Let's see what your mommy was hiding on here," he said.

He turned on the computer.

35

He pulled up various file folders on the computer's hard drive. There was a folder labeled "My Documents," and several subfolders within it such as "Salon Business," "Finances," "House Docs," and "Miscellaneous."

He scanned through the folders, but nothing jumped out at him.

He launched the Web browser. Her laptop, like his, was equipped with a wireless router connected to their home's DSL network. The browser loaded the Google home page.

He went to the browser's address bar and pulled down a list of the last few sites that she'd visited. Among the news sites and hair care-related pages, one link stood out.

The Illinois Department of Corrections Web site.

The page she had attempted to print the other day had come from there.

He surfed to the site. It had a menu for various options—"Inmate Search," "Facilities," "Visitation Rules," and many more.

He drummed his fingers on the table, thinking for a moment, and went to the Web browser's History folder.

It listed all of the links Rachel had accessed in the past several weeks, including the pages she had visited on the Illinois Department of Corrections Web site.

She had gone to a page entitled, "Most Wanted Fugitives."

Heart knocking, he selected it.

"Whoa," he said.

A man named Dexter Bates glowered at him.

36

Belle Coiffure was located in Camp Creek Marketplace, an outdoor shopping and dining complex off Camp Creek Parkway, a busy road that led to Hartsfield-Jackson International Airport. National chain stores and restaurants were represented there: Target, Lowe's, Circuit City, Barnes & Noble, Red Lobster, Longhorn. Dozens of local businesses were represented, too: wing restaurants, barber shops, delis, dentists' offices.

Belle Coiffure had a prime location between a Hollywood Video and a Publix grocery store. The name "Belle Coiffure Hair Salon," was spelled in elegant lettering in a big, luminous red sign. A red awning, emblazoned with the salon's name, offered protection from the elements that could ruin a fresh 'do. Large front windows gave a prime view of the action inside: women busy doing hair.

Dexter crawled past in the Chevy, clenching the steering wheel.

My goddamn money paid for this. The bitch took my money and opened a fucking beauty shop!

He saw several stylists at work, but none that he recognized as his wife.

He swung toward the far corner of the large parking lot. He had to be careful about being seen. His wife might have alerted her employees to the situation, circulated a photo of him, and instructed them to call the police if they spotted him in the area.

He parked in a location that gave him a clear line of sight to the salon. It was a quarter past eight, and according to the hours listed on the back of the business card, the shop closed at nine.

He dug a pair of binoculars out of his duffel. He had purchased them at the store yesterday, for basic surveillance needs.

He would watch, and wait. He was good at both. Stakeouts were mostly waiting and watching, and he'd done many, many of those in his day.

He passed the time thinking about how his wife was squandering his fortune, and how he could most savagely vent his displeasure when he faced her at last.

37

Joshua read the one-page profile of Dexter Bates.

The record included two mug shots: one from the front, another from the side. Wearing a dark beard, Bates was a handsome man, but with his I-wish-you-would expression, he looked like a guy you didn't want to screw around with.

His eyes were his most striking feature. They were dark, intelligent, cunning. The eyes of a predator.

Bates had been incarcerated at a medium-security prison. The vitals section stated that he was thirty-eight, stood six feet tall, and weighed two hundred pounds. He had no tattoos.

He'd been convicted for attempted murder, and taken into custody a little over four years ago. His sentence was for ten years.

But the red headline at the top of the profile announced the disturbing news:

FUGITIVE!!! DO NOT ATTEMPT TO APPREHEND.

CONSIDERED ARMED AND DANGEROUS.
CALL IDOC IMMEDIATELY.

The fugitive alert had been posted on Friday, December 15.

On Tuesday the 18th, Rachel had gone on the run.

Bates was unquestionably the one from whom she was fleeing. The mystery man from her nightmare.

When he considered Bates's attempted murder conviction, he felt a chill all the way down to his bone marrow.

Rachel had several faded scars on her body. She'd claimed, when he had asked about them, that they had come from an "old accident," and declined to elaborate further. He'd never broached the subject again.

Without a doubt, her "accident" was Bates.

Oh, Rachel. I'm so sorry.

Rachel would not have left their home without reason to believe that Bates could track her from Illinois. He remembered her sad tears shortly before her departure—Bates must've done something to compel her to run. Hadn't Tanisha said that Rachel had rushed into the back office to take what appeared to be an emergency call, and not long after had abruptly left the shop?

He pushed up his glasses on the bridge of his nose and continued to gaze at Bates's photos.

What had been Rachel's relationship to this guy? Ex-boyfriend?

Or maybe she had dated him only once, and he'd gone nuts and stalked her. Or maybe she hadn't known him at all, but he'd spotted her and gotten obsessed.

He could not imagine that she'd been in a serious relationship with a man like this, a man with such cold, unsettling eyes. The Rachel he knew was a shrewd judge of character.

He skimmed the remaining documents in the Recycle

Bin, looking for a file that might give him a clue as to where Rachel had gone into hiding. But he found nothing of interest.

All he had was the inmate profile of Bates. Rachel's enemy.

Their enemy.

If Bates was a threat to Rachel, he was a threat to him, too.

In fact, Bates might regard him as the bigger target, a more satisfying outlet for his violence. An undoubtedly jealous man like Bates would be enraged by his marriage to Rachel, would consider it a betrayal of the worst kind, and as a means of punishing her, would be eager to scrub him off the face of the planet.

He got up and took a cold can of Red Bull from the refrigerator. He took a long sip, glanced uneasily at the gun case on the counter.

After only a moment's hesitation, he removed the revolver from the box and loaded it, as Eddie had taught him. He placed it within easy reach.

Better.

Next, he picked up Rachel's cell phone.

38

He began his search in the cell phone's address book.

Scrolling through the list, he found the expected numbers. His own cell phone number. The salon's. Tanisha's cell and home numbers. Cell and home numbers for a handful of women whom he recognized as members of the salon staff.

He also found two numbers that he didn't recognize.

One was for Prescott Property Management. The number had an Atlanta area code.

The other was for someone named Thad H. The area code prefix of 314 was unfamiliar.

He turned back to the laptop, accessed the Internet, and found a site that listed nationwide area codes. The prefix of 314 was assigned to St. Louis, Missouri.

Thad, in St. Louis? Rachel had never spoken of a guy named Thad, or of knowing anyone in St. Louis.

Picking up the cell once more, he went to the call records. He checked incoming calls. Most of the calls listed in history had come from Joshua's cell phone, but two had come from Thad's number.

The first call from Thad had come that past Saturday. The second was yesterday afternoon, around the time Tanisha said Rachel had received what seemed to be an emergency call.

What had this Thad guy told her that had upset her so much? Something about Bates, maybe?

Frowning, he reviewed outgoing calls.

Most of the outgoing calls Rachel had placed to the salon, or to Joshua, but she had made one yesterday afternoon, to Prescott Property Management.

Did she own property somewhere? He knew nothing whatsoever about that, if she did. But what else was new?

He switched back to the address book. He hit the button to call the property management firm.

The line rang three times, and then a recorded message greeted him: "Thank you for calling Prescott Property Management. Our normal business hours are nine A.M. to six P.M., Monday through Friday—"

He terminated the call.

Next, he called Thad's number.

Voice mail picked up immediately. A man with a soft voice spoke, "Hey, you know who it is. Leave me a message and I'll hit you back. Have a blessed day."

He left a brief message stating his identity and asking Thad to call him back about Rachel, and then he hung up.

Settling in front of the computer again, he found the Web site for Prescott Property Management.

The company had a comprehensive, professional-looking site. They had locations in Atlanta, Macon, and Savannah, with the primary office based downtown on Auburn Avenue. They managed properties throughout the state of Georgia, specializing in rental management of houses, condos, and vacation homes on Georgia's barrier islands.

On the About Us, page, there was a photo of the president

of the company, LaVosha Prescott. She was an attractive black woman in her thirties, with shoulder-length braids and a welcoming smile.

He could not recall ever meeting her, seeing a picture of her, or hearing Rachel mention her name.

Yet Rachel had a business relationship with the company. They must have managed a property of hers. Why else would she have stored their number in her address book?

The place Rachel owned, wherever it was located, was where she'd gone. It was the only logical conclusion to draw from the available facts.

He remembered their drowsy pillow talk from a couple of nights ago.

"Love, do you ever think of going away?" she asked.

"Going away?"

"You know, like having a sanctuary . . . from the world. Somewhere you could be totally safe . . . without a care at all."

"Like a getaway or something?"

"Hmmm . . . like that."

"To get away from who?"

"No one in particular. Life . . . the world. Just the four of us—you, me, Justin . . . the dog . . ."

He looked at the profile of Dexter Bates. He thought about Rachel and their unborn child.

I'm going to find you, Rachel, whether you want me to or not. It's too dangerous for you all alone out there.

Coco pawed his leg. He glanced down.

"What's up, kid?"

Coco whined, tail wagging. He noticed that her small food bowl was empty.

"My bad." He rose from the kitchen table and retrieved the dog's food from a sealed plastic container in the pantry. "I've been so busy I forgot to feed you."

He dumped half a cup of kibble into the bowl. As he straightened, he had a line of sight from the kitchen into the two-story family room, where Rachel had hung so many pictures and pieces of artwork.

A revelation rose in his mind, like a deep-water sea creature swimming upward to poke at the ocean's surface . . . and then it swiftly plunged back into the murky depths of his subconscious.

He stood there, frozen, willing the thought to return. But the harder he strained for it, the farther it receded.

Coco was poised above her bowl, big eyes fixated on him, as if waiting for him to announce his great discovery.

"Never mind, it's gone," he said. "Maybe it'll come back."

39

By twenty past nine, the last customers had left the salon, and the stylists began going home for the night. Binoculars lifted to his eyes, Dexter watched as the women streamed out of the building, still running their mouths.

There was one person left inside. It looked like the co-owner, Tanisha May—she'd been in the photo on the card with his wife. She was sweeping the floor and talking on the phone.

He waited until the other stylists had gotten into their vehicles and driven off. Then he slid on a pair of latex gloves and left the car. Hands in his pockets, he crossed the parking lot, as if heading toward the video store.

When he hit the wide promenade, he made a sharp right toward the salon. Arriving underneath the awning, he cast a quick glance around the parking lot to confirm that no one was watching. He grabbed the door handle.

Although it was after hours, the door was open. As he'd observed the stylists leaving, he'd noticed that no one had locked the door behind them.

Sweeping the floor behind the front desk, Tanisha looked up, phone pressed to her ear.

"Sorry, we're closed," she said, and offered a tired smile.

"We sure are."

He twisted the dead bolt in the door. Turning back to her, he opened his jacket and showed the Glock stashed in his waistband.

Terror flashed in her eyes.

"Hang up the phone," he whispered. "Tell them something came up and you'll call them back."

Stuttering, she followed his instructions. Her hands shook so badly she nearly dropped the phone into its cradle on the front desk.

"Anyone else in here with you?" he asked.

She shook her head.

"Expecting someone to drop by, or pick you up?"

"N-no." She shook her head again.

He believed she was telling him the truth. Fear had dilated her pupils, and when people were afraid and caught off guard they tended to be honest.

"Let's go into the back office," he said. "You walk ahead of me."

She hesitated.

"We don't keep a lot of money here."

It took a moment for him to comprehend what she meant.

"You think I'm here to rob you?" He laughed. "Why would I want to steal from a salon that was opened with my money?"

"Your money?"

"Rachel never told you? Sweetheart, we've got a lot to talk about."

"I don't understand—"

"Move. To the back. Now." He brushed his fingers across the butt of the gun.

On shaky legs, Tanisha walked slowly down the center aisle. He followed a couple of paces behind, looking around.

Each of the stylists had a dedicated station with a styling chair, full-length mirror, shelving, and utility cart that held the tools of their trade. The name of each stylist was elegantly inscribed above their respective mirrors: Precious, Tanisha, Jordan, Ashley . . .

Rachel's station was near the middle of the shop, on the right. The space was clean, all of the brushes, combs, curling irons, clippers, scissors, and other implements put away. It looked as if she had gone home for the day.

"Stop right there," he said to Tanisha.

Tanisha halted. She looked hesitantly over her shoulder.

He moved closer to Rachel's station. There was a wedding photo on the shelf. His wife in her white bridal dress—as if this were her first marriage—stood beside a very tall, broad-shouldered brother with thick glasses. Both of them were cheesing for the camera.

"What's this guy's name?" He tapped the photo.

"Joshua."

"Joshua who?"

"M-Moore. Joshua Moore."

He grunted. "He looks like a pussy."

Tanisha stared at him, comprehension brightening her gaze.

"You're the man Rachel's running from," she said.

"I'm the one who's going to find the bitch. Keep moving to the back."

They reached the STAFF ONLY door. Tanisha opened it.

He shoved her through the doorway. She shrieked, staggered, tried to run.

He caught her by her mane of hair and slammed a hard fist into her face, busting her nose.

Crying out, she slumped against the wall and fell to her knees.

He calmly closed the door behind them and swept his gaze around the area, confirming that they were indeed alone.

Head bowed, Tanisha had her hands to her face. Blood trickled down her fingers, and she was weeping quietly.

"I'm Rachel's husband from Chicago," he said. "She stole my money and used it to open this goddamn shop."

Tanisha was shaking her head fervently. "We . . . we got a bank loan . . ."

He kicked her in the ribs. She gasped, buckled.

"A bank loan?" he said. "That's your cover story? No wonder she went into business with you, you're just alike. Lying, scandalous bitches."

"But . . . but it's the truth!"

He grabbed her by her hair and flung her across the room. Screaming, she crashed against a coffee table, and magazines and empty cups cascaded to the floor.

"Where did Rachel run off to?" he asked.

"I . . . don't . . . know . . . help me . . . Jesus . . ."

He hauled her off the floor and body slammed her onto a sofa. Her head banged against the wall, and her eyes swam dizzily. Copious amounts of blood drained from her smashed nose.

He flipped her over as if she weighed no more than a doll and mashed her face against the cushions. He sat on her outstretched legs.

She wailed, squirmed underneath his weight, but he was too heavy for her, and she was too battered to mount a real fight.

He lifted her work apron and the shirt underneath, exposing her smooth-skinned back. Almost tenderly, he massaged the skin with his gloved fingers, and located the tender area of her right kidney.

"Where do you *think* Rachel ran off to?" he asked quietly.

"I don't know!" Voice distorted by the sofa.

He clenched his hand into a fist and hammered it against her kidney. She went as rigid as if she'd been given an electrical shock, and released a high-pitched shriek that would have shamed Mariah Carey.

"Talk to me, Tanisha. Rachel's your girl, your partner in crime. She told you something. Where did she go?"

"Don't know . . . no . . . oh, Jesus . . ."

Using his fist like a mallet, he pummeled her kidney again.

"Don't hold out on me," he said. "It's a simple matter of respect, sweetheart."

She choked on her wails. Sobbed incoherently for Jesus.

Delivering sharp kidney blows reminded him of how he'd sometimes punished his wife. A punch to the kidney caused the kind of sickening, blood-in-the-urine agony that stayed with you long afterward. Members of his team had used it to force confessions from hardheaded suspects before they lawyered-up, and he'd brought the tactic home, unleashing it on his wife whenever she delivered his dinner lukewarm, neglected to launder and press his clothes just right, or pissed him off in general.

Good times, back then.

He raised his fist high and brought it down hard on her kidney once more.

She gagged, convulsed, and suddenly, vomited.

"Oh . . . God . . . oh Jesus . . . oh please . . ."

"Okay, maybe you don't know where she went," he said. "But you know where she and her husband live. I want the address."

Breathing loudly and wetly, she pointed across the office with a trembling hand.

He got off her and went to the desk she indicated. A black, leather-bound organizer lay beside the telephone.

He thumbed to the address section. Underneath the "M"s he found a hand-written listing for Rachel and Joshua Moore, in Fairburn.

He read the address aloud to Tanisha. "Is this current?"

Weeping. "Yes . . ."

He tore the page out of the book and folded it into his pocket.

Tanisha turned her head to regard him. Her face was smeared with blood, snot, and vomit. She looked to be in so much agony that she would consider death a blessing.

He picked up a fluffy throw pillow from a nearby overstuffed chair and brought it toward her.

She shrieked, flailed her arms and kicked, but weakly. He smashed the pillow onto her face. He pressed down with his full weight behind his arms.

"Crime doesn't pay, sweetheart," he said. "Not when you fuck with someone like me."

Her muffled screams soon ended, and so did her struggles.

He unlatched the ring of keys that dangled from a loop of her belt. In a supply closet, he found spray bottles of pine-scented disinfectant, and cotton towels. On the desk, he located a sheet of paper, tape, and a black Sharpie marker.

Working methodically, he sprayed and wiped down everything he had touched in the shop, even though he'd been wearing latex gloves this time. Old habit.

He cut off the lights, taped a hand-made sign in the front window that stated, "Closed Until Further Notice," and left the salon through the back service door, locking up behind him.

Back in the Chevy, he entered his wife's home address in the StreetPilot.

It was only fifteen minutes away.

40

A second can of Red Bull at his elbow, Joshua surfed to Google and entered search phrases that included the name "Dexter Bates," and the word, "murder."

Since the man had been convicted of a felony, he reasoned there should have been a document stored somewhere online—perhaps an archived news story—that included more information about the crime. Although it had taken place four years ago, the thing about the Web was that most of the data never disappeared. When he'd searched on his own name recently he'd found a description of a Photoshop project he'd completed in art school, almost ten years ago.

Google returned, surprisingly, about four hundred results. He clicked on the first link and was taken to a news page dated six years ago.

> Dexter Bates, a detective in the Narcotics Division with the Chicago Police Department, stated that the suspect, Manuel Ortiz, 29, was sought for murder and drug trafficking charges.

He sat rod-straight in the chair. Was Dexter a cop, for God's sake?

Rachel was from Chicago—that was what she'd claimed, anyway. But Chicago was a huge city. The Dexter Bates quoted in the article might have been a different guy than the one who had attacked her.

He returned to the search page and refined the search by adding the phrase, "attempted murder." The engine gave back a hundred and sixty results, which still seemed like too many. He selected the first one, another news article.

> According to Dexter Bates, a narcotics detective with the Chicago Police Department, the charging of the suspect, Tremaine Dixon, 24, with attempted murder is based on the evidence . . .

He went back to Google and narrowed his search further, including the words "attack," and "knife."

Google spat out seventeen results, and all of them appeared to reference the same incident.

He clicked the first link. It was a story from the *Chicago Sun-Times* published four years ago.

Chicago Narcotics Detective Faces Attempted Murder Charge in Attack of Wife

> Dexter Bates, a ten-year veteran of the Chicago Police Department accused of attacking his wife with a knife, will face attempted murder charges, a Cook County prosecutor said Tuesday.
>
> "We're doing everything we can to mete out the appropriate punishment,"

said Greg Young, first assistant state's attorney. "The fact that Mr. Bates is a police officer who took a vow to secure the safety of the public makes this case especially troubling."

Dexter Bates, 34, was charged Tuesday with aggravated battery and assault with a deadly weapon in a Sunday evening attack that left his wife of three years, Joy Bates, 26, hospitalized with serious injuries. She has since been treated and released.

Prosecutors stated that the victim admitted she had been subjected to domestic abuse throughout her marriage to Bates, but that she had been afraid to report the abuse because of her husband's respected standing in the Chicago Police Department.

"She feared that her cries for help would be ignored," Young said. "Her husband is a decorated narcotics detective, and she worried that the 'police brotherhood' would close ranks to protect him from prosecution."

During a court hearing on Tuesday, prosecutors and police said the victim fled her home on Sunday evening and sought shelter at a neighbor's residence, pursued by Bates, who proceeded to attack her with a switchblade knife in the presence of several witnesses.

"She was very fortunate to survive the attack," Young said. "We intend to prosecute this case to the fullest extent of the law. Domestic violence will not

> be tolerated, and being a cop doesn't grant you immunity from the laws the rest of us must abide by."
>
> Bates is currently being held without bond at Cook County Jail.

By the time he reached the end of the story, Joshua's brain had sputtered to a halt like an engine overloaded with electrical current. He sat for a long, breathless moment, staring at the screen with glazed eyes.

Then he exhaled, violently, and his mind started racing.

Rachel's real name was Joy? She'd been married to this cop Dexter?

Married?

Back when he was attending art school, he'd been in a car accident. It had been a rainy afternoon, with poor traffic conditions on the highway, and a pickup truck on his left had slewed into his lane, smashing against his SUV. Joshua's vehicle spun off the road and flipped over three times, and as the SUV tumbled over the earth, end over end, his life had quite literally flashed before his eyes. Miraculously, he'd sustained only minor injuries.

Just like back then, images of his life whirled before his eyes—the life he had created with Rachel.

Bumping into her while perusing an art exhibit at a local museum. Going out on their first date, coffee at a local cafe. Tentatively holding her hand. Kissing her, for the first time. The incredible anticipation, and eventual excitement, of making love to her. Declaring their love for each other. Purchasing the engagement ring. Proposing on bended knee. Getting married at his family church, and the hotel reception. Buying a house together, moving in, intermingling their lives, nurturing their love.

So, have you ever been married? he'd asked her on their first date.

She'd dipped her gaze into her coffee for a beat, and then met his eyes.

Never been married. How about you?

He pushed away from the table, knocking over the chair in his haste. Lying near his feet, Coco squeaked with surprise.

He charged back and forth from the kitchen to the family room. Hands balled into tight fists. Heart beating so hard it felt as though it were going to rupture.

Why the hell had she lied to him? Why?

41

Only two turns away from his wife's house, Dexter was about to hang a right when he saw the familiar signs of a police checkpoint set up farther down the road he was planning to travel: four police vehicles with flashing blue beacons, cops on foot in reflective orange vests, and a queue of civilian vehicles being stopped and checked.

Shit.

Without slowing, he passed through the intersection.

Although he had a full set of clean ID and didn't think the law had yet tracked him to Georgia, he could not take the risk. Police technology had advanced since his prison stint, with more interconnected databases and surveillance cameras than ever, and someone might have glimpsed his face, somewhere, and made the connection.

Or the checkpoint might have been set up solely to nab people driving without proper license or insurance. Some police departments had monthly ticketing quotas, and setting up checkpoints in certain parts of town was a sure way to boost the numbers.

At any rate, he'd come too close to finding his wife to risk losing it all. Patience, as ever, was advisable.

Continuing to drive, he flipped out his cell phone. He called Shakira, the saucy sister he'd met at his wife's former apartment.

"It's Brian," he said, easily falling into character. "Want to get together tonight?"

42

Still reeling, Joshua returned to the computer. He moved the laptop to the counter—he was too jittery to sit in a chair.

Online again, he located a Web site called Net Detective. With records on over two hundred million people, the database offered information on an individual's criminal, marital, motor vehicle, birth, and legal judgment history—everything that was already in the public domain anyway, but often housed by disparate sources. Net Detective collected all of the data under one virtual umbrella and made it easy to conduct research on almost anyone.

He opened an account and paid via credit card for unlimited database access.

He would investigate both Joy Bates and Rachel Hall. He wanted to know everything.

In hindsight, he realized that he should have done such a background check before he'd married Rachel. He should have paid heed to his intuition that had whispered to him from the very beginning that something wasn't quite right.

But willful ignorance, while it had lasted, had been bliss.

Later that night, eyes grainy from gazing at the screen, he shuffled to the sofa in the family room. He was exhausted, but didn't want to sleep on their bed in the master suite. The memory of the love they'd made in that bed, and the tender things they'd said to each other while lying there, would have only upset him all over again.

Instead, he fell asleep on the sofa.

For the second consecutive night, he dreamed about the beach. The glorious sun, the pristine white sand. Rachel's heart-rending smile. His son perched on his hip, his small finger pointing out to the sea and the ferry that plied the tranquil blue waters. The beach house ahead, and Rachel's seductive wink as she led the way inside.

43

For her, hell and the devil were not confined to a beautiful Jamaican resort. Hell and the devil were at home, too.

Every day.

She lived in a state of constant tension. She never knew what might set Dexter off and invite punishment. It could be anything. Too much salt on his eggs. Not enough starch used on his work shirts. An after-work beer delivered too warm for his tastes. Taking too long to answer the phone when he called.

Punishment could be a sharp, back-handed slap, though he tended to avoid touching parts of her body that were outwardly visible. Most routinely, he pinched her nipples hard enough to leave them sore, or pinned her to the floor and tickled her mercilessly and humorlessly, until she cried in agony.

Other times, he mashed a pillow onto her face when she was sleeping, long enough to cause her to asphyxiate and think she was dying. Or forced her head into a kitchen sink filled with ice cold water. Or cuffed her and then locked her in the guest room closet for the entire night, a space so cramped that when he released her in the morning her entire body would be aching.

When he was really angry—a couple of times a month at least—he handcuffed her, sat on her legs, and jabbed her kidneys. She had grown accustomed to the sight of blood in her urine.

And when he was most furious—this had happened twice in their three years of marriage—he threatened her with a knife, though he had yet to actually cut her deeply enough to leave a noticeable scar.

She thought about divorcing him, of course. But it was a fantasy, like a child might dream of walking the moon one day. If she dared to go through with it, he would kill her—after all, he had told her as much.

"You ever think about leaving me, divorcing me, baby, you might as well call the coroner and tell him to get your death certificate ready. You belong to me till the day you die, and you know I don't sell no wolf tickets."

She believed him. A man who bragged with his buddies about killing people in the line of duty would have no compunctions about murdering his wife, and with his cop friends backing him, he might even get away with it.

Running—stashing money and clothes, buying an airline ticket to some far off place and leaving—was an equally doubtful proposition. Dexter was a detective. He tracked people down for a living. She didn't have the resources to run.

There seemed to be no way out. The best she could hope for was that someone would mortally wound him or somehow maim him while he was working. Or gun him down in the line of duty.

Certainly, she'd heard the stories of long-suffering, abused women who snapped one day, and slit their husbands' throats while they were sleeping, but Dexter slept so lightly she was convinced he would wake up and seize her hand as she was leaning over him, and God help her then.

Every day, she asked herself why she had married him. She'd witnessed his taste for violence from the start, yet some sick part of her had been turned on by it, had swooned over his authority and brute display of might. She wondered if she believed she deserved to be treated like chattel, if growing up in a home without a father figure had ingrained in her some kind of damaged perception of what manhood was really all about, and left her ripe for the picking for a man like Dexter, who recognized in her a woman he could control. A woman he could trap.

That was exactly how she felt. Trapped.

Late one summer night, she lay in bed alone, actually thinking, God forgive her, about how she could kill him and make it look like an accident, when she rose to use the bathroom. They had gotten into a fight last night at dinner—she wanted to visit her aunt that weekend and Dexter didn't want to allow it—which had resulted in his pummeling her kidney again, and as a usual consequence, she needed to urinate with painful frequency.

She left the lights off as she went to the bathroom. Although Dexter was out, supposedly on police business, he hated for her to turn on the lights when he was sleeping, and she obeyed the house rules he'd decreed whether he was present or not.

She urinated—it was blessedly free of blood this time—flushed the toilet, and was pulling up her pajama bottoms when she heard his unmarked sedan rumble into the driveway.

Immediately, her nerves wound tight as guitar chords.

She hurried back to the bedroom and got under the blankets. If he believed she was asleep, maybe he wouldn't want to have sex. It worked about half the time.

Oftentimes, though, he would have his way with her anyway. She had awakened on many occasions to find him on top of her, sweating, grunting, and pumping.

Underneath the covers, eyes closed, she waited, and listened.

She heard the back door, in the kitchen, open, and the alarm system disengaged. A minute later, however, she detected an unfamiliar sound.

Something heavy. Sliding across the floor.

What was he doing? Moving furniture?

She slipped out of bed and padded across the bedroom. The door was partly open, and she pulled it open wider on silent hinges—as part of her extensive housekeeping chores, she had to oil the hinges every month.

From the end of the hall, a dim light burned in the kitchen. She heard a sound like stones being stacked.

She tiptoed along the hallway. She peered around the corner.

On the other side of the kitchen, Dexter, dressed in a dark suit, his back to her, was kneeling in the wall slot from which he had pulled out the refrigerator. A dark oil mat lay beside the refrigerator, along with a stack of several travertine tiles, as if he were digging up the floor.

On the kitchen table, there was a black leather briefcase, half open. It bulged with cash.

She placed her hand to her chest, as if to quiet her racing heart.

Grunting, Dexter twisted something in the floor. She caught a metallic gleam of some type of lever. It looked like a safe.

He started to turn. Holding her breath, she backed away

from the archway. Soundlessly, she retreated down the hall, into the bedroom, and returned underneath the covers.

There, she exhaled into her pillow.

She knew Dexter was a dirty cop. She overheard his conversations with his buddies of the badge. Although the stories troubled her, she never thought of doing anything about it, like going to tell his superiors. "What you hear and see inside this house stays inside this house," he had told her when she'd first moved in, and she hadn't dared to disobey.

Besides, if she did go to his boss, how could she be sure his boss wasn't complicit in his corruption? How could she be certain that Dexter had not somehow implicated her in his wrongdoing, too, to ensure that if he went down, she went down with him?

Those worries kept her lips sealed. But the sight of the money had shaken her. Where was he getting it from? Drug busts? Dealers? Murder for hire?

How much was he hiding in that floor safe?

When Dexter came to bed fifteen minutes later—she'd heard him move those stone tiles and roll the refrigerator across the floor again—she had buried her face in the pillow and was forcing herself to draw slow, deep breaths, to give the impression that she was in a deep state of slumber. She feared that if she looked into his eyes, he would know what she had seen, and would be so furious that he would give her the worst beating of her life.

He took off his clothes and dropped into bed without touching her. Soon, he was snoring.

But she laid awake the rest of the night, thinking about the money.

And how, if she ever got an opportunity, it could help her escape.

44

"So Rachel's been married before," Eddie said. He shook his head as he spooned sugar and cream into his coffee. "Damn, I don't what to say. I'm sorry."

That morning, Joshua and Eddie had met at a café on Abernathy in the West End called Buzz Coffee. Buzz had some of the best java in the city. With its New Age industrial design and minimal frills, it wasn't somewhere you went to luxuriate in sensory impressions, but a Starbucks had opened a short distance away and Buzz was still packing in customers, so they obviously knew their stuff.

"Sorry is about all that can be said," Joshua said. He sipped his double latte. After his late-night data mining session, he needed the massive caffeine dump to stay awake. "What I don't understand, Eddie, is why did she lie to me? I wouldn't have stopped dating her if she'd said she'd been married before. I wouldn't have cared at all."

Joshua had brought print-outs of the records he'd found. Eddie pointed at the inmate profile of Dexter Bates.

"If I'd been married to a crazy brother like this, someone

who'd tried to kill me, I might not have told you about it, either," Eddie said. "It's gotta be tough for her to live with those memories, dawg. She probably wants to forget it ever happened."

"I can understand that, but still, she should've told me."

"She was trying to cover her tracks, I guess. Make it harder for him to find her if he got out. She couldn't do that if she told the whole world about her past."

"I'm not the 'whole world'—I'm her *husband.*" Joshua set down his coffee cup so forcefully that liquid slopped over the lip.

Eddie raised his hands defensively. "Hey, you're right. She should've told you the truth. I'm not agreeing with what she did. I'm only trying to see the situation from her perspective."

"Joy Bates," Joshua said, and the name felt like a four-letter word coming from his mouth. "That was her married name. Her maiden name back then was Joy Williams. Rachel is actually her middle name."

"Where did Hall come from? That was her last name when you met her, right?"

"It's her mother's maiden surname," Joshua said. "I found it on her marriage records."

"I hate to ask, but you think she might've had any kids by this dude?"

Joshua thought about the child of his that Rachel claimed she was bearing. He wanted to believe that Rachel, in spite of all the lies she'd told him, hadn't lied about her pregnancy, and that their child would be the first for her. He couldn't explain why that last point was so important to him, but it was.

"I hope not," Joshua said. "None of the records I looked at made any mention of a child."

Eddie stirred his coffee. "What else did you find, then?"

"Basically, she married this guy Bates seven years ago, when she was twenty-three."

"Pretty young to be getting hitched. Most people don't know their heads from their assholes at twenty-three."

"Three years into the marriage—an abusive marriage—Bates snaps and tries to kill her with a knife. She's still got some scars from him attacking her. She told me they came from an accident."

"An accident." Eddie let out a grim laugh.

"Bates is nailed on attempted murder and gets a ten-year sentence. He's in for barely a month when she files for divorce."

"Good for her," Eddie said. "Hell, good for you, too. Your marriage is legal."

"For what it's worth," Joshua said sourly. "She was born in a suburb of Chicago called Waukegan. Both parents had passed by the time she was five. That lines up with what she told me before."

"What else do you know about this dude, Bates?" Eddie asked. "Other than the fact that he's crazy as hell and escaped from prison a few days ago?"

"He was a hotshot narcotics detective in Chicago. I looked up a few news stories about him. Had a great arrest record."

"Meantime, he was beating his wife."

Joshua glanced at Bates's photo on the print-out, nodded tightly.

"There's another thing," Joshua said. "Rachel told me she was raised by her aunt Betty. I think Bates killed her."

"Are you serious?"

"Rachel never told me much about her aunt—I knew she was alive, but Rachel sort of gave me the impression that the woman was up in age and never got around. But I found a news story that ran in a Waukegan-area newspaper. Betty Leonard, an elderly black woman, was found murdered in her home this past Tuesday. She'd been cut up with a switchblade."

"Jesus," Eddie said. He looked ill. "That was the same day Rachel took off, wasn't it?"

"Based on an anonymous tip, Bates was named as a person of interest in the murder," Joshua said. "He's still at large."

Eddie looked warily around the coffee shop as if he would find Bates lurking nearby.

"Where's your piece?" Eddie asked.

"Left it at home. I don't have a permit. If I get pulled over for speeding or something and the cops find me with a gun in the car, I'll be the next one in jail, man."

"I wouldn't go far without it. Not while this guy is running loose. Why the hell would he kill an old woman?"

"Maybe he thought she could tell him where Rachel had gone," Joshua said.

"You think he's in ATL?" Eddie asked.

"I don't know if Rachel's aunt knew where she lived. It seems to me that if Rachel had gone through all this trouble to change her name and all that she would've kept her address secret from everyone."

"But Bates was a cop, Josh. A good one, like you said. If Rachel skipped town as soon as she found out about her aunt, you can bet it's for a good reason. Be careful."

"I'll be careful. But I'm not running away like some punk."

"I've never heard you talk like that." Eddie made a show of looking underneath the table. "You grow a pair of steel balls in the past couple of days?"

Joshua didn't laugh.

"Listen, this guy scared my wife so badly that she ran

away. I'm pissed at her for lying to me—but I'm even more pissed at him for what I think he did to *her,* and what he probably thinks he's gonna do to me, and to her again." *And to our unborn child,* Joshua thought, but didn't say. "So hell no, I'm not running. This is my life, Rachel's life. I'm not gonna back down and let this son of a bitch take it all away. If he wants to throw down . . ." Joshua squeezed his hand into a fist as massive as a sledgehammer. "Let him bring it."

45

After spending the night with Shakira, the next morning Dexter drove to his wife's house.

The checkpoint he'd seen last night was gone. Not a cop in sight.

His wife lived in a subdivision called The Lakes at Pine Trace, a neighborhood of spacious homes with attached garages, brick fronts, and Hardiplank siding. Expansive lawns, many featuring holiday decorations, lay wheat-brown and dormant in the winter weather. Dense forestland bordered the perimeter of the community, giant pines stood like silent sentries, and the main road bended around a trio of modest lakes the color of gunmetal.

Her house was in a cul-de-sac at the end of the block. It was a two-story model standing on perhaps a third of an acre, with white siding and green plantation shutters. A Christmas wreath hung on the front door, and a tree was visible through the partly opened blinds on the bay window.

Cozy-looking house. He wondered if the bitch had used part of his money for the down payment.

There were no cars in the driveway, but the blinds on the other windows were closed, preventing him from ascertaining at a glance whether anyone was home.

A sign advertising a home security company was posted in the mulch-covered flower bed beside the walkway. Of course, she would have insisted on an alarm system.

He swung back to the prior intersection and veered around the corner. He parked in the driveway of a ranch house with a FOR SALE sign in the yard, a lockbox on the front door, and bare windows. Passersby might assume he was a prospective buyer.

For additional cover, that morning, he'd swiped a Georgia license plate and tacked it into the Chevy. Police often targeted out-of-state tags, and last night's checkpoint had reminded him that he needed to be ever vigilant.

Rummaging in his duffel, he extracted a few pieces from the tool kit he had purchased. He slipped them into an inner pocket of his jacket and hiked back to the house.

Cold wind skirled down the streets, stirring up phantoms of dead leaves and debris. A fine drizzle had begun to fall from the tumorous gray sky.

There was a black wrought iron mail box at the corner of the driveway. The red arm pointed skyward. He opened it and found a payment envelope addressed to the city water department.

She might have gone on the lam, but it looked as if her new husband had stayed behind. He was paying bills, like a responsible spouse.

Using my money.

He crossed the driveway to the left side of the house. A big plastic trash bin stood over there, behind a small bush. The gray phone box, gas meter, and satellite TV dish were affixed to the wall of the house.

The house next door was quiet, the blinds shut, the residents surely at work.

Using his tools, he opened the phone box and disconnected the wires, effectively disabling the home security system from notifying the police via the landline. Although it was possible that they had cellular backup installed, which would transmit an alarm even if the regular landlines were severed, in his experience, most people settled for the basics and didn't bother with add-on services, trusting mostly in the *appearance* of high security to ward away intruders.

He crossed to the rear of the property. A large wooden deck was attached to the back. It was furnished with patio furniture: a table, four chairs. A big barbeque grill, covered with a blue tarp, stood off to one side.

He imagined his wife and her punk-ass husband on the deck, grilling burgers and hot dogs and then sitting down to eat, like a happily married suburban couple. Burning through *his* goddamn money.

Fire licked his heart.

Beyond the perimeter of the backyard, the land was given to woods: pine trees, skeletal elms and oaks, bone-thin shrubbery. Wind howled through the forest and nipped at his earlobes.

A French-style patio door opened onto the deck, the square segments of windows covered with blinds. He tried the knob. Locked.

Inside, a dog started yapping. Annoying, high-pitched barks that could have only come from a small dog.

His wife had always wanted to get a dog. He hadn't allowed it. A dog demanded time, money, energy, attention. A married woman had no business taking care of a dog; she ought to be taking care of her husband.

The dog pressed its nose to one of the lower window

panes, parting the blinds. He glimpsed the animal's small, bulbous head. It looked like one of those ugly little Mexican dogs.

No one came running to check out the reason for the barking, a good a sign as any that no one was home.

He knelt and put his lips to the door.

"Keep up that barking you fucking mutt, and I'll crush your head under my boot like a grape when I get inside."

The dog whimpered. He heard the patter of tiny feet as it skittered away.

He applied duct tape to one of the window panes and broke the glass with a hammer. Although no one was home and he had killed the security hookup, why get careless? Success was a matter of developing good habits.

He stuck his gloved hand through the jagged maw. His fingers found the dead bolt lock, and twisted.

The door opened, and the alarm didn't make a peep.

46

Prescott Property Management was located downtown, on Auburn Avenue. Auburn Avenue, known as "Sweet Auburn," was a stretch of roadway that once had been called "the richest Negro street in the world." In the segregated, pre–Civil Rights era, it had been a showcase for black-owned financial institutions, churches, markets, professionals, entertainers, and politicians.

After desegregation allowed black businesses to spread across the metro area, the money left, and economic turmoil settled in for a decades-long stay. In the past several years, however, as urban revitalization projects swept the city, Auburn Avenue was on the upswing, too, with new office buildings, mixed-use developments, and condos springing up regularly.

Joshua swung his Explorer into the parking lot beside the company's office. Wind slashed at his face as he trudged toward the building, and the mottled gray sky spat an icy drizzle that weather forecasters predicted would soon become a full-fledged winter storm. He hoped to conclude his business downtown and get home before conditions worsened, because everyone knew Atlantans couldn't drive in bad weather.

Prescott Property Management operated out of a one-story, red brick building, sandwiched between a law firm and a realtor's office. An OPEN sign hung on the glass entrance.

Inside, there was a small waiting area and a receptionist, a grandmotherly woman, at a front desk. Behind her, there was a work area with a woman and a man sitting in cubicles, and an enclosed office in which the woman whose photo he'd seen on their Web site was talking on the phone.

"Good morning, young man," the receptionist said. "How may I help you?"

He'd been hoping to fabricate a story he could use to uncover clues about Rachel's relationship with this company, but nothing had come to mind.

"I'd like to talk to someone about managing a rental property of mine."

"Certainly. What is your name?"

"Joshua Moore."

She slid a clipboard and pencil across the desk to him. The clipboard bore a sheet of white paper that listed questions about his property.

"Please complete this form, Mr. Moore. Mrs. Prescott will be with you shortly."

He sat in the waiting area and skimmed the questionnaire. It asked for his property address, whether it was a single-family home, condo, duplex, or town house; whether it was currently leased; the rent that he charged or wished to charge; if he ever intended to use the property himself; and other questions.

Reading through the inquiries failed to give him any ideas. He twirled the pencil in his fingers, glanced around the area. Color photographs of properties for rent were tacked to the walls, but none of them sparked inspiration.

"Mr. Moore?" a woman asked.

It was LaVosha Prescott. She strode toward him, smartly dressed in a double-breasted plum-colored pantsuit and black pumps. She offered a professional smile and extended her hand.

He stood, dropping the clipboard in his haste. He picked it up, and shook her hand.

"Hi, nice to meet you."

"You can give that to me," she said. "Have you filled it out yet?"

"Not exactly."

"No problem. We'll review everything in my office. Follow me, please."

In her office, he took one of the leather wingback chairs in front of her desk. On the desktop, she had a photo of a handsome man that he took to be her husband, and a shot of a young girl that was probably her daughter. No pictures that gave him any clues.

LaVosha sat in a high-backed executive chair and laced her fingers on the burnished oak desk. "Tell me about your property, Mr. Moore."

"It's a place that my wife and I own jointly, actually," he said, wondering where the lie came from. "She's already had dealings with your company. I was dropping by to check up on things."

LaVosha gave him a quizzical look.

"And your wife's name is?"

The office had been pleasantly warm, but it suddenly felt like a furnace. He was no good at lying.

"Rachel Moore. I think she called you earlier this week?"

LaVosha's expression was guarded.

"Yes, she did call me."

The woman didn't offer anything else. Why? What had Rachel said to her? Had she warned this woman about him?

"Rachel sort of kept me in the dark about the property," he said. "Matter of fact, it was all her idea to buy it. I wasn't involved in the purchase. It's not until recently that I found out that your company was managing the place."

"We may be."

"I'd appreciate anything you can tell me about your business arrangement with Rachel," he said.

"I'm sorry, but I can't tell you anything, Mr. Moore. My dealings with your wife are confidential."

"Is that your company policy, or is that by her request?"

"Does it matter?"

"Please, ma'am. This is important. This could be a matter of life and death—I'm not exaggerating. I need to know where my wife has gone, for her safety."

LaVosha firmly shook her head.

"Mr. Moore, you're asking me to divulge information that my client explicitly asked me to keep confidential. I can't jeopardize her trust. It would be unethical, and I don't do business that way."

"But I have to help her!"

LaVosha pushed back from her desk, eyebrows arched. "Excuse me?"

"Look at this." He placed the manila folder he'd brought inside on her desk and opened it to the inmate profile of Bates that he'd printed. "See this guy here? He was in prison for trying to kill Rachel, and he escaped last week. He's already murdered her aunt, in Illinois."

"Good Lord, that's horrible." LaVosha put her hand to her chest.

"He's coming for Rachel next. He used to be a detective in Chicago—he'll know how to find her. Wherever she is, *I have to be there to protect her.*"

"You need to call the police, Mr. Moore. Seriously."

"They're already looking for him. But he's still at large. I don't know where this guy is—all I know is that he's looking for Rachel."

"Which means that the fewer people who know where she's staying, the better." Sighing, LaVosha rose from her chair. "I'm sorry, Mr. Moore. I can't help you."

Slumping forward, he removed his glasses and pinched the bridge of his nose.

"Can you tell me *anything?*" he asked.

LaVosha glanced at the photos of her family on her desk, brow knitted in thought. When she turned back to him, her eyes softened.

"I can tell you that Rachel loves her property dearly," she said. "It's been . . . a part of her for a very long time."

He frowned.

"I don't understand."

"If you love her as much I think you do, then you will soon enough."

47

The patio door opened into the kitchen. Dexter closed the door behind him and brandished the Glock.

The little dog was nowhere to be found. It had gotten the hell out of the way, apparently. Smart mutt.

He stood on the threshold for a moment. Trembling with a degree of excitement that he rarely felt.

Four years of thinking about his wife. Four years of imagining how it would feel to get his hands on her again. Four years of fantasizing about the terror he'd see in her big, pretty eyes as he choked the life out of her.

His wife and his money were so close his anticipation was almost painful.

He walked deeper into the house. Thick shadows lay everywhere around him. Rain drummed on the roof, tapped the windows like insistent fingers.

It was a roomy home. Big kitchen with Corian countertops, stainless steel appliances, an island, and a large eating area. Hardwood floors in the entry hall. Dining room and living room furnished with nice pieces. Laundry room with washer and dryer. A home office with a desk, comfortable chair, computer, and filing cabinet.

A tray of business cards on the desk read MOORE DESIGNS, LLC. Was hubby self-employed, too?

The two-story family room was furnished with microfiber sofas and chairs, and a large, flat-screen television bracketed by shelves full of DVDs like *The Color Purple, Love and Basketball,* and *Friday.*

The rooms were painted an array of colors, soft reds and greens and earth tones. There was no clutter. The place was as clean as if a crew of maids had visited that morning.

The lessons he had taught her about keeping a proper home had remained with her.

There were pictures everywhere, too. Photos of his wife. Photos of her posing at her wedding with her pussy husband. Photos of people that he took as their family and friends. A photo of a beach somewhere.

She'd taken the pictures after she divorced him. They were a literal shrine to the deceitful life she'd built.

There were no recent pictures of her family, which supported her aunt's claim that she didn't know where her niece had gone. Looked like his wife had relocated and hadn't told her new man anything about her true, scandalous past.

Dexter would be happy to give him the 411.

The two-car garage was empty. It contained the standard implements of suburban living: lawn mower, weed trimmer, edger, rake, shovel.

After checking the bathrooms and closets, he ascended the staircase, and entered the room on the left.

A study with a desk, a bookcase displaying dog figurines and more pictures. This had to be his wife's area.

He flipped through the file cabinet, but found nothing of interest.

The study opened into a sparsely decorated jack-and-jill bathroom. The bathroom led to another room that had a futon and a small television: a guest bedroom.

He reentered the hallway and headed toward the doorway at the end.

It was the master suite. King-size bed draped in wine-colored sheets, and a thick, matching comforter. Classic, cherry wood furniture: nightstands, armoire, wide dresser with an oval mirror. More goddamned photos.

He checked the bathroom—it had a dual-sink vanity, garden tub, and glass-fronted shower stall—and the walk-in closet, too. All clear.

He was not only habitually securing the scene. He was seeking clues to where she had gone—and the most likely hiding place for a safe.

She would have stored his money in a safe. She couldn't have deposited one point seven million in a bank account without having to face a lot of questions she would have been unprepared to answer.

He returned to the kitchen. It had a tile floor. Holstering the pistol in his waistband, he approached the refrigerator.

He pulled it out of its niche.

No mat underneath. He knelt, and did not feel any loose grooves between the tiles, either.

He'd been half-hoping for an ironic conclusion, that she would have hid his money in the same place he'd stashed his. No luck. Devising his hiding place, after all, had required a level of intelligence and cunning that she didn't possess.

He had to think like her. Dumb it down several notches. Look in obvious places.

He moved to the cabinets and began to fling open doors. Dishes, glassware, canned goods, containers of seasonings and spices. No coffee cans full of cash.

In the dining room, he tore open the china cabinet doors, but they contained only dishes, place settings, and tablecloths.

Catching sight of a painting, he grabbed the frame and ripped it off the wall. No safe behind it.

He snatched all of the other painting and photographs off the walls, too, tossing them to the floor, their protective glass fronts shattering. Nothing.

Sofas. Rip those cushions off and look underneath.

Nothing.

You fucking bitch, where the hell did you hide my goddamned money?

Chest heaving, he withdrew his knife and hammer.

And got down to serious work.

48

A freezing downpour bombarded the city. In typical Atlanta fashion, that meant everyone, from natives to area transplants to visitors, suddenly forgot how to drive. Joshua found himself mired in traffic on I-75/I-85 South barely a mile removed from downtown, an ocean of red taillights surrounding him.

He swore under his breath. A traffic update on the radio told of a major accident a couple of miles ahead that had resulted in the closure of three out of the six interstate highway lanes. He could try to take surface streets to bypass the wreck, but in circumstances like this, about a thousand other drivers usually had the same notion, guaranteeing gridlock at every turn.

He was going to be stuck on the road for a while.

As he inched forward, windshield wipers ticking across the glass, he reflected on his conversation with LaVosha. *I can tell you that Rachel loves her property dearly. It's been . . . a part of her for a very long time.*

A profound remark, yet he had no idea what she could be

talking about. He felt that he should, however. It was as though the gears of his brain had locked up, preventing him from reaching a revelation that danced around the edge of his thoughts.

Maybe the answer would pop into his mind later that day. As an artist, he'd learned that inspiration could be cajoled and encouraged, but never forced. He had to give his subconscious a chance to work out the solution.

But he was eager to get to the bottom of things. He felt as if time were running out.

To distract himself, he switched to an R&B music station. "This Christmas," by Donnie Hathaway, was playing. It was Rachel's favorite holiday song. Such a hard knot formed in his throat that he had to change the channel to talk radio.

Almost an hour later, he finally turned into their subdivision. Although it was only a few minutes past noon, the storm had brought a premature twilight, which normally triggered the community's street lamps. But the lights were dead. A power line must have been down somewhere in the vicinity.

He pulled into his driveway. The rain was coming down in sheets. He hit the remote control button to open the garage door, but nothing happened.

His home was without power, too. He would have to go inside through the front door.

Cold rain beating onto his head, he raced from his truck to the door, unlocked it, and stepped into the foyer, dripping wet.

He had activated the alarm system when he'd left, but the system did not beep when he'd opened the door. Probably due to the loss of power.

Droplets had spattered the lenses of his glasses, blurring his vision. He took off the spectacles to take them to the bathroom and wipe them dry with a tissue.

Without benefit of glasses, his surroundings were a colorful blur.

Walking through the foyer of his shadowy home, he did not immediately sense that anything was wrong. The house was quiet; the only sound was the driving rain. Coco usually greeted him at the door, but she might have been asleep upstairs.

He turned to the left, where the powder room was located. His shoulder thumped against the wall. He was even clumsier than usual without his glasses.

When he walked into the bathroom, his boot crunched across something scattered on the tile floor. It sounded and felt like glass shards.

He looked down. Squinting, he could make out pieces of broken glass.

Still squinting, he looked up at the mirror above the vanity.

It had been smashed.

Someone broke inside our house, he thought, with sudden clarity. And in the next breath: *Bates.*

The sound of a shoe squeaking against hardwood made him spin around in the bathroom doorway.

Just in time to see the fist crash into his jaw.

49

His head snapped sideways. He stumbled and banged against the wall, and his mouth lolled open.

In his dazed state, he could think only that he had never been hit so hard in his life.

He had dropped his glasses while reeling from the blow. But he didn't need them to see that Bates was close, looming near him.

"Welcome home, punk motherfucker," Bates said. He had a deep, sandpaper-rough voice.

Glass crunched. He realized that Bates was grinding his spectacles under his heel. He had a backup pair in the bedroom, but Bates was blocking the hallway.

The gun was in the bedroom, too.

Using the wall for support, he forced himself to stand. Bates watched him as coolly as a tomcat watching a hobbled mouse.

Unlike his appearance in the mug shot, Bates was clean shaven. He wore a dark jacket, jeans, black leather boots.

He did not have a weapon, but with fists as powerful as his, he didn't need any.

"Know who I am?" Bates asked. "You ought to, 'cause you've been fucking my wife."

It took a moment for Joshua's stupefied brain to process the man's comment.

"S-she's not your wife . . . any more." Joshua's jaw was swelling painfully; his voice sounded as if he had a mouthful of marbles. "Divorced . . . you."

Bates grunted, flashed a hard grin.

"So you know. Two questions I got for you, then. Where's the bitch? And where's my goddamn money?"

"M-money? What money?"

"Right," Bates said, voice thick with disgust. "What money?"

Snarling, Bates came at him. Joshua lunged and threw a wild punch.

Bates nimbly evaded the blow, and Joshua's miss left him exposed. Bates landed a punch to his gut that felt like a detonating bomb.

Joshua gasped, gagging on the pain. Bates grabbed him by the lapels of his jacket and swung him around, slammed him against the wall hard enough to chip the plaster.

A quick uppercut to Joshua's chin clapped his teeth together, made him bite his tongue. A jab to Joshua's throat ripped a garbled scream out of him and sent him sliding to the floor on useless legs.

Tears wetted Joshua's cheeks. His body was a symphony of agony. He had never been in so much agony in his life.

Bates stood over him. He wasn't even breathing hard.

I can't fight this guy. What the hell was I thinking?

It was tempting to lie there and take the beating. To give up. That was what he did in life when situations got difficult—gave up. He wasn't a fighter, in spite of his tough talk to Eddie that morning. He was a big, clumsy guy with poor vision and untrained fists and instincts, and how could he ever stand up to a guy like Bates, a former cop, an ex-con?

It was hopeless.

Bates knelt. The inmate photo didn't do him justice. Gazing into his dark eyes was like staring into the depths of the grave in which you would one day be buried.

"The bitch," Bates said, "and the money. Where are they? Start talking, chief—else this only gets worse for you."

"I don't . . . know," Joshua said in a ragged voice.

Bates seized Joshua's ring finger on his left hand, adorned with the titanium wedding band. He savagely bent the finger back.

Joshua shouted, tried to pull away, but Bates didn't relinquish his hold. Lips twisted, he only pushed back further.

Joshua's finger snapped like a pencil. He howled. Wanted to black out. Blacking out would have been a blessing.

But he remained wide awake, his entire left hand feeling as if he had soaked it in a flesh-dissolving acid.

"Punk-ass," Bates said.

In the act of breaking Joshua's finger, he had removed his wedding band. He glanced at it with disdain and dropped it into his pocket.

Cradling his limp hand to his chest, Joshua scooted backward down the hall.

"The bitch," Bates said. "The money. Where?"

Bates spoke in a flat tone, like a murderous robot programmed for a single brutal mission. The laundry room was at the end of the hall, behind Joshua. Joshua clambered to his feet and made a run for it.

Bates didn't chase after him. He had a bemused expression, as if this were a game.

Joshua hustled into the laundry room, slammed the door behind him with his shoulder.

It was a small, shadowy room, the majority of the space taken up by the washing machine, electric dryer, wire shelving packed with detergents, laundry sheets, and cleaning agents, and a plastic basket on the floor heaped with towels that needed to be laundered.

Murky light sifted inside through a tiny window on the wall opposite the door. The window was much too small for Joshua to squeeze through.

He also might have pushed the washing machine against the door, to bar Bates from entering, but he needed the use of both hands to move the heavy machine, and with his broken finger, such a task was all but impossible.

He unclipped his cell phone from the holster. But when he saw the "Network Busy" signal on the display, he dropped the phone on top of the dryer. Bates was coming, and he couldn't waste his precious time waiting to squeeze a 911 call through a network that was probably overloaded due to the inclement weather.

Bates's footsteps creaked toward the door.

Squinting, Joshua surveyed the items on the shelves. He spotted a cleaning agent in a spray can; the formula contained ammonia. He twisted off the cap, nearly fumbled the can to the floor.

The door exploded inward.

Gripping the spray can in his good hand, Joshua surged toward Bates. He mashed the button.

The jet of spray found Bates's eyes. He roared, raised his arms to shield his head.

Joshua charged through the doorway and smashed the blunt bottom edge of the can against the man's skull. Bates sank to the floor, cursing, wounded and temporarily blinded, but not out of the fight. A guy like him would never give up.

Joshua raced past him, back into the main hallway.

Through squinted eyes, he could see that Bates had trashed

the house. Broken glass was everywhere: ceramic figurines, framed photos and artwork, vases. Furniture was overturned. Ripped cushions spilled their stuffing like disemboweled corpses.

There was a landline in the kitchen, mounted on the wall beside a bank of cabinets. The cabinet doors had been flung open, and dishes and glasses and canned goods had been swept out and onto the floor.

Joshua avoided the broken glassware glittering on the floor, and grabbed the handset.

The line was dead.

Bates emerged from the hallway. His eyes were swelling, nostrils crusted with snot.

He now held a switchblade with a nasty, razor-sharp edge.

They circled slowly around the kitchen table, like boxers in a ring.

Joshua wanted to get upstairs, to get the gun and his backup pair of glasses. Bates seemed to intuitively sense Joshua's goal, and barred the way.

"The bitch, and the money," Bates said. He twirled the knife in his fingers.

"I don't know where she is, and I don't know anything about any money!"

"One point seven million," Bates said. "She stole it from me, and don't tell me you don't know all about it. You married the bitch."

"You're crazy," Joshua said, shakily.

Growling, Bates grabbed a chair and heaved it toward Joshua. Joshua moved to dodge the object, but as he did, Bates tossed another chair at him, heaving them as if they were as weightless as tennis balls, and the second chair hit Joshua in the chest. As he staggered backward across the kitchen, Bates came at him, murder in his eyes.

Joshua backed up against the refrigerator, which had been pulled out of its normal spot. He grabbed the door handle of the freezer and jerked it open.

The door smashed into Bates's face. Bates bellowed and dropped down as swiftly as if a trapdoor had opened beneath his feet.

Joshua sidestepped to rush past him. On his knees, Bates swung the blade in a wide arc. The knife tore through Joshua's calf.

Shouting, Joshua stumbled against the counter.

Behind him, Bates was getting up again.

Joshua lurched out of the kitchen and into the family room.

Bates had swept all of their wedding photographs off the walls and smashed them. He'd knocked over the Christmas tree by the fireplace, crushed all of the multicolored ornaments. They lay scattered across the carpet like broken eggs.

Why had he ransacked the house? Had he been looking for the money he claimed Rachel had stolen from him? One point seven million?

It was so unbelievable it was almost certainly true.

Joshua reached the staircase. In his pain-wracked condition, climbing the fifteen steps seemed as daunting a task as scaling the summit of a mountain.

Bates was stalking across the family room. Blood poured from his nose, which was probably broken, but he seemed oblivious to the pain.

Joshua grabbed the railing and started ascending the steps. He used his long legs to take them three at a time, risking a nasty fall if he lost his balance, but he didn't slow, and, miraculously, didn't fall.

He made it to the second floor. Bates had wrought destruction up here, too. Smashed photos and artwork covered the hallway carpet, and black smears and deep dents marred the walls.

Bates was halfway up the staircase. Coming fast. Knife gleaming.

Joshua ran into the master bedroom, slammed the door, and locked it. He braced his back against it.

He expected Bates to attempt to kick the door down, as he had done in the laundry room, but after a few seconds, nothing had happened.

Warily, Joshua moved away from the door.

50

The bedroom was trashed, too.

Shards of glass from the busted dresser mirror covered the dresser and floor. The drawers had been pulled out, and clothes thrown everywhere. The mattress was torn and gouged, stuffing leaking out. The television tube had been smashed, and the DVD and cable box were dented.

Bates had also hammered the nightstand lamp bulbs to smithereens, upended the nightstands themselves and dumped their contents on the floor.

Joshua found the gun case on the carpet, underneath a pile of socks and T-shirts. The lid was badly dented, but it was still locked.

Bates clearly hadn't known what was inside, and hadn't thought it contained anything of use to him.

He knelt to retrieve the box, wincing at the pain that fanned through his body.

He heard a soft whimper from underneath the bed. He looked, squinting.

It was Coco. She cowered far under the bed, large eyes glimmering in the shadows. She looked fine, just scared.

"You stay under there, okay?" he said softly. "Everything's going to be fine."

He found his backup pair of glasses in a case beside one of the dumped drawers. The lenses were intact.

He slid them on. The world came back into vivid view.

He opened the gun safe and loaded the revolver. It was a challenge: his broken finger hampered him, and his hands were shaking.

Somehow, he managed to plug all of the rounds into the chambers without dropping any of them. In the heat of battle, he'd discovered a dexterity that he hadn't known he possessed.

He disengaged the trigger lock and rose into a shooter's stance, holding the gun firmly in his good hand.

Bates hadn't tried to force his way into the bedroom, but that meant nothing. He wasn't going to leave the house.

Carefully, Joshua opened the door, quick-stepped backward.

The hallway was full of shadows. And empty.

He didn't hear Bates, either. He heard only the plinking rain, water gurgling through gutters.

He crept down the hallway. Finger poised on the trigger. Muscles tensed for the slightest noise.

He moved to the guest bedroom, on the right. A glance showed no one inside. Just more chaos—a futon ripped to shreds and an upended TV.

He moved into the jack-and-jill bathroom, checked behind the door and shower curtain. The vanity mirror was smashed and the cabinet hung open, rolls of toilet tissue and cleaning supplies spilling out.

Next, Rachel's study. Bates had destroyed the laptop and printer, swept the photos and figurines off the bookshelves and crushed them, and yanked out the file cabinet drawers and torn through the paperwork.

Joshua edged back into the hallway.

He heard a whispery inhalation of air behind him.

He whirled to see Bates coming at him with the knife. There was blood on his lips. Hatred in his cold eyes. He must have circled through the rooms via the shared bathroom and flanked Joshua. He was leading with the switchblade, thrusting the knife at Joshua, intending to deliver a fatal wound, and he would have succeeded, would have gored Joshua right there in the hallway, if Joshua's reflexes had not been faster than his.

Joshua squeezed off three shots at point blank range. The first round slashed through Bates' shoulder. The next two hit him squarely in the chest.

Bates's eyes widened in apparent surprise. He staggered, lost his balance, and tumbled end over end down the staircase.

He lay at the bottom of the steps, immobile.

Joshua's ears were ringing. His wrists burned from the gun's recoil.

Rain pinged on the roof. A burst of wind blew around the house.

Realizing that he had been holding his breath, he let out a loud exhalation.

He aimed the muzzle downward, and descended the steps on watery knees.

Bates lay on the floor, eyes closed, legs sprawled, one arm contorted behind his back. Dark blood soaked his shoulder, and ghostly ribbons of sour smoke rose from the bullet ruptures in his jacket.

His chest rose and fell almost imperceptibly. He was not dead, but nearly so.

Joshua felt his gorge rising. He clapped his hand over his

mouth, but he couldn't stop the rising column of nausea. He hurried into the kitchen and vomited in the sink.

He turned on the faucet and ran cold water to wash his face and clean out his mouth.

He returned to Bates with a wad of paper towels. Covering his fingers with the towels to keep the blood from getting on them, he dug into Bates's jacket pocket and fished out his wedding band.

"I'll be taking this back," he said.

He washed off the ring in the sink. He couldn't put the ring on his broken finger, so he slid it onto a finger of his right hand.

Then he went to get his cell phone, to call the police.

51

Joshua had left his cell in the laundry room. Keeping hold of the gun, he plucked the phone off the dryer.

He dialed 911—he didn't get a "Network Busy" message this time—and calmly reported that he had shot an intruder in his home, and that he had been injured during the attack. He ended the call without answering any further questions.

When he came back into the kitchen, the patio door was swinging open, rain pattering inside. A trail of blood droplets led from the doorway, across the family room, and to the bottom of the stairs.

Bates was gone.

52

Less than ten minutes later, the police and an ambulance arrived.

Feeling lightheaded, Joshua explained to the cops what had happened. He gave them Bates's name and showed them his inmate record. The officers noted his bruises and wounds, and the destruction wrought in his home, and told him that he was lucky to be alive.

He knew how fortunate he was, but the enormity of his battle with Bates hadn't completely sunk in. He guessed that he was suffering a mild case of post-traumatic shock.

The paramedics treated his injuries, applying a splint and a bandage to his broken finger, an ice pack to his swollen face, and a bandage to his slashed calf. They encouraged him to seek X-rays and additional medical care from his physician.

Broken finger or not, he had no intention of wasting time in a doctor's office until this was over. To dull the edge of the pain, he swallowed a handful of Advil.

Although he had shot Bates in self-defense, the police

forced him to ride with them to the local station. There, he gave an official account of what had transpired.

The cops wanted to know where Rachel had gone, of course. He told them he didn't know—but that he did know Bates had escaped prison and was wanted for a murder in Illinois.

They said they would issue an APB on Bates, and would notify area hospitals to be on the lookout for anyone matching his description seeking treatment for gunshot wounds. With these action steps in place, the police felt assured of collaring Bates soon.

Joshua wasn't so confident. As long as Bates was alive and mobile, he was a threat.

When he asked the cops how Bates could have gotten away after sustaining three gunshots, two of them directly to the chest, they stated it was possible he had been wearing body armor. A former cop, they said, had likely taken such a precaution, and the blood Joshua had seen might have come only from a minor flesh wound on his shoulder.

It was all the more reason he was convinced that Bates was nowhere near done. He remembered the savage, determined glint in the man's eyes.

One point seven million. She stole it from me, and don't tell me you don't know all about it.

He didn't mention Bates's comments about the money to the police. What could he have said? He knew nothing whatsoever about any money, and bringing up the subject would have only led to another frustrating series of questions and possibly shifted suspicion to him.

The only one who could tell them about the money was Rachel—and she was going to have to tell him first.

Could the money explain how she'd been able to open the salon? She'd told him that she and Tanisha had gotten a bank loan, but he wasn't sure what to believe any more.

In spite of everything that had happened, he'd wanted to maintain hope in Rachel. He could understand her fear of Bates, and why she had run and apparently started her life anew. He even could imagine how her anxiety about her past had made her feel as if she needed to lie, though her deceit deeply angered him.

But the revelation about the money was too much. Bates had no reason to lie. Although he couldn't fathom how a narcotics cop had come to possess close to two million dollars, Bates had been fanatically determined to turn their house inside out to find it, and he didn't seem like the kind of guy who chased false leads.

Rachel either had the man's money, or had information about where it might be. And she had told him nothing whatsoever about it.

His loss of trust in her depressed him. If he managed to find her, he didn't know what kind of marriage they'd have left. Or if he'd even want one at all.

Unfortunately, the police confiscated his revolver. In spite of his claims that Rachel probably had a license for it, since he couldn't produce the permit, they took the gun.

He decided that he would purchase his own firearm as soon as possible. He wasn't going to be caught defenseless again.

53

It was midafternoon when the police released him. He called a taxi to pick him up from the station.

The rain had abated, and the clouds had cleared. The storm that had pummeled the city only a short while ago was only a bad memory, like everything else that had happened.

As the taxi approached his house, he spotted a car parked in the driveway beside his Explorer: a smoke-gray Cadillac sedan with a bumper sticker that read, I'M SAVED. ARE U?

"Oh, no," Joshua said.

It was his mother. She had dropped in for one of her unannounced "inspections." He had been avoiding her lately, but she would not be ignored.

This had to be the worst possible time for him to see her. He almost told the cabbie to turn around and drop him off at Eddie's. Eddie's house was twenty minutes away, but he'd rather pay a thirty-dollar cab fare than face his mom.

The taxi parked in front of the driveway. He paid the fare and slowly climbed out of the car.

As the cab sped away, the Cadillac's passenger door opened. He saw his father's small head behind the wheel, but his father wouldn't get out of the car and participate in this conversation. During his mother's inspections, Dad served as little more than her chauffeur.

With much effort, Mom rose out of the vehicle. She wore a long, black woolen jacket, a scarf, gloves, and a dark hat with a floppy brim. A gigantic purse dangled from her shoulder. Although the rain had passed, she gripped an umbrella like a walking stick.

"Where you been?" she asked. "We been waitin' out here in the cold for half an hour!"

When he had been a bachelor, Mom never waited outside his apartment. She'd had a key to his place and would enter at her leisure and make herself at home.

Rachel had refused to give anyone a key to their house, and though it had enraged his mother—it was one more reason Mom despised Rachel—he was thankful that his wife had refused to bend.

"I've been taking care of some business, Mom." He went to the mailbox and removed the day's mail, which appeared to consist of the usual bills and junk.

Mom slid on her bifocals and shuffled down the driveway. Shock brightened her eyes.

"What the hell happened to you, boy? Your face is all swoll and purple, you got that bandage on your finger—"

"I got in a fight. I really don't want to talk about it. I'm fine."

"You don't look fine. You look like somebody beat the hell outta you! Who was it?" Her eyes gleamed with curiosity. "It was that heifer's boyfriend, wasn't it? I knew it! That low-down, triflin' bitch!"

He sighed. "Mom, please, this isn't the time."

She hooked her hand around his arm, her fingers like talons. Her voice was soft, lulling. "Come on home with us, baby. Let mama take care of everything."

"Thanks, but I can take care of myself." He paused, and then added, "I'm a grown man, you know."

Her gaze was muddy, uncertain—but only for a moment. Her eyes quickly sharpened like darts, and her lips drew into a stern line. "Get in the car, Joshua Earl, right this minute. Don't make me tell you again."

She tugged at his arm. He stood firm.

"I'm not going home with you, Mom," he said. "I've got business to handle here."

"The only business you been handlin' is gettin' your ass beat! Now get in the damn car!"

Immobile, he shook his head.

"You a damn fool, boy." Blinking quickly, she rooted frantically in her huge purse. She soon found what she was looking for: a handkerchief. She had started to cry.

He folded his arms across his chest as she dabbed at her eyes. He recognized the tears for what they really were—another weapon in her arsenal of manipulative tricks.

For his entire life, she had manipulated him into doing whatever she wanted. Sometimes she used syrupy kindness, sometimes cruel remarks, sometimes tears. That he'd eventually figured out how she was manipulating him had never stopped him from doing what she wished. He'd always been the obedient son and, by extension, the soft-hearted boyfriend, the pushover husband, always avoiding confrontations, always going with the flow, always giving in whenever someone turned up the heat.

No more. He had battled a coldblooded killer and survived. Surely, he could handle his mother.

His mother's tears succeeded in summoning his father.

Dad got out of the car, looked at Mom and then at Joshua. "What you say to your mama, boy?"

"I told her that I'm staying home, Dad. I appreciate your stopping by, but I'm in the middle of something here."

"That bitch is gonna get him killed!" Mom said, fat tears streaming down her face. She honked into her handkerchief. "Look at our baby, Earl. *Look at him!* Some man his wife's been keepin' up with done did this to him!"

Dad scrutinized Joshua as if seeing him for the first time. He grunted. "Gotta say, you do look like you done took a lickin', son."

"It's not like that at all, Dad," Joshua said. He turned to his mother. "And please do me a favor, Mom. Don't call my wife a bitch again. Or a heifer, or a jezebel. She's the woman I married, and whether you like her or not, you need to respect her as my wife."

Blotting her eyes, Mom scowled. "Respect her? Hmmph."

"Enough," Joshua said. "Please."

Mouth turned up scornfully, muttering under her breath, Mom stuffed her handkerchief back into her purse. Her tears had ceased as quickly as if they had been produced by a water faucet that you could turn on or off at will.

"I don't mean to be rude," Joshua said. "But I have to go inside and work on some important things. I can't have any company right now."

"You ain't even gonna let us in?" Mom looked toward the front door. He could see her desire to pick apart whatever she found in the house gleaming like hunger in her eyes.

"Not today," he said.

"Our door's always been open to you, baby," she said. "You gonna turn us away like we strangers?"

"Mom, give it a rest, all right? I'll call you when things settle down again."

She glared at him, jaws set like stone.

He matched her angry stare without blinking.

Finally, she shrugged.

"Fine. Whatever you say, Mr. Man. Earl, let's go, since we ain't been *invited.*"

Dad grunted. "All right, Bernice."

He helped Mom get into the car, and shut her door. He approached Joshua.

Surprisingly, he shook his hand. "I'm proud of you, boy. You done needed to stand up to your Mama a long time ago."

"I know."

"Be careful out there, son, whatever you doin'. Call me if you need somethin'."

"Actually," Joshua said, "I was wondering if you still have that handgun you used to keep in the house?"

"That .357? 'Course I do. Man gotta have his guns. Wanted to teach you all about that, but your mama . . ." Dad cast a look toward the car. "Well, you know how she is."

"Can I borrow it? I wanted to pick up a piece myself, but I doubt a gun shop would sell me anything if I walked in looking like this."

"Stop by the garage later tonight. 'Round ten. She'll be sleep."

Joshua smiled, though it hurt his bruised face to do so. "I'll be there."

54

He was still smiling when his parents drove off. He tilted his head backward—the movement aggravated his sore jaw—and let the afternoon sunshine warm his face.

Lucky to be alive, the cop had said.

The winter sky was a gorgeous, cobalt blue. Like a becalmed sea.

The image caused an idea to sputter like a wavering flame in the back of his mind. He opened the cargo door of the Explorer. An aluminum baseball bat was wedged in the back of the cargo space, from when he'd played in the softball league at his former job. He pulled it out with his good hand.

He doubted Bates would be so bold as to return to the house so soon after the cops had left, but better safe than sorry.

Armed with the bat, he went inside.

Coco was barking her welcome-home bark when he entered. He had confined her in her kennel in the bedroom upstairs until he had a chance to clean up the damage in the house, but the little dog's yaps were as good a sign of any that Bates wasn't there. When Bates had been around, the dog had been silently hidden beneath the bed like a kid taking refuge from a hurricane.

Keeping the bat balanced on his shoulder, he walked to the family room.

Bates had ripped the photos and artwork off the walls and smashed the glass fronts. He had slashed some of the canvases to tatters, too.

He found the picture he wanted beneath a heap of broken frames. The glass was cracked in the center, but it was largely intact.

It was the panoramic photo of the beach. A curve of white sand. An ocean of clear blue water beyond the shore. A boat in the distance, cresting the waves.

He took the picture to the kitchen counter. As he examined it closer, the idea that had flickered in his thoughts slowly gained substance.

Two consecutive nights, he had dreamed of walking a beach with Rachel and their child. He hadn't thought the dream had any particular connection to the photo. He didn't even know where the beach was located. There was no title scrawled on the border of the picture, no indication of where it might be.

But Rachel would know.

Because that was where she was hiding.

A chill of wonder stepped along the ladder of his spine.

I can tell you that Rachel loves her property dearly. It's been . . . a part of her for a very long time.

This had been the first photo that Rachel had hung in their house. She kept miniaturized versions in her study, and in her office at the salon. She had a screensaver of the beach on her laptop and cell phone, too.

When he'd asked her once about the photo, she'd said only that she loved all beaches, and that it was a picture that made her happy whenever she looked at it. *I think I was a beach bum in a former life, sweetie.*

The property management company operated exclusively in Georgia. They had a branch office in Savannah. Where could you find a beach in Georgia?

On the southeastern coast of the state. Or on the barrier islands off the coast.

He turned the photo facedown on the counter, and used a knife to pry loose the picture from the frame. He carefully peeled out the photograph.

He checked the back side. There was a processing inscription from Wolf Camera dated three years ago, but that was all.

He flipped over the photo. He brought it closer to his face.

There was text scrawled on the side of the boat. But it was much too tiny for him to read.

He stepped across the kitchen, avoiding the debris on the floor. He rummaged through their junk drawer—it was full of miscellaneous items that didn't seem to fit anywhere else—and found a small magnifying lens underneath old Chinese take-out menus.

He held the lens above the boat in the photo. No good. The text was still blurry. He needed more powerful magnification.

He took the picture into his office. At the doorway, he stopped, cursed. He'd forgotten that Bates had banged up his computer, printer, and scanner. His work files were safe—he backed them up daily to an online file storage site—but his equipment was worthless, and he remembered that Bates had destroyed Rachel's laptop and other devices, too.

He rolled up the photo like a poster and went to visit Tim.

55

After the divorce was finalized, she returned to Dexter's house—she'd never thought of it as her house—with a locksmith.

The past several months, she'd been living with Aunt Betty, until she got on her feet again. She'd quit her job at the salon on the South Side, and found work at a small beauty shop in Zion. She was keeping her expenses low and saving money, in hope of making a much bigger move sometime soon.

Dexter had been sentenced to ten years, but what if he got paroled sooner? What if he even escaped? He had so many cop friends that she would never be safe unless she got far away. Unless she started over with a clean slate.

The money he was hiding in that floor safe could help her.

The locksmith was a white-haired gentleman from Lithuania who spoke broken, heavily accented English and wore faded denim overalls. She'd intentionally gone to someone who would be unlikely to tell what he was going to witness to persons Dexter might know.

She helped him drag the refrigerator away from the wall. He bent on creaky legs, glasses perched on the tip of his long thin nose, and pulled away the oil mat.

He tapped at the stone tiles. "Here?"

"Yes, under there."

He felt around the tiles for a moment like a blind man reading Braille, took a flat-bladed tool from his toolbox, and loosened a tile in the corner.

She got down on her knees with a butter knife she'd taken from the drawer. "I'll help you."

Together, they removed all of the tiles in the area where the refrigerator had stood, exposing a gray floor safe sunk in concrete. The locksmith ran his long, nimble fingers across the combination lock.

She watched, heart thudding.

"Can you crack it?"

He gave her a grandfatherly smile.

"One hour or sooner."

At first, she tried to wait sitting at the kitchen table, but wound up pacing through the house. She had taken nothing from Dexter's home but her clothes. Her divorce attorney had advised her that because of the circumstances of her situation, a judge very well might have awarded her the house, but she was adamant that she didn't want it. It held nothing but painful memories.

She took bitter pleasure in the dust and cobwebs that had accumulated in the rooms. Let Dexter clean the house his damn self when he got out of prison. Her cleaning days were over.

After about a half-hour, the locksmith called her into the kitchen.

The hinged door of the safe was open. She peered into it.

It was full of cash. Dozens and dozens of bundles of cash

held together with rubber bands. More money than she had ever seen in her life.

The locksmith looked from the money, to her. His face was somber.

"Please, sir," she said, "I would be deeply appreciative if you don't ever tell anyone about this."

He smiled, and made the motion of zipping his lips shut.

"Thank you," she said.

He gathered his tools and presented her with the bill. She paid with some of the money she had saved, and offered to pay him extra, but he declined with a firm shake of his head.

"Do a good thing," he said.

He shook her hand and left the house.

Alone, she locked the doors and pulled all of the blinds shut. She returned to the open safe.

Working slowly, she removed all of the bundles and stacked them on the table. She counted them all, couldn't believe it, and counted them again.

The cash totaled one million, seven hundred ten thousand, and three hundred and sixty dollars.

It was a lifetime of earnings, and more than enough to guarantee a fresh, successful start almost anywhere in the world.

But that required her ignoring where this money had surely come from. Dexter's dirty cop exploits. Blood money.

The locksmith's remark echoed through her thoughts: Do a good thing.

Didn't she deserve the money for what she'd suffered at his hands? Wasn't she worthy of a windfall? She might never have another shot at this kind of fortune.

She took a packet of bills and riffled her thumb across it, the distinctive, alluring smell of money blowing into her face. She could go anywhere with this, do anything she wanted.

Help out Aunt Betty. Open a salon of her own. Buy a home. Buy a car.

Buy a new life.

Or do a good thing.

She decided that she would think about it for a while, and then make her decision.

56

Tim was on a stepladder hanging a colorful sign advertising a new PDA from the ceiling when Joshua entered the shop. At the sight of Joshua, Tim almost lost his balance.

"Dude, what the hell happened to you?" he asked. "Your lady kung fu you when she found you snooping, or what?"

Tim wore a rumpled, black Megadeth T-shirt with a faded skull on the front, a shirt Joshua was quite sure Tim had used to wear in high school. His jeans had gaping holes in the knees, and he had on a pair of combat boots that looked as if they had trudged through two world wars.

"No," Joshua said.

"Do tell, dude." Tim hopped off the stepladder.

Joshua shrugged.

"I got in a fight."

"No shit, Sherlock. How's the other guy look?"

"I shot him three times."

"Whoa! Fuckin'-A, dude." Tim suddenly squinted at Joshua. "Wait, you're shitting me, right?"

Joshua only looked at him. Then he unrolled the photo on the counter.

"My scanner and computer are trashed, Tim. I want to scan this and magnify the boat image."

Tim came around the counter. He rotated the photo toward him. "Where the heck is this beach? Looks cool."

"That's what I need to find out," Joshua said.

"Let's go in the back." Tim snatched the picture off the counter.

Joshua walked around the counter and followed Tim through a beaded curtain into a cramped, windowless room full of lopsided boxes, CPUs, monitors, keyboards, and unnamable spare parts.

Tim settled into a squeaky, spring-backed chair in front of a battered metal desk that held a notebook computer that appeared brand new. He lit a cigarette.

"Just ease yourself on that box right there, dude," he said, pointing.

Joshua sat. Tim placed the photo in a scanner on the edge of the desk and turned on the machine.

"You really cap someone three times?" Tim asked. "I always figured you for the nonviolent type, like Martin Luther King."

"Can you please pull up the imaging program, Tim?"

"Guess you don't wanna talk about it."

"You've always been a smart guy."

Tim tapped on the keyboard and opened the imaging software. After a few seconds, the image of the beach photo filled the screen.

"Focus on the boat," Joshua said.

Tim centered the cursor on the boat and entered a command to magnify the image.

Joshua leaned forward on the box. His heart had begun to pound. "Keep going."

The text on the vessel was blurry at first, but it gradually became clearer as Tim continued to increase the magnification. Soon, the digitized boat was the only object on the screen, a reddish blur.

"Voilà," Tim said.

Joshua pushed up his glasses on his nose and read the now-huge, blocky words across the boat's hull.

"*Hyde Island Queen*," Joshua said. "I've never heard of Hyde Island. You?"

Tim shook his head.

"Google it?"

"Please. Use Georgia in the search, too."

Tim pulled up Google, typed in the search phrases, "Hyde Island," and "Georgia," and was rewarded with over five hundred links.

"You mind if I surf back here for a little while?" Joshua asked.

"*Mi casa su casa*, dude." Tim bounced out of the chair. "I actually gotta do work today. Knock yourself out."

Joshua sat in the chair, and started reading.

57

Hyde Island, Joshua learned, was a barrier island off the coast of Savannah. It was only about seven miles long, and had a population of less than a thousand. Most of the island was under the control of the Georgia State Parks Department, which operated a marine institute there in conjunction with the University of Georgia. The southernmost tip, however, called Hall Hammock, was a historic community of Geechees who had lived on Hyde Island for over two hundred years.

He had once viewed a cable documentary about the Geechee and Gullah people. They were a small subculture of blacks on the sea islands of Georgia and South Carolina, brought there to work the cotton plantations during slavery times, who had managed to preserve significant elements of their African heritage. They had their own customs, rituals, and way of life. In the past few decades, encroaching beachfront development and lack of a stable economy had caused their numbers to dwindle as they left their island homes and integrated into life on the mainland.

How had Rachel come to find out about this place? Did she actually own property there?

Hall Hammock, in particular, interested him. Her mother's maiden name was Hall. Was there was a family connection to the island?

The mystery surrounding his wife kept deepening. The marriage to Bates . . . the large sum of money she potentially possessed . . . now maybe an island property.

He was angry that she had hidden so much from him, but he couldn't help being intrigued, too.

Hyde Island was accessible exclusively by ferry. On a tourism site, he found a ferry schedule: the boats ran four times a day, from seven in the morning through five in the afternoon, Monday through Saturday. Since it was a four-hour drive from metro Atlanta to the coast, it was too late for him to catch the boat that day.

But he could get there tomorrow.

PART THREE
Day of Reckoning

58

Rachel burst out of sleep with a strangled scream and the feeling of strong hands crushing her windpipe.

Springing upright in bed, she grabbed the .38 revolver that lay on the nightstand. The gun was already loaded. She clutched it in trembling hands and swept it across the bedroom.

The lamps were off, but a nightlight burned on the side of the bed, radiating a greenish glow that cast the room in an unsettling, alien light. The dresser, the bookcase, and the leather club chair might have been mysterious artifacts beamed into the room by an advanced civilization.

She was alone. The house was quiet but for a soft wind whispering through the eaves.

She cleared her throat and drew in several deep, relaxing breaths. She placed the gun back on the table.

The digital clock read a quarter past seven in the morning. She had gotten into bed around midnight, but she felt as if she had barely slept at all.

Dexter haunted her sleep just as he did her waking hours.

She swung her legs to the side of the mattress. Her sneakers sat beside the bed, ready to be slipped on at a moment's notice. She'd gone to bed fully dressed in a pink sweatshirt and matching pants.

Although she was safer there than she was perhaps anywhere else on the planet, she needed to be prepared for anything, at any time.

She slipped into her shoes. Standing, she clipped a leather gun holster to her waistband, fit the revolver snugly in it, and pulled her shirt over the gun.

The weight on her hip comforted her. She didn't dare to go anywhere without the .38. Not even to the bathroom.

She padded across the creaky floorboards to the balcony door. She disengaged the double-bolt lock, unlatched the security chain, and stepped outside onto a broad balcony constructed of sun-and-salt weathered pine. A rattan table and a pair of matching chairs stood in the center.

There was a chill in the salty air; the thermometer beside the door read fifty-two degrees. She shoved her hands into her pockets and moved to the railing.

Beyond the balcony, there was the beach, white, and flat, fringed on the landward side with tall Spartina grass.

Beyond the shore lay the Atlantic Ocean. The moon rode the predawn sky, giving the crashing waves a pale, eerie radiance.

This time of day, the delicate interval between light and darkness, her aunt Betty had called "dayclean," for the night sky was being cleansed to make way for the sun and the promise of a new day. It was a sacred period, a time for prayer and reflection.

Since she was a child, no matter the time of day, the ocean had tended to soothe her spirit. When she stood on the beach and gazed at the seemingly infinite body of water, she felt as if she lingered on the brink of unraveling all of life's mysteries, of understanding her ultimate purpose in the greater scheme of things.

At other times, however—times like then—when she stared at the water, she felt insignificant in the face of such vastness. As if she could walk down the balcony steps, shuffle across the shore, and wade into the sea until completely submerged and the water took her life, and the universe wouldn't give a damn, because she was as meaningless as the conch shells that dotted the sand.

No, she was not meaningless. She was condemned. Aunt Betty had been killed because of her. Maybe other innocent people, too. All because of her.

If she had never married Dexter, no one would have ever gotten hurt.

If she hadn't run away from Illinois and started a new life founded on deceit, she wouldn't have met Joshua, wouldn't have broken his heart with her lies.

Condemned.

Fifty paces would carry her down the steps and into the water. She could put an end to it all. She deserved a watery grave for all the damage she had caused.

She faced the staircase. But she couldn't make her feet move.

There was the baby to consider.

She touched her abdomen, rubbed gently, and imagined that she could feel her child's beating heart, though it was much too early in the pregnancy for the baby to have developed that vital organ.

Although she herself deserved punishment for all she had done, she couldn't sacrifice their unborn child on the altar of her guilt. Joshua might not want her any more, but he would want their child—and a baby was the least she could give him since she had failed to give him the truth.

Hand pressed against her stomach, she turned back to regard the ocean.

It was, truly, a postcard worthy view. She'd surrounded herself with photos she'd taken of the beach, and had used to feel joy and peace whenever she looked upon them.

But with Dexter at large and searching for her, her private paradise had become a beautiful prison.

59

An hour before sunrise, Joshua was ready to go.

He'd had fewer than four hours of sleep, and his lack of rest had little to do with the assorted aches and pains that wracked his body. He'd been busy.

Last night, he'd stopped by his parents' house and picked up his dad's .357, a leather holster, and a box of ammo. When his dad offered to show him how to load the gun, Joshua shocked him by adeptly plugging the cartridges in the chamber.

He'd spent hours cleaning up the house, too. Sweeping up the broken glass. Righting the furniture. Putting away the contents of the ransacked cabinets and drawers. Getting the bloodstains out of the carpet. Trying to make the house livable again.

It would take days of work, fresh paint, and new furniture to get their home back to its former state, but he did the best he could with limited time. Allowing it to remain in a state of chaos seemed the equivalent of letting Bates win.

He'd packed an overnight bag that held the gun and ammo, toiletries, and enough clothes for a couple of days.

Coco waited in her pet carrier on a chair in the kitchen. Eddie had agreed to keep the dog while he was away. As Joshua picked up the kennel and started for the garage, Coco made an inquisitive whimper.

"You're going on a vacation, kid," he said. "You'll be staying at Uncle Eddie's house. When Daddy comes back Mommy will be with him."

Although he spoke those comforting words to the dog, he had no idea how he would feel when he saw Rachel. Would he hate her? Would he want her to come home with him? Would he want to resume their lives, as before? Would he want a divorce?

During his brief period of slumber, he'd dreamed, for the third consecutive time, of walking the beach with Rachel and their son. Upon waking, he'd been too disturbed to return to sleep.

In the garage, he placed the dog on the SUV's passenger seat. He clipped his driving directions to the sun visor.

It was a four-and-a-half hour trip to Darien, where the island's ferry dock was based. He hoped to catch the noon boat to the island.

He pulled out of the garage.

Driving in the pre-sunrise darkness, he kept an eye out for any vehicles that might have been following him. As he didn't know what make of car Bates might be driving, all vehicles were suspect.

He also reminded himself that as a former cop, Bates might be capable of tailing him without detection.

After fueling up at a gas station, he moved Coco's kennel to the backseat and the overnight bag to the passenger seat, with the half-open compartment that held the loaded gun in easy reach. It automatically made him feel better.

In a matter of a few short days, he'd gone from a man who avoided confrontation to a man who had shot a person in his home, from a man who would capture spiders in his house and transport them outdoors to avoid stepping on them, to a man who drove around with a lethal weapon close at hand and an eager trigger finger.

He glanced in the rearview mirror. His face bore purple bruises, and his eyes were webbed with red—but they glinted with iron resolve.

He missed the soft-hearted, innocent Joshua, the one he'd seen in the mirror before chaos and violence had taken over his life.

But that man was gone, perhaps never to return.

60

Wearing a wrinkled T-shirt and sweatpants, Eddie opened the front door.

"Damn, dawg," he said, staring at Joshua's bruised face. "I'm feeling pain just *looking* at you."

"Good morning to you, too," Joshua said. He held Coco in her pet kennel in one hand, and a canvas bag containing dog food, her blanket, and favorite treats in the other.

Eddie quickly took the bag from him.

"You get that finger x-rayed yet, man?"

"I haven't had time for that."Joshua looked past Eddie's shoulder. "Ariel and the kids here?"

"Just woke up. I have to help her get the kids ready in a sec." Eddie filed inside.

Joshua entered the house behind him and gently set Coco on the foyer floor. Coco scratched at the bars of her cage. Eddie knelt and waved at her.

"Thanks for letting her stay here while I'm gone," Joshua said.

"No prob." Eddie straightened. "Any sign of Bates?"

Joshua shook his head. "He's gone—for the time being."

"I still can't believe you shot him. Damn, I only showed you how to use the gun like two days ago. I've known guns most of my life and I've never pulled the trigger at anyone."

"Hopefully you never will." Joshua moved toward the doorway. "Give Coco a half cup of food, once a day, and she'll be fine. She'll mostly sleep all day anyway."

"Got it." Eddie followed him to the door, as if reluctant to let him leave. "You're serious about checking out this island?"

"She's there, man. I know it."

"You find her listed in the phone book for this place?"

"I checked the phone book, but she wasn't in there. It doesn't matter. I know it here." Joshua tapped his heart.

"I hope you're right, dawg. Hope you aren't driving all that way for nothing, either."

He knew what Eddie meant. He wasn't talking about Joshua traveling to the island merely to find that Rachel wasn't there. He meant Joshua finding Rachel there as he believed she was, only to discover that their marriage was over, and all hopes for their future dashed.

"I don't know what's going to happen between us," Joshua said. "But I have to get there. We talked about how far I'd go to protect my family, remember? Isn't this what it's all about—putting it all on the line for the ones you love?"

As if on cue, Eddie's children released shrieks of laughter from one of the bedrooms, and Ariel's voice followed shortly thereafter, admonishing them to get dressed.

Eddie glanced from the back of the house, to Joshua. Grim-faced, he clasped Joshua's hand.

"Go take care of yours," he said.

61

From a distance of well over a mile, Dexter tailed the Ford Explorer.

He wore a bandage on his shoulder from where the bullet had grazed him. He'd sustained worse injuries in the line of duty, and had been able to treat the wound on his own with a simple first aid kit—a good thing, since the law would have been paying close attention to ERs around the city.

He wore the concealed body armor under his jacket, as he'd been wearing from the beginning. Basic cop common sense. When you were out on the street, you geared up.

The two shots to the chest he'd sustained, though stopped by the body armor, had stunned him, and the tumble down the stairs had briefly knocked him unconscious. His eyes were red and grainy from the cleaning agent that had been sprayed in them, his nose was swollen, his wrist was sprained, and some of his tendons were sore, too.

It had been by sheer dumb luck that the guy had whirled around before Dexter had slit his throat in the hallway at the house. He had been toying with the guy, taking his time, enjoying the ass-whipping he'd been delivering, and the guy had gotten lucky. It happened sometimes.

It wouldn't happen again.

Sunrise was brightening the horizon, chasing away the last vestiges of the night. Dexter rolled along Highway 16 at the posted speed limit, cutting southeast through Georgia, an old school soul station on the radio and a Styrofoam cup of hot, strong black coffee in his cup holder.

He sang along with the music. Drummed his fingers on the steering wheel in time with the beats.

Although conducting a tail on a suspect usually involved a team of undercover vehicles switching off periodically, without the benefit of backup, he had to do all the work on his own, which was fine, when you had technology on your side.

During his ransacking of his wife's house yesterday, he'd swiped an extra set of house keys he'd found on a pegboard in the kitchen. The set included a key to open the roll-up, sectional garage door.

After he had cleaned himself up and attended to his wounds, he'd visited a local electronics store. He purchased a GPS tracking kit, good straight out of the box.

In the wee hours of the morning, he'd returned to the house, used the key to get into the garage, and affixed the miniscule transponder to the undercarriage of Moore's Explorer. The transponder would transmit GPS location data to the handheld component of the device—a gadget barely larger than a cell phone with a color LED screen that displayed a virtual map—every five minutes. He had hung the handheld to the dashboard with the included Velcro strip, to keep his target's path in plain view.

Meanwhile, he sang, and savored the pain that simmered in his body. He hadn't used painkillers to take the edge off. Pain, as one of his instructors at the academy had used to say, was weakness leaving the body. It would keep him sharp. Focused. Eyes on the prize.

And the big prizes were yet to come.

Moore had lied to him. He knew where the bitch was hiding, and he knew where she was keeping the money, too. He was going to lead Dexter straight to both of them—he sure hadn't awakened before dawn that morning to take a leisurely drive through the state for the hell of it.

He gazed through the windshield. The Explorer was so far ahead that it had faded from view, but that mattered not at all.

"Lead on," he said. "Lead on."

62

At ten minutes past eleven, Joshua pulled into the asphalt parking lot of the Hyde Island Visitor Center in Darien.

As he got out of the Explorer, draping his overnight bag over his shoulder, he surveyed the parking lot. It was less than half full. Winter was probably a slow season for island visitors.

Then he saw a vehicle in the far corner, under the long, limp leaves of a palmetto tree, that made his breath catch in his throat.

Rachel's silver Acura sedan.

At first, he thought he was mistaken. He'd seen plenty of similar Acuras the past few days, and every time, his heart jack-hammered and he looked to see if his wife was driving, and he was always wrong.

He walked closer, rocks crunching under his boots. A seagull wheeled overhead, screeching, and in a fluttering of wings landed atop the car's roof.

The Acura had Rachel's rear Georgia license plate. The other giveaway was the red-and-white bumper sticker. It gave her salon's name, and included the shop's phone number and Web site address. In a city like Atlanta, where everyone had a hustle, you had to promote yourself constantly to stay competitive.

He walked around the car, peering inside. The seagull, perched like a weathervane on the roof, didn't flee at his approach. The bird followed him with a penetrating, almost challenging look.

Streaks of salt, from the ocean breezes, filmed the windows, but he could see that she hadn't left any belongings inside. It was typical of her. She always kept the car showroom clean.

He placed his hand on the vehicle's flank, needing to make sure it was solid and wouldn't evaporate like a figment of his imagination. His fingers tingled on the cool surface, as if the car were a live wire running directly to Rachel.

The seagull shrieked and took flight. It glided toward the sun-jeweled ocean, as though daring him to follow.

He gave the Acura another glance, and then he went toward the visitor center.

The visitor center was a small, red-shingled building standing atop a four-foot high slab of wind-sculpted stone. Winter-sapped palmetto trees dotted the property. A set of wooden steps led to the front door.

Inside, a middle-aged black woman with wild hair that made her resemble Chaka Khan in her heyday booked his passage on the ferry for ten dollars, and gave him a laminated plastic "Visitor" badge to pin to his jacket.

The dock was behind the building. The ferry was tied at the end of the dock, and shrimp boats and other sea-faring vessels bobbed gently in the water, too. Overhead, seagulls cawed and banked through the clear sky.

Walking along the dock, he noted with satisfaction that the ferry was the same boat he'd seen cresting the waves in the photographs that Rachel kept in the house. The vessel was the red of autumn leaves, and *Hyde Island Queen* was scrawled across the hull in eggshell white.

Seeing it up close gave him an oddly surreal feeling—like stepping into a picture, or a dream.

But the hard lump of the handgun in his bag, and the thought of why he needed it, kept him tethered to reality.

63

At a quarter to noon, the ferry began boarding. The first mate was a short, dark-skinned black man with a fuzzy goatee fringed with silver.

Politely ignoring Joshua's bruises, he nodded at Joshua's guest pass and showed a gap-toothed smile. When he spoke, it was in an accent that reminded Joshua faintly of a Caribbean patois. "Visiting a friend?"

Joshua cleared his throat. "Actually, uh, my wife."

Secret knowledge gleamed in the man's bright eyes. "Ah, we will speak shortly, my friend."

"Oh, well, okay."

The ferry had a few rows of bench seats that ran the length of the vessel. Joshua sat at the end of a bench and braced his overnight bag between his legs.

The only other passengers were a trio of college students with bulky backpacks and University of Georgia caps and jackets.

At precisely noon, the ferry cast off into the marshy channel. Seagulls circled the boat, like escorts. Cool, salty breezes swirled over the deck, tickling Joshua's nostrils.

He got off the bench and leaned against the deck's metal railing, watching the dark water churning underneath as the vessel surged forward. A pair of dolphins swam off to the side, gray fins cutting the water's surface.

He thought about his dream. Walking the beach with Rachel and Justin. Gazing at the beach house, the ferry, and the sea. He felt an almost painful swell of yearning in his chest.

"It be a scenic ride, no matter the time of year," a man's voice said, from behind him.

It was the first mate.

"Yeah, it's pretty out here," Joshua said. "You said you wanted to speak with me?"

"My name is Jimmy." He offered his hand.

Joshua shook it. "I'm Joshua. You got a look in your eye when I said I was going to visit my wife."

"A look?"

"Like you know who she is."

Jimmy smiled gently. "There not be many of us, my friend. All us know each other, from way, way back, yeah."

"You're talking about her family, the Halls?"

"Yeah. Has she not told you?"

Joshua shook his head, his face hot with embarrassment. Jimmy touched his arm sympathetically. "When we dock, I drive you to her, 'kay?"

"That would be great."

Jimmy excused himself to attend to ship operations.

About twenty minutes later, a lighthouse, striped with fat red bands, came into view. Joshua could make out old wooden houses on high timbers along the shore.

He thought he could see the house he'd seen in his dream, but it was too far away for him to clearly discern it.

If that's the same house out there on the shore, that would mean my dream was a vision of the future, wouldn't it?

A chill played down his spine.

The main dock was ahead, crowded with shrimp boats and smaller boats secured to the pilings. He took out his BlackBerry to call Eddie and let him know he'd arrived, and received a message on the display: NO SERVICE.

The lack of a service carrier wasn't surprising. With the island's remote location, it most likely fell into one of those infamous cellular dead zones.

The ferry docked, and the passengers disembarked. Joshua waited at the end of the gangplank for Jimmy to finish his duties. He tried to use the BlackBerry again, with the same frustrating result.

When Jimmy was done on the boat, he and Joshua loaded into a battered black Ford pickup that was parked in a dusty parking lot on the outskirts of the dock. Jimmy steered out of the lot and onto a narrow, bumpy road.

"How far away is her place?" Joshua asked, shouting to be heard above the roaring engine.

"Two miles, yeah. Not far."

"Did my wife's people found Hall Hammock?"

That brought a grin. "Ask her. Maybe she tell you, yeah."

The ride was rough; the road there might have been the same one used during the antebellum era. Numerous rusty cars sitting on sagging tires lined the grassy shoulder. The sun-spangled ocean was on the left, visible through the palmettos and moss-draped live oaks that bordered the road.

Soon, they neared a white sign with blue text: HISTORIC HALL HAMMOCK. ESTABLISHED CIRCA 1857. 445 ACRES. POP. 72.

They entered a community of mostly old, modest homes and faded trailers that sat on high wooden foundations. A large brick ranch house had a sign out front that advertised a bed-and-breakfast. A tiny cinderblock store sold groceries, and there was a white stucco church with a large bell.

He didn't see anyone in the street, or in the yards, though winking Christmas lights decorated several of the residences.

"Quiet place," Joshua said.

"Not always this way." Jimmy shook his head sadly. "Everybody's moved to the other side. Ain't no jobs here, no nothing. Place be dying."

He steered around a bend, stopping at the mouth of a long, gravel driveway that led to a two-story Cape Cod. The clapboard house had a fresh coat of white paint and burgundy trim, and was in good repair.

A row of palmettos ran along the back of the house, the silvery ocean visible between their narrow trunks.

Joshua's heart rammed. "This is it?"

"The Hall place," Jimmy said.

Pulling his eyes away from the house, Joshua dug in his pocket for his wallet, but Jimmy waved his hand.

"No, no, I be doing you and you wife a favor. You go on in there and see her. She need you, yeah."

"Thank you, Jimmy. I appreciate it."

He climbed out of the truck and slung his bag over his shoulder. Jimmy honked, and grumbled away the way they had come.

For a moment, he stood at the edge of the driveway. As he gazed at the house, the hairs at the nape of his neck stood on end.

In his dream, he hadn't seen the place from the front, but this seemed to be the same model—a white, two-story Cape Cod on the beach.

Would it have a patio and a balcony, too?

Slowly, he started down the driveway. He reached the front walk, went to climb the porch steps, and then paused.

On a clear, sunny day such as today, Rachel would not be

inside. She would be on the balcony, taking in the panoramic view of the sea.

He walked around the side of the house, brushing drooping palmetto leaves out of his face.

At the rear corner, he looked up. He saw a patio, and above, the moss-braided balcony that he knew would be there.

Rachel was up there, too.

64

He climbed the balcony staircase.

She stood in the far corner, arms folded on the railing, contemplating the ocean. She wore a white velour jogging suit and sneakers. Her hair was tucked underneath a baseball cap.

He noticed a bulge on her hip, concealed by her jacket. A gun. Although she had retreated to her hideaway, she was still afraid Bates would find her. He couldn't say that he blamed her.

She didn't turn at his arrival. She continued to gaze at the water. She was so beautiful that his heartbeat stuttered, but in many ways, she was as mysterious as the vast sea that claimed her attention.

He lowered his bag to the floor. He had considered his opening line for this conversation over a hundred times, and now, when the moment had finally come, he didn't know what to say.

She spoke first, without looking at him: "So. You found me."

"It wasn't easy."

At last, she turned. She looked him up and down as if seeing him for the first time. Anguish flashed in her eyes.

"Oh, God, you're hurt," she said. She started to come toward him, and then stopped herself. "What happened?"

"Bates came to the house. We had a fight. I shot him with the gun you left for me—three times."

"You shot him three times! What? Is he—"

"Don't get excited. He's still alive. He had on a bulletproof vest, I think. By the time I called the cops he had already gotten away."

"Jesus." She nervously tucked a strand of hair behind her ear. "I-I never thought you could deal with him, Josh. That's why I ran. I was afraid of what might happen to you if you had to face him."

"Thanks for the vote of confidence, Rachel. You think I'm a wimp?"

"I didn't say that."

"But that's what you thought about me. I was a pushover. I avoided conflict. You didn't think I could handle Bates."

She shook her head. "You don't know him, Josh."

"You don't know me, either!" He slammed his fist onto the railing, and the entire balcony creaked.

"Okay," she said softly. Eyes wary, she edged into the corner as if to escape. "Calm down, please."

She had a cornered animal look in her eyes that made him think of Bates, and how she must have often looked at him when he had abused her, and Joshua didn't want her to ever look at him like that, as if fearful that he was going to raise his hand to strike her. That a display of anger was enough to send her cowering in fear was evidence of how deep her wounds ran.

He blew out a chestful of hot air, and unclenched his fist.

"Look," he said. "Just because I'm pissed off doesn't mean I'm going to hurt you, Rachel. I'm *not* him."

"I know you aren't." But her eyes held a trace of anxiety.

"Part of my problem is that I don't get angry often enough. I keep things bottled in. I need to learn how to express my feelings more openly, before they explode out of me."

Nodding, she hugged herself.

"I'm not a violent person," he said. "I would never treat you the way he did."

"I know, baby, I know." She pressed her fingers to her eyes, which were starting to get teary.

"But I was willing to die for you, Rachel. I believe in our marriage vows. I would lay down my life for you . . . and when you stand here and tell me that you were afraid I wouldn't stand up to Bates, that's about the biggest insult you can give me."

"I'm so sorry. I . . . I don't know . . ."

"You said you ran because Bates escaped from prison, but I don't think that's the whole truth. There's a lot more to it than that."

She dropped her gaze. "Maybe you're right."

"You were running from me, too. From giving me the truth."

"Do you hate me?" Her eyes searched his face, desperately. "I would understand if you do. After what I did to you . . . I deserve your hate."

"I don't hate you." Folding his arms across his chest, he leaned against the railing. "I hate what you did to me, but I don't hate you."

"You should."

"I've done some research. I know how Bates got thrown into prison for attacking you. The guy's a certified nut job. Your leaving Chicago and changing your name is probably the only reason you're still alive."

"It was a living hell," she said. Tears wove down her cheeks, and she wiped them away with the heel of her hand. "Leaving behind my family, my friends, my life. All because of him. When I first moved to Atlanta, I would cry myself to sleep every night. Giving up everything . . . it didn't seem worth it. But all that changed when I found you." Through her tears, she managed a slight smile.

His throat got tight, and it was difficult to speak.

"If you felt that way about me, why didn't you tell me the truth?"

"Because I was scared! I was scared to tell anyone I met in Atlanta about Dexter. Dexter was a cop, well connected . . . he knew people everywhere, and you know how folks talk. I slip up and tell someone, and word begins to travel, and the next thing you know, as soon as he gets out of prison—or escapes, like he did—he's coming to Atlanta and showing up at my front door. I couldn't risk telling anyone."

"I'm your husband, damn it! I deserved to know."

"You did." She blotted her eyes. "But I was scared to tell you, most of all."

"Why?"

"Come on, baby. What would you have thought of me, knowing that I'd been married to a terrible, abusive asshole who was in prison because he'd tried to kill me? Would I have been as attractive to you? Would you have wanted to be with me, knowing that when Dexter was released, he was going to track me down and try to finish what he'd failed to do the first time?"

"It wouldn't have changed anything with me. I would've wanted to be with you, regardless."

"Now don't *you* start lying to *me.*" She laughed hollowly. "Think if I'd shared all of these things with you after we'd been dating for a couple of months. You would've run for the hills."

"Give me a little more credit."

"And then you would've told your mother," she said, rolling her eyes. *"She* would've talked so bad about me to you that the shit she says about me now would've been no comparison. She would've made it her mission to drive you away from me, and you might have given in and ended it."

"You were assuming way too much, you know, way too much."

"But on top of everything, you were so . . . nice, so damned *decent."* Her eyes were watering again. "I was coming out of a situation where I'd been married to the devil incarnate, and I mostly blamed myself for getting involved with him, for letting him do the things to me that he did. I honestly didn't believe that I deserved to meet a good man. But there you were." She smiled wanly. "I guess I wanted to be a woman who was worthy of you."

"You wanted to be worthy of me?"

"I wanted to be worthy of you—not some scared woman on the run coming into your life with all this crazy-ass baggage."

It was perhaps the most revealing answer he'd ever received from her. She wanted to be worthy of him? With her beauty, intelligence, and charm, he'd lain awake many nights worried that he didn't deserve her, that her professed love for him was only a passing fad, that she would wake up one day and realize how thoroughly unremarkable he was—and would want out.

"We never see ourselves as others see us, baby," she said. "You're a good man, Joshua. Honest to a fault. Considerate. Gentle. Hardworking. Dependable. And need I say, fine." She laughed lightly. "I almost couldn't believe that we had a chance to build something together. I was scared to let my skeletons out of the closet and risk screwing it up."

"So you lied," he said. "About everything."

She cringed as if slapped. "Not everything."

He stared at her.

"But far too much, I admit," she said.

He turned away. She hesitated, and then crossed the balcony and touched his arm. Her hand was warm, electric.

"I never lied about loving you." Tears glimmered in her eyes. "I'm sorry for everything. I hope . . . I hope you can find it in yourself to forgive me."

He clasped his hands together. His heart felt as if it were on the verge of imploding.

"We have a lot more to talk about," he said. "Bates told me some pretty shocking things."

"About money," she said.

"There's that, and then this house—something I never knew anything about."

"I'll tell you everything. But will you be able to forgive me?"

He gazed out at the ocean, the waves gilded with sunlight. "Leave me alone out here for a little while."

"Of course." She squeezed his arm. "I'll be inside."

She went inside the house through a sliding glass door, her figure folding into the shadows within.

He remained on the balcony. He watched the waves crashing on the beach, the seagulls screeching overhead, the fleet of clouds gathering on the horizon. The gentle cycles of nature that would continue long after he and Rachel were gone and forgotten.

Their time on this world, together, was precious. He knew she loved him, and he loved her more than he'd ever dreamed of loving another person. Her dishonesty had wounded his heart, and it would take him time for their marriage to recover from the emotional damage, but his feelings for her, in light of the suffering he had undergone to find her again, had only deepened many fathoms. Like the sea before him.

This was what commitment was all about, he realized. Braving heartache and disappointment, in order to keep a union intact. It wasn't easy, wasn't painless, wasn't convenient. Commitment was work.

And staying committed was a conscious choice.

He remained on the balcony for perhaps a half hour. Then, he picked up his bag, and went inside.

65

Entering the house via the balcony door placed Joshua in a bedroom. A large, cleanly swept space, it was sparsely furnished with only a queen-size bed, dresser, and a small bookcase packed with several old Bibles, as if Rachel had come there to do penance. Her suitcase lay open beside the bed, clothes with the tags still on them lying inside.

He entered the hallway. There were three more doors off the hall, but they were closed.

"Rachel?" he called.

"Downstairs," she said. "In the kitchen."

She sat at a dinette table, drinking coffee and reading a newspaper. She had removed her cap, and from the strands of hair that stood in disarray, he knew she had been scratching her scalp, one of her nervous habits.

She looked up from the paper, smiled hesitantly. "Coffee?"

"Please, thanks."

She went to the counter. As she was opening a cabinet to retrieve a cup, he came behind her and rested his hands on her shoulders. She flinched at his touch, as if expecting a blow, and then she relaxed, her body becoming pliable in his hands.

He gently turned her around. She looked up at him.

Hope and anxiety flickered alternately in her eyes.

"I forgive you," he said.

She closed her eyes and released a sigh that seemed to come from the depths of her soul. "Thank you."

"There's no way I'm leaving you. You're my wife, the mother of my child. I pledged to stay with you till death do us part, and I'm not changing my mind now. I hate what you did, but I love you."

Tears streamed out of her eyes, rolled down her cheeks. "I love you, too."

He flicked away her tears with his finger. "But you have to promise me something."

"Anything," she said.

"No more secrets between us."

"No more. I promise."

He wrapped his arms around her and pulled her close. She slid her hands across his back and nuzzled against his chest.

They stood in the kitchen, holding each other, for a long time.

66

Over coffee at the kitchen table, he said, "You know I've got a lot of questions."

"I know you do." She looked at him over the rim of her cup. "Like about this house, for example."

"That's a good place to start. Do you own this place?"

"The property's been in my mother's family for many, many generations. My aunt Betty placed it in a trust to avoid the hassles of probate . . . in the event of her death."

"I heard about your aunt." He reached for her hand. "I'm so sorry."

Clenching his hand, she pulled in a shaky breath.

"Anyway, she designated a bank as the trustee, but I'm the only beneficiary. I've been responsible for taking care of things here for the past few years, ever since Aunt Betty has gotten up in age."

"You never told me much about her. I knew you were close to her, but not much else."

"She was like a mother to me." She sighed heavily, closed her eyes.

"You don't have to talk about it right now if you don't want to."

"I can't talk about this house and not talk about Aunt Betty." She looked around, a wistful smile surfacing through her grief. "I've got so many happy memories of this place. Growing up, I used to spend summers here with her—she was a teacher back home in Illinois and would come here for summer vacation. It was an annual thing we'd do, up until the time I graduated from high school." She shrugged. "When I left Illinois and came to Georgia, to start fresh, I lived here for a few months, trying to get my head right again."

"Does the name of this area, Hall Hammock, have something to do with your family?"

"Back in the 1870s, my great-great granddad, Frederick Hall, got together with two friends and bought this part of Hyde Island from a white plantation owner." Her voice was rich with pride. "Seven hundred acres—a huge land purchase now, and practically unheard of for black people back then."

"Right after the Civil War? Most definitely."

"He and his buddies kept about a hundred acres apiece for themselves, and then divvied up the rest in tracts that they sold to other freed families who had lived as slaves on Hyde before the war. Free Geechee folk from all over the rest of the island poured into Hall Hammock. It was a new beginning in a place they could call their own."

"That's pretty amazing," he said.

"We've lost some of the land to the state parks department—they operate a big marine institute on the North End—and a lot of people have moved out, too, to live on the other side where they can have jobs, 'cause there aren't many jobs here any more. But some of us are still here, hanging on to our roots."

"How long has this house been standing? It doesn't look that old."

"An awful hurricane came through here in the early seventies. It destroyed a lot of homes, including ours. Aunt Betty and Uncle Sammy took the insurance money and built a new house, the one we're sitting in now."

A frightening thought occurred to him.

"Does Dexter know anything about this place?"

"Are you kidding? I never dared to tell him a word about it."

"But you were married to him. How did you hide . . . well, never mind."

"No, it's a fair question. I kept it secret from Dexter because I realized on some level, even then, that he didn't have my best interests at heart. This house has always been a very personal, important place for me and my family."

"You never told me about it, either. You hinted about it, though, I recall."

She touched his hand. "But I was planning to tell you, baby. I really was. But with Dexter being around . . . I was afraid. This is the one place in the world where I've always felt safe."

"I can understand. You've got your own private hideaway here."

"Now let me tell you about Dexter. If I'd told him about this house when we were married, he would have demanded that I try to take it out of trust and sell it. That man didn't want me to have anything that I cherished—outside of him, that is."

"Did you ever love him?"

"Never," she said plainly. "But I was only twenty-three when we got married, naïve, and Dexter is ruthless about getting what he wants. He wanted a trophy wife, and he decided I was the one. When I met him, it was like getting swept away by a deadly tidal wave. We got married within three months of our first date."

"Three months? We got engaged after six months, and some people told me that was too fast."

"Every relationship is different. In the case of you and me, we'd developed so much chemistry that after a few months, it was a given that we were going to get married."

"True," he said. "Actually, by the third date, I had a pretty good idea."

"With Dexter, though, it was like being forced into a corner. He started talking about marriage on the second date, and he went all out with the flowers, chocolates, jewelry, designer clothes, expensive dinners. He wanted to see me every single day. He would tell me, 'My job is to make you marry me.'"

"His job?"

"Right, his job. Nuts, huh? But I was scared to death of him—he's not the kind of man who takes no for an answer, and at that point my life, I was unsure about what I was looking for in a man, didn't know what a *good* man was all about. So I gave in."

"But you never had a child with him."

"Lord, no. Dexter can't have kids, Josh. He tried to get me pregnant almost immediately after we tied the knot—I think he wanted me to have a baby so he could have another way to pin me down, control me. But we did some fertility testing, and the doctors told us that he had a low sperm count."

"Seriously?"

"Oh, yeah. Dexter was pissed, let me tell you. I thought he was going to tear apart the doctor's office. He went to two more doctors, and both of them told him the same thing. So of course, Dexter turned it all around and laid the blame at my feet. He said that the doctors who tested him were jealous of him, and that I was the one who had a fertility problem."

"He's a real piece of work."

"It's all part of the nutty package that's Dexter."

"Why did he attack you that night? I read the story of his arrest in a Chicago paper."

"Big shot narcotics detective arrested for attempting to murder his wife," she said, with a rueful smile. "Well, Dexter's always had this nasty jealous streak."

"So I've seen."

"We'd gone out to dinner that night. Some favorite steakhouse of his—we always went wherever he wanted to go. I saw this guy I'd gone to high school with, and he stopped by our table and made small talk for a minute, then went on his merry way."

"Was he someone you'd used to date?"

"Never. He was only a friend from school, like years ago. But Dexter got real quiet afterward, which I knew was a bad sign. When we got home . . ."

"He went ballistic."

"Accused me of seeing this guy on the sly, of being the biggest slut in the world . . . we had the battle royale of fights. I ran out of the house, to a neighbor's, he chased me with a knife." She let out a bitter laugh. "Now you know how I got these scars, huh?"

"He should have gotten the death penalty," he said, hands fisted. "So when he went to prison, how did you go about starting over?"

"First thing I did was get an uncontested divorce. Then I went to court for a legal name change—I changed my middle name to my first name, and then took my mom's maiden name, Hall. I knew Dexter would get out of prison one day and come after me, and I wanted to have a last name that I didn't think he would know, or remember. At the same time, I didn't want to totally cut my family ties, you know?"

"Makes sense," he said. "Although something tells me he probably figured it out."

"Yeah, he probably did—he's got a mind like a steel trap." She chewed her lip. "Anyway, because I was a victim of domestic violence, I was able to get a new social security number, tied to my new name. I bought Coco—he never allowed me to have a dog—and moved down here for a little while, to get my affairs in order. I'd been to Atlanta several times before, for hair shows and whatnot, so . . ."

"You relocated to ATL," he said. "And started working at a hair salon in College Park."

"Yep. And after a while, we bumped into each other at an art museum."

"I bumped into you, actually." He chuckled. "You know how clumsy I am sometimes."

"How do you know I didn't make sure that I happened to be in your way?"

They smiled at each other, and it was a good smile, even better than the ones they had shared before Dexter had invaded their lives, because now, the veils of the past were being blown away and they were seeing each other as they really were—two people who had somehow managed to hook up and fall in love in a crazy world that often seemed dead set against ever allowing such a thing to happen.

She got up and refreshed their coffee from a stainless steel carafe.

"Baby, I've got a question for you that's been burning a hole in my brain," she said. "How the heck did you find me here?"

"This might sound kinda crazy, but . . . I dreamed about this place."

"You did?"

"I dreamed about it every night after you left."

"What exactly happened in this dream?"

"We were walking on the beach out there." He pointed toward the shore, a slice of which was visible through a nearby window. "I was holding our son, Justin, too. He was maybe a year old."

"Wow." She was grinning, rubbing her belly.

"Our lives, in the dream, seemed just perfect. Our lives probably weren't really perfect, but they sure felt perfect because we were together, a family . . . just enjoying each other."

"Sounds perfect to me," she said.

"Honestly, I was pretty broken up when you left. But that dream made me want to find you all the more—made me want to get to the bottom of things. I found out that you'd hired a property management company. I found their number in your cell phone."

"How'd you get into my cell? I always kept it locked."

"You know my boy Tim's got hacking skills."

"Oh, I forgot about him," she said.

"I met the woman at the property management place, LaVosha. She didn't really tell me anything, except that you'd gone somewhere that was very dear to you. She was pretty adamant about preserving your privacy."

"Go, LaVosha. She's good people. She sends a crew here once a month to do upkeep on everything."

"After she gave me that hint, it finally hit me: all the photos of the beach that you kept in our house. You were *here*."

She was nodding.

"Every time I look at them, I think of being here, and I feel at peace."

"Tim magnified one of the photos on a scanner, we deciphered the words on the ferry, *Hyde Island Queen*, and we did a search online . . . and voila. Here I am."

"Bravo." She clapped. "Now where is Coco? You didn't bring her."

"Left her with Eddie. Speaking of which, when I got here I tried to call him from my cell and couldn't get connected. Do you have a landline in the house?"

"It's not in service. One of the main reasons I come here is to be isolated—from everything."

"What if you have an emergency?"

"Some of my neighbors have phones in their houses," she said. "Anyway, remember, we're on an island. Nothing gets here fast. It would take even an emergency helicopter a while to reach us here."

"There are no cops, no hospitals?"

"None of that. Any emergency services would have to come from the other side. Some people here have boats, but they're not exactly rapid transit."

"So if we get into a bind while we're here . . ."

"We're on our own," she said. She frowned. "Why're you asking these questions? You think Dexter followed you?"

"He's still alive."

"Which means there's always the possibility." She glanced worriedly out the window, scratched her scalp.

"Especially when he believes you've stolen one point seven million dollars from him."

"I was going to get to that," she said.

He leaned back in the chair, sipped his coffee.

"I'm all ears," he said.

67

Afterward, Rachel prepared a lunch of tuna salad sandwiches on wheat, iced tea, and chips. They took their meal on the balcony.

The previously clear sky had become overcast, and the strength of the wind was gradually building. According to Rachel, forecasters predicted a storm to arrive by nightfall.

In the midst of lunch—they were talking about New Year's Eve plans as if purposefully avoiding the gravity of their situation—she asked, "Did you bring the gun I gave you? We're going to need all the firepower we can get, Josh."

"I didn't have the permit for the gun, so the cops confiscated it."

"Damn. I forgot about that. Sorry."

"But I brought another one with me."

"You did?"

"Of course I did. Did you think I would come here to protect my wife and child without bringing a weapon?"

"Well excuse me" she said, and laughed. "Guess I was wrong."

"Damn right you were wrong."

A gust of wind blew their napkins off the table and sent them whirling across the balcony to the beach below.

"Maybe we should get inside," she said. "Then you can show me this gun."

"I'll show it to you, all right."

They cleaned off the table and returned inside to the kitchen. He placed his overnight bag on the table and took out the stainless steel .357, the holster, and cartridges.

"Whoa." She gawked at the firearm. "Now *that's* a gun. Makes mine look like a damn peashooter. Where'd you get it from?"

"My dad." He began to carefully insert rounds into the chamber.

"Your dad? I thought he only cared about cars. Every time I'd see him, he'd ask if I needed an oil change."

"Cars are his main thing. But he always kept guns in the house, too. Mom never let him bring them around me, though."

"Big surprise there. Does she know he gave you this one?"

"No, but only because Dad wanted to keep it secret from her. I could care less if she knows. I'm a grown-ass man."

She eyed him curiously.

"Did you cut Mama's apron strings after I left or something?"

"You could say that. Long story short—we had words yesterday. I was respectful, but I made it clear that I wasn't going to allow her to be in my business any more. I wasn't going to tolerate her bad-mouthing you in my presence, either."

"Hallelujah." She snapped her fingers and did a little happy dance beside him. "I'm proud of you, baby."

He finished loading the revolver. After double-checking that the safety was engaged, he fit the gun securely into the holster, and attached the holster to the waist of his jeans.

"Now we're a pair." She patted the holstered piece on her hip.

"How long have you had that gun, anyway?"

"I bought both of them—the one I gave you and the one I have here—shortly after I moved to Georgia. Why?"

"You any good with it?" he asked.

"I'm a decent shot. I've taken lessons at a firing range."

"One thing we need to keep in mind, though—Dexter was wearing body armor."

"So we need more weapons, you think?" she asked. Hands on her waist, she looked around the kitchen. "Hmm, I've got a couple ideas. Ever made a Molotov cocktail?"

"You have the ingredients for one?"

"There's a can of gasoline in the shed outside. Probably some oil, too. And I know I've got some rags and empty bottles somewhere in the kitchen here."

"Then let's get to work. Might as well do it now so we'll have it ready whenever we need it."

68

He found gasoline and oil in the shed and used a portion of both to concoct a combustible mixture in a vodka bottle, employing an oil-soaked rag as a wick and securing it to the bottle with a strip of duct tape. He fit the Molotov cocktail snugly in a knotted pillowcase that he could sling over his shoulder for easy carrying.

They also took all of the candles and kerosene lamps out of the cupboards and distributed them throughout the house, to be lighted as needed. With the building wind, there was the risk of a power outage, a common occurrence on the island according to Rachel. There was a backup power generator outside the house, but it had to be manually activated, and if they lost electricity after nightfall, Joshua wasn't too keen on going outdoors to fool around with the generator, not when Dexter could be skulking around in the dark.

For general lighting needs, the candles and lamps would have to suffice. Rachel had a couple of utility flashlights, with fresh batteries, that they would carry on their persons.

In the powder room on the ground floor, he switched his

glasses for contact lenses. During his last fight with Dexter, the loss of his spectacles had rendered him almost helpless. He had no intention of letting it happen again.

"Can you come here for a sec, baby?" Rachel asked from the kitchen. "I need your help with something."

"Just a minute."

He gazed at his mirror reflection. His face was still swollen and bruised, his finger ached, and his eyes were as red as an insomniac's. Based on his outward appearance, he had no reason whatsoever to feel good about himself.

But he actually felt a building sense of optimism. Optimism about their chances to end this, once and for all. Optimism about resuming their lives with a fresh new outlook. Optimism about everything. It was such an unusual feeling for him that it was a bit unfamiliar, like walking in a new pair of shoes, but he liked it.

"Baby?" Rachel asked again.

"Coming."

She was at the kitchen counter with the roll of duct tape, a small paring knife, and a plank of cardboard she'd cut from a box. She'd taken off her jacket and T-shirt, and wore only a pink sports bra underneath.

He tried mightily not to be aroused by the sight of her body, but the growing bulge in his pants betrayed him.

He cleared his throat.

"Umm, what are you trying to do?"

"I want to tape this knife to my lower back." She turned, showing him the smooth plane of her back. With her fingers, she indicated the area just above the swell of her derriere. "Right here."

"Okay. Looks very doable."

"Does it?" She glanced at him over her shoulder, winked. "You want to prove that?"

"I wish we could."

She twirled around to face him, hooked her fingers into the belt loops of his jeans. Standing on her tiptoes, she kissed him lightly on the lips.

"We'll have plenty of time later," she said.

"Of all the times for us to start feeling horny, why now?"

"I think it's because we feel so alive. I mean, I've hardly gotten any sleep in the past three days. I should be passed out on the floor. But I'm positively crackling with energy." She snapped her fingers. "Aren't you?"

"I'm hyped, ready to roll."

"Even though we know Dexter is probably coming soon, I wouldn't want to be anywhere else in the world right now."

He reached for the tape, cardboard, and the knife.

"Nice secret weapon," he said.

"Dealing with him, we can't be too prepared." She turned around. "Tape this knife to the cardboard, and then fix the whole thing to the small of my back, please."

He did as she asked. She put on her jacket and tested it a few times. She was able to tear the knife away from the cardboard backing with only a quick, forceful tug.

He checked his watch. It was a few minutes to five. Darkness was stealing over the island, and the strengthening winds were battering the palmettos and live oaks that surrounded the house.

The lights flickered for a moment, and then came back on.

"Time for the lamps," she said. She lit two of the kerosene lanterns, and double-checked that their flashlights were functional.

He sat on the sofa in the living room. He had the .357 on his hip, a flashlight dangling from his belt, and the Molotov cocktail strapped over his shoulder in a pillowcase.

She sat next to him and turned on the television to the local news. A storm warning flashed at the bottom of the screen.

"I think we're ready for anything now," she said. "Storms—and Dexter." She uttered a humorless laugh. "Not much difference between the two."

"So now," he said, "we wait."

69

The wind continued to increase in strength and velocity. It swept over the house, tearing at the eaves, howling around the walls, and hammering the windows like a barrage of fists.

Sitting on the sofa, Joshua kept his finger on the flashlight, waiting for a blackout. The lights flickered several times, but remained on.

Rachel put her hand on his arm. "What time is it?"

"Almost six," he said. "You think the ferry would've still run in this wind?"

"It would take something much worse than this to keep the ferry on the mainland. A lot of people depend on it for their livelihood, you know. Children go to school on the mainland, all of the jobs are there . . . trust me, the boat ran, and if Dexter was going to come today, he would have been on that last one."

Quietly, he nodded. He happened to glance at her hair, and on impulse, touched it.

"I found out that your natural hair color is auburn," he said.

She gave him a curious look. "How'd you find that out?"

"Tanisha told me."

"She would know, she dyes it for me. My hair used to be halfway down my back. I cut it and started to color it after I left home. It was part of my disguise, along with the glasses."

He ran his fingers through her soft, dark curls. He thought about his dream of the beach, and her auburn mane flowing in the sunlight.

"I'd like to see it how it used to be," he said.

She started to answer, but then the electric lights dimmed, quieting her. Another gale shrieked around the house.

Adrenaline sizzled through his veins.

"This is it. Lights out."

As soon as he finished the sentence, the lights died, the TV screen fading to black. The power didn't come back on.

She had placed one of the kerosene lanterns in the living room and the other in the kitchen, giving them pale light, but the blackness that devoured the rest of the house was so thick it might have been a solid substance.

On a sparsely populated, mostly undeveloped island, there were no street lamps to light the neighborhoods, no big buildings blazing in the night. He had lost power at their home in Atlanta yesterday, but that had been nothing compared to this.

Here, the darkness was breathtaking.

70

They switched on their flashlights.

After a short bout of tense waiting, Joshua removed the .357 from his holster and thumbed off the safety. Rachel followed suit with the .38.

The wind wailed for a few seconds . . . and then faded. In the well-deep silence that followed, he thought he heard a soft tinkle. Like breaking glass.

It came from somewhere outside.

"That's him." His pounding heart felt as if it had crawled into his throat. "Rachel, I want you to go upstairs."

"What? No way."

"You'll be safe up there. You're the one he really wants. Hide in one of the bedrooms. *Please.*"

The wind spoke again, an insistent keening. The house creaked, groaned.

Guns drawn, they moved to the staircase. She paused on the first step.

"What're you going to do?" She had lowered her voice to a whisper.

"I'm going to stay down here and hold him off. Cut him down, if I can."

"You sure about this?"

"Totally. Go on."

She gnawed her bottom lip. Then, holding the gun and the flashlight in front of her, she climbed the stairs.

He watched the darkness above swallow her. He stepped away from the staircase, sidled into the hallway, and extinguished the kerosene lantern in the living room. He slipped into the kitchen and doused that lamp, too.

From outside, though the blinds were drawn, Dexter might have glimpsed light. He wanted Dexter to think that they had left the living room, to lure him into attempting to enter through the front door.

Angling the flashlight beam to the floor, he returned to the hallway. There, he waited in darkness. Heart knocking. Finger curled around the trigger.

71

She hated being separated from Joshua. His strength and clarity of purpose had bolstered her confidence, and leaving his side brought back all of her old fears and worries about Dexter.

She would've run, if there was anywhere else to run to. She understood running was not a solution, but it would have delayed the inevitable confrontation.

Her old scars itched, as if remembering her last violent encounter with Dexter.

I won't have to fight him this time. Joshua's going to keep him away from me.

She wanted to believe that was true, but her nightmares were fresh in her thoughts. Nightmares were not necessarily prophetic—they were sometimes only manifestations of deeply held fears—but it was impossible for her to push them out of her mind. This entire evening had the quality of a terrifying dream.

The second-floor hallway was pitch black. She'd spent some of the best times of her life in this house, but her fear was so sharp that she might have been wandering through a foreign place, where every shadow held a latent threat.

She panned the flashlight around. Joshua had asked her to hide. But no room—nowhere on the entire planet—was safe from Dexter.

She was so damn tired of running, of living in fear. She wanted to kill the man. She'd never wanted to harm another human being, but she would hurt him, eagerly and gratefully.

Don't think like that, girl. You'll lower yourself to his level, and then where will you be?

A spare bedroom was on the right that her aunt had often used for prayer and Bible study. It was a chamber of peace that held nothing but comforting memories.

She would hide in there.

72

Joshua's finger twitched on the revolver's trigger. Dexter was outside—he'd heard him. But the asshole hadn't tried to break in yet. What was he doing?

Perhaps he wasn't going to come through the front. Perhaps he was looking for another way inside the house.

Joshua cut off the flashlight. He moved to a window on the right of the doorway.

With one finger, he lifted one of the slats in the blinds, giving himself a narrow side view of the porch.

A large tree branch had landed at the bottom of the steps, in the midst of glittering glass shards and dead leaves.

Where had the glass come from?

He backed away from the window.

Then, he cocked the hammer of the .357 and flung open the front door.

Cold wind gusted inside and struck him like a many-armed beast. But there was no attack from Dexter.

Silvery moonlight illuminated the porch. Checking both

ways, he went down the steps. At the bottom, his shoe crunched on the blend of glass slivers and leaves.

He kicked aside the offending branch, swung around, and looked up.

The dormer window, which led to the attic, was broken.

73

On the threshold of the spare bedroom, she played the flashlight beam around. It was bare but for a chair, bookcase, and desk. All clear.

She locked the door, leaned against it.

Then, she pulled the chair from the desk and levered the top of the seat back underneath the doorknob, for a little extra reinforcement.

Beyond the white cone of her flashlight, the room was tomb-dark. Earlier, they had closed the Venetian blinds on the big window, which gave a stunning ocean view.

She decided to open the blinds. It would make her feel better to be able to observe the ceaselessly rumbling tides. As if she weren't trapped.

She pulled the lift cord, raising the blinds to the top of the windowpane. Pale moonlight fell inside. On the beach below, the waves, lashed by strong winds, crashed violently on the shore, as if some gigantic sea creature were thrashing to the surface to devour her.

Disturbed by the sight, she was about to close the blinds

again, preferring the comfort of the flashlight to this, when she heard a sound behind her. Like creaking metal hinges.

In the far corner of the room, there was a rectangular ceiling panel that granted entry to the attic. As she watched, it opened slowly, a set of retractable wooden stairs lowering from the attic to the floor, like the widening jaws of an immense beast.

He's already in the house, oh, Jesus . . .

Terror bolted her feet in place. She wanted to run. But she couldn't order her muscles to work.

There was a thud: the weight of a body dropping onto the hardwood floor.

"I kept my word, baby," a familiar voice said, which had an effect on her like an ice pick piercing her spine. "I found you."

Run, she thought, wildly. *Run, run, run.*

But she couldn't. She wouldn't.

Not any more.

She aimed the flashlight in front of her.

Dexter looked mostly the same, like the man who had haunted her nightmares for so long. The only difference was that he appeared crazier, if that were at all possible.

Madness and blood thirst gleamed in his eyes.

"Aren't you going to run?" He nodded toward the doorway. "There's the door. Make me chase you, baby, make it sweeter for me. You know I love it when you run."

"Then I'm happy to disappoint you, asshole."

She dropped the flashlight, raised the gun, and pulled the trigger.

74

He got in through the attic, Joshua thought. *Why didn't I think of that?*

Dexter had out-foxed him. The man had a singular, twisted brilliance.

He rushed up the porch steps and through the front door. Like a fool, he had sent Rachel upstairs thinking that he was going to protect her from harm.

But he might as well have sent her away to die.

"Rachel!" He took the steps two and three at a time. "Rachel! Where are you?"

From a room upstairs, gunfire rang out.

75

Joshua had told her that when he'd fought Dexter, Dexter had taken two rounds point blank from a .38 and had gotten up only a few minutes later and walked away, because he was wearing a bulletproof vest. She should have known that shooting him anywhere but in his head would be a waste of energy and ammo.

But terror trumped rational thought.

She fired, scoring a direct hit in his chest, and he only rocked backward on his heels, as if she'd merely punched him.

"Try again." He thundered forward.

Outside the room, Joshua was shouting her name.

She aimed again, but Dexter was charging forward so fast that he got within range and swiped at her, knocking the gun out of her hand.

She screamed, spun to the doorway.

He seized her arm and threw her across the room as if she weighed no more than a doll. She smacked against the wall, rapping her head hard against the plaster, and slid to the floor.

As if from a great distance, she heard Joshua pounding on the door, calling her name.

I'm sorry, baby. I'm so sorry for everything.

Dexter descended on her like a spider that had trapped a fly in its web. He put his cold hands around her neck, and started choking.

76

The gunshots came from a bedroom. Joshua tried frantically to open the door, but it was locked.

"Rachel! I'm coming!"

He took a few steps backward, and then lowered his shoulder and rammed against the door like a bull. He hit the door hard enough to rattle his teeth. Wood splintered, and the door buckled in the frame, but it remained intact.

She screamed.

He thought of using the .357 to blow the door open, but his father had warned him that the .357 was such a powerful caliber that a round could punch through walls and kill someone inadvertently. What if he shot at the door, blew away the lock, and hit Rachel, too?

He couldn't risk it. He had to knock the door down. He was strong, a big man. He could do this. He had to. She needed him. His baby needed him. His future lay in that room, his only hope of lasting happiness, and this was his last chance, his only chance, to take hold of the future and blast away the darkness forever.

He slammed against the door again. And again. And again. . . .

77

Dexter was choking her.

"Where's my fucking money, bitch? Where did you hide my fucking money?"

Through her dimming vision, she could see the murderous intent in his lunatic eyes, could feel his overwhelming desire to kill her in his powerful hands.

Across the room, Joshua was banging against the door, attempting to knock it down, but the chair wedged under the doorknob was holding him back.

Above her, Dexter grinned maniacally. Darkness pulled at her, a fathomless darkness that would never relinquish her once she surrendered to it.

"Gonna fucking kill you . . ." he said, his hot breath washing over her. "Give me my money . . ."

Her arm was twisted behind her. Her fingers brushed against the handle of the knife she'd had Joshua tape to the small of her back. Her secret weapon.

"Simple matter of respect, bitch . . ."

Using the last of her remaining strength, she ripped the

knife away from her back, brought it around, and plunged the blade deep into Dexter's throat.

Dexter bellowed like a speared lion.

Struggling to breathe, she screamed at him.

"I gave away all of your money, asshole! All . . . of it! Every. Last. Penny!"

Blood arched from the wound in his throat. He fumbled to tear out the blade, and when he did, more blood spouted.

She coughed violently, scooted away, and shakily rose to her feet.

Still, she shouted at him, her voice raw. "Battered women shelters . . . domestic violence centers . . . churches . . . I gave it all to them. I thought hard about it . . . and decided I didn't *want* your filthy blood money."

He tried to rise. Screaming, she kicked him in the ribs, and he doubled over, groaning.

"And I didn't need it!"

78

On Joshua's seventh or eighth try, the door gave way. He stumbled inside, a chair spinning away from the door.

Dexter and Rachel were on the other side of the room, revealed in the pale moonshine and the backsplash of the flashlight that lay on the floor. She was on her feet, hunched over, chest heaving. Dexter lay on his side, gasping, bleeding copiously from a knife wound in his throat.

She'd stabbed the bastard. Joshua felt a flash of savage triumph.

Dexter saw him, and hatred twisted his face. He struggled to his feet.

And drew a gun.

But Joshua had already honed the .357 on him, clutching the weapon in his good hand.

He fired, and the gun's report was like an explosion in the small room. A round blasted Dexter's shoulder, and he swayed.

But he did not fall.

Joshua fired again, and this one shaved across Dexter's head, ripping away half his scalp and shattering the glass on the big window behind him. Another round in the head drove Dexter backward, reeling.

But he didn't fall, didn't die. His dark eyes held on stubbornly to life.

The man had the strength and determination of the murderously insane.

Stepping forward, Joshua fired the last two cartridges. They tore through Dexter's throat and chest and sent him hurtling through the window, and falling to the beach below.

79

Standing at the shattered window, cold wind swirling around him, Joshua peered down at the sand. Dexter lay sprawled on the ground, bits of glass sprinkling him like party glitter.

He wasn't moving. He appeared to be dead.

Joshua went to check on Rachel. She leaned against the wall, breathing laboriously and massaging her throat.

"You okay?" he asked.

She nodded, and asked in a raw voice, "He dead?"

"He hasn't moved."

"Better make sure."

He had left the Molotov cocktail in the hallway. He retrieved it and returned to the window.

Lying on the beach, Dexter appeared to twitch, but that might have been due to the brisk wind.

Rachel made her way to the window. She had picked up her gun.

"Let's end this," Joshua said.

He waited a moment for the wind to subside, and then he thumbed the Bic lighter, conjuring a flame, and touched it to the oil-soaked wick of the hand grenade. The fire tasted the rag, and began to devour it hungrily.

He let the bomb drop, the flaming wick fluttering like wings as it arced through the air. The bottle struck Dexter and exploded in an orb of flames and glass shrapnel, the heat so intense that Joshua felt it sear the sweat on his face from his vantage point fifteen feet above.

Dexter howled. He rolled across the sand and clambered to his feet, covered in rippling flames from soles to crown, but somehow, still alive.

He lurched blindly toward the ocean.

"Oh, shit," Joshua said. "He's gonna jump in the water and put out the fire."

"No, he's not." Rachel raised her gun, teeth gritted in concentration.

Stumbling, Dexter was less than ten feet away from the roaring tide, perhaps thirty feet away from them.

Rachel pulled the trigger.

Dexter wobbled as if slapped upside the head. He dropped to the sand, out of reach of the tide.

At last, he lay still.

"That was for everything you took away from me," Rachel said softly.

She lowered her head, whispered a prayer, and cast the gun onto the floor.

Joshua put his arm around her and pulled her close.

On the beach, the wind fanned the flames, keeping the dark of night at bay.

80

Two years later

They strolled barefoot along a curve of pristine white sand, hand-in-hand. A summer sun smiled down on them, and a cool, salty breeze ruffled the comfortable white shirts and shorts that both of them wore. They were alone on the shore, the ocean on his right stretching to a hazy horizon.

"Dad-dee."

He looked into the eyes of their son, Justin. He was a beautiful, healthy boy with soft skin the color of nutmeg, Rachel's eyes and nose, Joshua's lips and cheekbones, and a full head of dark, curly hair.

"Hey, little man." Joshua bounced him on his hip.

Walking beside them, Rachel looked at their child, then at him. She smiled—an expression of pure joy, utterly free of worry and fear. Sunlight filigreed her long, curly, auburn hair, giving it the appearance of spun gold.

He brought Rachel's hand to his lips and kissed her fingers.

"Let's go to the house." She winked. "Justin looks like he needs a nap."

The house was a short distance ahead, on the left. Justin tugged at his ear, drawing his attention. His son pointed excitedly at something in the distance: a ferry that bobbed on the waves like a child's bath toy.

A powerful sense of déjà vu gripped him. Had this happened before? Or had he dreamed of it?

He couldn't remember, and soon, the odd feeling passed.

His son was gesturing at the ferry, babbling.

"That's the ferry, little man," Joshua said. "You've been on the ferry before, remember?"

Justin only giggled, and tugged his ear again.

Rachel had walked ahead and waited at the open patio door. Coco sat beside her, tail wagging.

"Come on in here, baby," she said. "We've got some grown folks' business to take care of."

"Is that so? You must want another one of these." Joshua kissed Justin's forehead.

"Hmmm, how about a girl? We can name her Jasmine . . . Jasmine Elizabeth Moore."

He kissed her, and she took his hand.

"I'm all for it," he said. "Lead the way."

The family went inside the house together.

Subscribe to Brandon Massey's *Talespinner*

Readers of Brandon Massey now can subscribe to Brandon Massey's free *Talespinner* e-newsletter by visiting his Web site at www.brandonmassey.com. *Talespinner* subscribers get a quarterly e-mail newsletter, opportunities to win prizes in exclusive contests, and advance information about forthcoming publications. Go online today to www.brandonmassey.com and sign up. Membership is free!